Confession

Coming in March 1999
from Elizabeth Gage and MIRA Books

THE HOURGLASS

ELIZABETH GAGE
Confession

MIRA

MIRA

ISBN 1-55166-465-8

CONFESSION

Printed in U.S.A.

To Maile

My heartfelt thanks go to
Dianne Moggy of MIRA Books
for her interest in my work.
Sincere thanks also to
Amy Moore and Laura Shin
for invaluable editorial advice.

I also wish to thank Karen Daam
for her generous help in my research.

Prologue

Snow was everywhere.

The drifts were six and seven feet high. The piles left alongside the roads by the country plows were almost as tall as the street signs.

At its height, on Saturday afternoon and evening, the storm had stopped everything. Only plows or snowmobiles could make their ways through the center of town, and the county roads were officially closed. Mercifully, the power hadn't gone off, but all normal activity had ground to a halt. A few local people in snowshoes had explored the hills over the lake. Everyone else had stayed home.

By Sunday the snowfall had ebbed enough for the streets to be cleared, and today people were back at work.

The little girl was home with Pam, the baby-sitter, because her mother was out at a job interview. Pam was inside watching TV and the little girl was building a snowman when the stranger came up.

He was tall. His hair was dotted with flakes of snow. He had a handsome face, the cheeks a bit red from the cold.

"Hi," he said. "What's your name?"

"Natalie," she said.

"What are you doing?"

She smiled. "Building a snowman."

He stood back with his arms folded. "You've got a long way to go, don't you?" The ball of snow she was rolling was hardly a foot in diameter.

She said nothing.

"Don't you have anyone to help you?" he asked.

"Pam," she replied. "But she has her show until two."

"Oh," he said, glancing at the house. "Well, I'll help you."

He knelt down to get his hands under the ball of snow and rolled it quickly across the yard. The packing was good, for the temperature had risen a little overnight, and before long the ball was at least three feet high.

"There," he said. "That's a good start, don't you think?"

The child cocked her head and folded her arms, consciously striking a pose. "I guess so," she said.

"Now for the next ball," he said, warming his hands under his arms. "That's for the middle part of his body. Do you know what that's called, by the way? The middle part of a person's body?"

The child shook her head. "Do you?" she asked.

"Yes, I do. It's called the torso."

"Torso! That's a silly word."

"Yes." He smiled. "I guess it is. Anyway, let's roll ourselves a torso. Okay?"

They were kneeling down together when Pam came out of the house. She was a plump girl of fourteen, with blond hair and a complexion that made her self-conscious. She had pulled on a down jacket in haste.

"Can I help you?"

The man stood up, leaving the child kneeling in the snow. Pam's face hesitated between suspicion and girlish interest, for he was very good-looking.

"I hope so," he said. "I'm looking for a house. I don't know the town at all, so I'm kind of lost."

"Which house?" the baby-sitter asked. Lake Geneva was a tiny town, and she had been here all her life. She knew every family and every house—except for the fancy places owned by the part-year people and the new condos near the resort hotel.

"Here's the address." The stranger took a folded piece of note-paper from his pocket and handed it to her. He was smiling, and she couldn't help smiling back.

"Oh, sure," she said. "That's on the other side of the lake. I'm glad you asked me. You would have had a hard time finding it."

She glanced down at Natalie, who was pulling at the stranger's coat.

"I'll draw you a little map," Pam said, turning toward the house. "Be right back."

"I'll stay here with Natalie," the man said. "We have a torso to make, don't we, Natalie?"

The child smirked at the silly word.

Pam hesitated for a moment at the thought of leaving the little girl outside with a strange man. After all, Natalie was her responsibility. But now she noticed that he wasn't wearing gloves. His hands were red from the snow.

"You need gloves for that," she said. "And look at your pants!"

His slacks were far too nice for this weather. She could not see his shoes, for they were under the snow. He didn't seem properly dressed at all. The coat he wore was more stylish than anything sold in this region.

She went inside and got a pair of men's gloves from the closet and tossed them to him from the front stoop. Then she found paper and a pencil in the kitchen and drew the map. When she returned he was lifting a second ball onto the first while Natalie watched in obvious delight. It was easy to see that the little girl had missed her contact with a man since her father left.

"The first thing you have to do is go back through town," Pam said, showing him the map. "Take Center Street right through to Elm, then go left. That will take you around the lake."

She thought briefly of offering to go along as his guide. But he was a stranger here, and she couldn't risk getting into a car with him. And there was Natalie to think about.

"After about a mile and a half you'll come to a little roadside restaurant called the Pine Top," she said. "You turn right at the next stop sign. There's a neighborhood there with about four streets. Just keep going up the hill until you can't go any higher, then take your first right."

He was nodding, smiling at her.

"Did I go too fast?" she asked.

"Not at all," he said. "Let me just help Natalie roll a snowman's head here, and I'll be on my way."

He quickly helped the little girl roll a head for the snowman and lifted it on himself. The figure was quite tall.

He leaned down to shake the little girl's hand. "Be sure to find him a nice hat," he said. "And a pipe. Does your daddy have a pipe in the house somewhere?"

Pam gave him a significant look. "She lives with her mother," she said. "But we'll manage. Won't we, Natalie?"

The little girl nodded.

The man stood up, brushing the snow from his knees.

"You're going to be soaked," Pam said. She wished she could invite him in. If it were her own house she would have put his pants in the dryer and made him some coffee.

"Are you—just visiting?" she asked.

"Well, that depends," he said. "We might meet again." He seemed amused, in a nice way, by her interest. "Anyway, I'd better be going." He handed her back the gloves.

"Thanks for helping Natalie."

"It was a pleasure. I haven't built a snowman in a long time."

She watched as he went down the shoveled walk and got into his car. The top and hood bore shiny droplets of water, but no snow. He must have been driving a long time, she thought. All the cars in town still had snowcaps on their roofs.

The car edged soundlessly along the road, the tires sinking into the new-fallen snow, which was thick on trees and rooftops everywhere. Pam waved, and so did Natalie. An arm waved from inside the car, which gathered speed as it headed down the hill. Pam squinted to look across the lake. She could see the neighborhood where he was headed. There was a break in the trees where the new street had been cleared. She realized she had forgotten to ask him which family he was going to see. Oh, well, she thought. She would find out eventually. It was a small town.

She turned to Natalie. "Let's find a hat and a scarf for your snowman, okay?"

He followed the girl's directions, driving through the center of town, where Christmas decorations were hung on lampposts and stoplight wires. It was a quiet town with little traffic. The resort guests stayed in the hotel, so the only cars on the roads were the pickups and sedans of the local residents.

He found the roadside restaurant—closed until spring, the sign read—and headed up the hill. The neighborhood was an old one, with small frame houses, a few of which had boats on trailers in the yards. But the street at the top of the hill was new, with vacant lots as well as houses.

He found the address he wanted and drove past it. He stopped the car a hundred feet farther on and turned off the engine.

As he got out of the car he realized how cold his hands and feet were. He put his right hand under his coat to warm it. The street had a beautiful view of the lake. The water near the shore was frozen over and covered with snow, but the middle of the lake was blue and very pretty.

He felt a brief pang of worry as he paused in front of the house. He wondered if he could really do this. Then he reviewed the thoughts he had pondered during the journey here. After following them from premise to conclusion, as his mind was trained to do, he relaxed. He knew he was right.

He saw tire tracks leading from the driveway down the street over the still-falling snow. He walked slowly up the walk and looked in the front window.

There was a fireplace, and an old couch on which the woman lay. There was a book open on her breast. She seemed to be asleep.

He went to the front door and reached for the doorbell. Then, on an impulse, he tried the knob. The door was unlocked. No wonder: this was a small town.

He stepped inside quickly and closed the door behind him.

He did not want to make a noise, but he knew the sudden breath of cold air could betray him.

There was no danger, though. She was lying before the fire, which warmed the whole room despite the fact that the logs were only embers now.

Her face was at peace; sleep made it prettier. But as he came closer he saw her brow furrow. She was probably having a bad dream.

The gun was in his hand. His heart went out to her. This was not going to be easy.

Cause and effect, he thought. *Crime and punishment.*

The gun was pointing at her, steady, motionless, as though on a wire. The cold in his hands had gone. He wanted her to be awake, but he hesitated to break the silence.

He didn't have to. Her eyes fluttered open, as though his mere presence were all the summons she needed. She was smiling through her perplexity.

"You did this," he said.

She did not seem to have understood. She was still half asleep, or mostly asleep. But she knew who he was.

The gun wanted to tremble, but when he saw her eyes focus on it, he derived strength from her own recognition. That was the important thing, he thought. She had brought him to this. Let her help him even now.

And she did. She smiled dreamily, accepting him as the gun fired.

Part One

1

Eighteen months earlier

On a hot July evening in New York, Rebecca Lowell stood in the bedroom of her Upper East Side apartment, looking in the mirror.

It was not a task she relished. It required too many adjustments. There were changes to be made to the real face that stood before the glass, of course. Little touches intended to make herself presentable to others. But also changes to be made inside, so that when she walked away from the mirror she could take with her an image of herself that she could live with. This was a far more difficult job.

Rebecca was not considered an attractive woman. She never had been. Not even when, as an undergraduate, she had been slim and active, before childbirth had thickened her figure and her face.

It was not that her features themselves were bad. The nose and chin were finely modeled. The large, intelligent eyes dominated her face, wistful and sometimes sad. Her hair was kept short, the curls frosted a bit against encroaching gray by her hairdresser. The skin was pale. It would wrinkle eventually, like her mother's, but for the moment it still looked fresh.

She had an undeniable dignity of bearing. An air of maturity. The warmth of a woman who has lived and felt and yearned. But not the other thing. Not the daring that makes some women desirable, and others beautiful. Even in those interesting eyes one sensed possibilities unexploited, a brink never tested. And no one saw this more clearly than Rebecca herself.

She turned away. A dozen times a day she turned away from that same look in her eyes, that look in which she met herself and thought, *You're not what you could have been.* She put it out of her mind, squared her shoulders and faced the world outside the mirror with a firm self-respect that made others depend on her, and almost made her forget the truth.

"Rebecca, help me with this, will you?"

Her husband came briskly into the dressing room. At fifty he was everything he should be. Tall, tanned, quick of movement, a tennis player still, and a good one, as well as a corporate golfer, with silver around the temples and eyes that flashed precisely the same smile in every photograph that had ever been taken of him, Damon Lowell was by far the handsomest man of his circle, and the envy of all his friends.

He looked the part of power and prestige, and he had played it with aplomb for more than twenty years. A partner in the firm, a member of every club and social organization that mattered, he was a pillar of the society he moved in. He had accomplished everything his Harvard degrees promised, and a lot more. He had an assurance that almost frightened Rebecca, though he was, and always had been, solicitous of her to a fault. He was quick to pull out her chair, hold a door for her, and often touched her or hugged her in public. Little proud remarks about her humor, her spirit were a regular part of his conversation. Their truth value was less important to Damon than the image they created of his marriage.

His father, according to the family, had behaved almost the same way toward Grandma Lowell. Rebecca could not testify to this personally, since old Dr. Lowell, who had been an M.D. as well as an attorney, specializing in patenting new drugs and medical treatments, had been on his deathbed when she was introduced to him. But the family albums showed an uncanny resemblance between Damon's hard, engaging smile and his father's. And indeed, as Damon shot along the trail of success blazed for him a generation before by his father, it almost seemed he was polishing away the last traces of his own personality in order to fit the mold. Curiously, this only increased his power in everyone's eyes.

"Darling, thanks," he said as she tied the tie. The grainy tanned skin of his neck came close to her as she worked, and she smelled his fresh, earthy scent. She watched his eyes dart about the room. He was always on the alert, never really at rest. She used to wonder what thoughts were hidden behind those glinting eyes. Now she didn't.

"There." She patted the tie. He leaned forward quickly to kiss her.

"You look elegant," he said. "Better hurry, though. Roy will be all over me if we're late again."

They were going to a party at Roy Minter's house. The partners would be there—Bob Krieg, Evan Gaeth and the others—as well as some government people. The firm was doing all the legal work for the Hightower Land Development Project, on which the mayor was gambling his political future, and Damon had been chosen as point man to work with the City. This was not the first time the firm had played a role in city and state politics—the governor had relied heavily on Bob Krieg, a college classmate and former roommate, for advice and influence since his days as a councilman—but the Hightower project was very expensive and had attracted enemies as well as friends on all sides.

It was a feather in Damon's cap to be the firm's representative on something so controversial. His picture had been in the papers nearly every week since he got involved. Even *New York* magazine had done a feature on him last spring. His work on Hightower might well lead to a federal appointment one day, for the project, when completed, would change the face of Midtown as Rockefeller Center had done before it.

Damon would be spending a lot of time running back and forth from New York to Albany and Washington. This did not mean he would be home less than before. It simply meant he would be in a different place.

"Meet you out front," he said, striding quickly from the room. An instant after he left, their daughter Dusty came in. She replaced him as quickly and smoothly as an actor who darts from behind the curtain just as his predecessor has left the stage.

"Mother, would you help me with this?"

Dusty was going out on a date with her new boyfriend and had come home today to get an outfit she had forgotten to take back to her apartment downtown. The dark slacks and silk blouse were casual but looked expensive. Rebecca had bought them for her earlier in the summer.

"Let me see," Rebecca murmured, squinting as she clasped her daughter's gold neck band.

Dusty was blond, well-formed, only a little thick in the calves, with pretty shoulders and hands, skin that tanned like her father's, and beautiful, complicated eyes. Everyone always said that she had Damon's eyes, but it was Rebecca's expression that shone in them—quiet, a little worried, a little evasive.

She looked like what she was—a rich girl accustomed to fine things, designed for success, bred for happiness. Yet she did not seem entirely comfortable in that role. And in this she was, again, her mother's daughter.

"I've got to rush," Dusty said. "I forgot about the traffic."

"Can't we drop you?" Rebecca asked.

"No, thanks. It's out of your way."

Not for the first time Rebecca noticed that Dusty had not greeted her father on the way in. She waited for him to be out of sight.

For years she had been in the habit of giving Damon a wide berth. At least since she hit adolescence, and maybe even before that.

It wasn't that Dusty didn't like Damon. She admired him, she enjoyed showing him off to her friends, and she seemed flattered when the family said she had inherited his good looks. But she was in awe of him; she did not seek him out.

Damon, busy with his own plans, either ignored this distance from his daughter or chose not to complain about it. Rebecca said nothing to either of them about the situation. She wished they communicated better, but felt she could not do anything about it without irritating either or both of them.

The new boyfriend, whose name Rebecca always forgot, was the latest in a long line, but Dusty had been talking more and more seriously about him in the last month. He was a law student at Columbia, a Harvard graduate like Damon, and he came from a fine family. What was that name again? Rebecca could never recall it.

"How do I look?" Dusty asked, turning to have her mother examine her outfit.

How does anyone look at twenty, with eyes like that? Rebecca thought.

"Come here," she said, and she pulled out a loose strand of thread from the silk blouse, noticing the scent of her daughter's hair spray as she did so.

"Your ends are splitting again," she observed. "Why don't you go to Sally this week? I can call her for you if you like."

Sally was Rebecca's hairdresser, and a treasure. For some reason Dusty had refused the invitation to use her, and clung to the girl near campus that she had been using for the past couple of years. Rebecca thought Dusty's hair always looked too full, but she was too tactful to make an issue of it. The girl was bursting with life and would have looked wonderful even in pigtails.

"Don't worry about it," Dusty said.

"You're right."

There was no point in being at odds with her daughter. Rebecca was at that stage in life where everything seemed to be slipping away at once. Her mother was ill, some of her friends were, too, and it seemed that with each passing day a cherished hope grew dimmer or was forgotten. Dusty was growing up fast, and the closeness between her and Rebecca was straining to adjust itself to the rapid changes in their lives. It was important to keep the door open for Dusty without making her feel trapped by her mother's love. That was why Rebecca never criticized Dusty's clothes, her use of time, or her boyfriends. She sometimes affected an air of amused tolerance about Dusty's choices; she carefully hid the deep concern and protectiveness behind it.

Dusty was glowing as she met her mother's eyes in the mirror. "Mother, I want you to meet Tony."

Tony! Of course. Tony Delafield. Every time Rebecca was reminded of the first name the second one came along in its trail. It was a fine old name, and she knew several Delafield branches through her own family and through Damon's.

"Really?" she said. "I thought you were shielding him from us."

"No, he's just busy."

Rebecca had been wondering about this Tony, because Dusty had made a great point of not inviting him home. She behaved as though she was saving him for something. This made Rebecca suspect she was serious about him. Dusty was free and easy about bringing her more casual boyfriends home. But she had never brought Brandon, the Baltimore boy from college, or Michael, the fellow she had met through her friend Susan. Something in the way she talked about those two had made Rebecca take notice. And after the breakup with Brandon, Dusty had seemed upset for a whole month.

"I'd love to meet him," she said. "Your father, too."

Dusty was silent for a moment. She was looking at herself in the mirror.

"Mother, do you think my face is too wide?"

Rebecca smiled.

"What does *he* think?" she asked.

"Oh, he says I'm perfect in every way," Dusty replied. "But you know men." A slight blush colored her cheeks.

Rightly or wrongly, Rebecca took this as a hint that Dusty was sleeping with the young man. But she put the speculation out of her mind. She had long since decided she didn't want to know anything about her daughter's sex life except what Dusty might want to tell her. And, mercifully, Dusty had told her nothing.

These were not easy times for mothers. Sex was not what it had been only a decade ago. Promiscuity was no longer a matter of pregnancy and propriety, but of life and death. But Dusty was a safe girl. She had never been particularly adventurous or headstrong as a child, and she showed every sign of having inherited her mother's caution now that she was older. She would do the normal things, the things that would not hurt her. Sexually, and in other ways.

Rebecca felt a mixture of regret and relief about this. Regret that her pretty, intelligent daughter would probably do nothing more remarkable with her life than be a suburban wife and mother, like Rebecca herself and all her friends; relief that this relatively tranquil destiny was better than all the heartaches so many women faced today. This was no time to be reckless, even if one had to pay a price for caution.

So Rebecca asked no questions. And Dusty appreciated this. Mother and daughter spent happy, easy times together, knew each other as far as they wished to be known, and liked each other.

And now Dusty was to bring home a young man about whom she was serious. Rebecca suspected that an engagement might be in the works. Dusty was about to start her senior year. A June wedding might be at the back of her mind.

Again that mixture of relief and sadness tugged at Rebecca's heart. She looked at her smiling daughter.

"I've been saying to your father that it's about time we met this paragon," she said. "Do you want to bring him to dinner?"

Her little reference to Tennessee Williams was lost on Dusty, as Rebecca had known it would be. One of Rebecca's quirks was that she was literary. It was a habit she had picked up in college and never renounced, perhaps because it reminded her of her youth. Literary references sometimes crept into her conversation, but neither Damon nor Dusty nor anyone else ever noticed them.

"No. I want him to come out to our place at Sands Point next weekend," Dusty said. "His parents have a home in Kings Point, so he can come over and still get home early. I want him to come swimming. We can have lunch...."

"What about your father?" Rebecca asked. "Won't he feel left out?"

"I thought it would be nice for you to meet him first," Dusty said. "He's a little—well, you know how boys feel about Daddy."

Rebecca gave her daughter a little smile.

"Well, be sure to tell him not to dress up," she said. "We're just simple folks."

"Mother, I love you." Dusty hugged her quickly. "Have a good time tonight."

"You, too, sweetie."

Damon would be in the city this weekend and would not be available. Later he would listen with interest to whatever Rebecca had to say about the young man. Damon affected a proprietary concern about Dusty's boyfriends and wanted to approve of whomever she chose. He had been annoyed never to have met Brandon and Michael and had occasionally wondered out loud whether they really existed.

So it would be an important lunch, an important day. All the more reason to treat it as the opposite, at least within Dusty's hearing.

Dusty had left the dressing room, and Rebecca was alone, staring at her dress in the mirror and thinking about the evening ahead. The partners and their wives were as familiar to her as the oldest clothes in her closet. But the presence of the political people, including the mayor's top aides, would add spice. Rebecca would have to try to seem interesting. Damon would be watching her out of the corner of his eye.

"Rebecca, are you coming?" It was Damon's voice, carrying with knifelike ease from the living room. He didn't want to be late tonight. Too many important people were waiting for him.

Later he would bring her home and go back out. She would sleep alone again. When he finally returned, in the wee hours, she would pretend to be asleep. The smell of a recent shower would be on his skin, and under it another aroma, the one she had come to accept over the years, realizing that she could do nothing about it. A scent she could inhale at her leisure, for Rebecca slept little nowadays.

Trying to avoid this thought, Rebecca made the mistake of looking in the mirror once more. She saw her eyes and turned away.

2

The party was as deadly as Rebecca feared. A few of the wives spoke to her. Doreen Blackman, already slurring her words a little, complimented Rebecca on her hair. Barbara Krieg spent twenty minutes comparing notes about the academic careers of their respective daughters. (Cindy Krieg was going to be a senior at Wellesley and had been pushed into relentless competition with Dusty since seventh grade by Barbara.) Caron Minter, the most notorious snob among them, didn't even greet Rebecca.

The men, of course, couldn't be bothered. From long years of familiarity with Damon, they knew he did not require that they pay attention to his wife.

Everyone knew Damon was unfaithful. Worse yet, the partners and their wives knew who his current mistress was. This was Rebecca's great chagrin, and the principal reason she abhorred the firm's parties.

Damon's mistress was a lobbyist named Alison Shore. She worked for some sort of textile company, and Damon had met her years ago. She was not a terribly beautiful woman, but she was vivacious, as lobbyists tend to be. She wore her hair long—it was rather too black, but striking—and liked cocktail dresses with tiny straps. She had attractive, straight shoulders that made her stand out in a room. Her laugh was arrogant, sensual.

Miss Shore (never married) was not Damon's first mistress, but he had stuck with her for a long time now and by all accounts— what an irony!—was faithful to her. He had no other mistresses to Rebecca's knowledge. Twice a year he took a solitary trip to Chicago on business; Rebecca knew he was spending the time with Alison at a resort hotel in Wisconsin.

They were probably like an old married couple after all this time,

Rebecca sometimes mused. And that, of course, was the unkindest cut of all.

That trip to "Chicago" was coming up in September, and this made the party a little more painful than it would have been otherwise. One of the partners, Evan Gaeth, even mentioned it to Damon right in front of Rebecca.

"So you're off to Chicago in the fall, are you?"

Damon smiled, not thrown off balance at all.

"Who knows if I'll even have the time this year, with all this Hightower business going on." He shrugged fatalistically. Evan nodded and, with a sidelong glance at Rebecca, drifted away.

After the party, Rebecca passed a sleepless night. Somehow the waiting for Damon's return was too much for her. After he finally slipped into bed she lay beside him, trembling slightly, for half an hour and then got up.

The fatigue of that long night stayed with her all week. She spent Thursday and Friday answering cards and making plans with the caterer and florist for the party Damon was to give next month for the mayor. She spoke twice with her mother, who lived in Florida and who had recently undergone surgery.

Irene, Rebecca's mother, was twice widowed and dying of cancer. Or perhaps *dying* was not the word for it. She had been diagnosed when her estranged first husband, Frank, was still alive. Since then she had married and buried a second husband, Roger, and was "keeping company' with a new fellow named Wes, who accompanied her on her pleasure trips when she was well enough to travel.

Irene was a demanding, indomitable woman, and though the cancer had been pronounced incurable by her specialists, it did not seem to limit her in any way that Rebecca could see. She had now lived with the disease for a decade and a half, had made a fortune on the Florida real estate market since her second operation, and traveled more than ever. Rebecca could not help thinking that even cancer was no match for her mother. Now that her death sentence had been given by the doctors, the disease had done its worst. The old lady would win out over it in the end.

Wes, her boyfriend, was as docile as Roger had been, and followed in the wake of Irene's energy like an acolyte. Frank Winthrop, the first husband, had had more gumption. He had married

Irene because their families were closely linked in Boston society, but had never liked her. He abandoned Irene when Rebecca was still a child, giving her a generous divorce settlement in order to "get her out of his hair." Rebecca had only seen her father twice more before his death. He had attended her college graduation— seeming somewhat the worse for liquor, and for not having been invited—and her wedding to Damon (whose family, the Lowells, were allied by numerous links to the Winthrops). An older man by then and already afflicted with the illness that was to end his life, Frank showed a great liking for Damon, and rather little enthusiasm for Rebecca, who was like a stranger to him after all those years of separation.

On Friday night, Rebecca and Damon went to dinner at the Parkers' house, down the street. The Parkers were old friends, and Damon played tennis every Sunday with Judd at a local indoor tennis center. Rebecca sometimes had lunch with Mimi, but this week there was no time.

Mimi had asked her about Dusty's new beau.

"Have you seen him yet?"

"I'm going to, tomorrow."

"Is Dusty really taken with him?"

Rebecca nodded. "I think so. But she's had serious beaux before. You can't tell what's serious with these children."

"Do you think they're—doing it?" whispered Mimi eagerly.

"I really don't know," Rebecca replied wearily. The prurient curiosity of her friends was a cross she hated to bear. She lived in a society where the entire intellectual capacity of women was devoted to gossip. Rebecca had never been cut out for that sort of thing. Not that she was so much above everyone else, but she did her thinking about things, felt her feelings in a part of herself where the amours and tragedies of friends and neighbors were irrelevant. She had only met one other woman who was thus immune to the lure of gossip—her college roommate, Katie, who later married a stockbroker and left him to move in with another woman in Old Town, in Chicago.

But why was she thinking of Chicago? Ah, yes—Damon's upcoming trip.

Now it was Saturday, and Rebecca was putting the finishing touches on the table for lunch. It was a beautiful day in Sands Point, and they would be able to eat on the veranda, which was shaded by the overhanging roof. Ruta, the cook, had made a clever little roast with Mexican seasonings that they would eat cold, along with a potato salad from Rebecca's own recipe. The wine was chilling, there were plenty of snacks for the young people, and the table had been set to look as informal as possible.

She would have done it differently if Damon were going to be here. The silverware and china would have to be their best, the wine a Montrachet or Pommard of fine vintage. Damon always expected a show of class. He never forgot who he was.

He had told Rebecca to get a good look at Dusty's beau and report back to him. "I trust your judgment," he had added flatteringly.

Privately Rebecca was relieved. Damon's presence always made her edgy. He would of course have put the young man through the wringer, for he thought no young man was good enough for Dusty. It never ceased to amaze Rebecca that Damon could muster so much possessiveness about a child in whom he had actually taken so little interest throughout her life.

She knew that Dusty had been affected by this. Rebecca was no psychologist, but she could easily imagine that the decision whether to marry a man like Damon or a lesser, quieter man must be weighing heavily on Dusty's mind. Her previous boyfriends had all seemed like compromises with the model of Damon. They were strong, confident, apparently destined for great success in life. Always Dusty had broken it off. Rebecca thought she sensed relief in her daughter each time, as though the painful experiment of choosing a man like her father was over, at least for the time being.

Rebecca stood looking out the back windows at the Sound. Sailboats were everywhere, and the day had a festive feel to it. Though it was July now, the sun seemed to have the crisp, heady optimism of June about it. Everything sparkled.

Rebecca had, as usual, planned too far ahead. There was still an hour before Dusty and the boy would come. She drummed her finger on the counter, looking out the window.

"Do it yourself this weekend!" The voice of a radio announcer, borne mysteriously from somewhere beyond the lawn, came in the window with startling clarity. A gull floated toward the house on an updraft and was gone. A dog barked.

Abruptly Rebecca decided to go out on the beach and enjoy some sun before they arrived. After all, she herself had insisted on informality. She might as well set the tone by taking off these clothes.

She went upstairs, put on the two-piece suit that was the least unflattering to her figure—this much coquetry she allowed herself in anticipation of a man's visit—threw on a silk cover-up and went out across the lawn with a blanket, a folding chair and the copy of Paul Bowles' short stories she had been reading all week.

Her house was the only one within a mile that had a stretch of actual beach behind it. Those fifty yards of sand had cost Damon a pretty penny when they bought the place, but he had insisted that the investment value more than justified the outlay.

It was indeed a glorious day. Rebecca sat on the chair with the book in her lap, then abruptly dropped the idea of reading. She spread the blanket on the sand, left the book on the chair and lay down. The sun was behind her, so she could gaze directly up into the sky, which seemed amazingly blue.

She lay staring into the intensity of color, blinking now and then. The sun warmed her like a heavy hand massaging her skin. She heard distant sounds—a child's eager shout, the sputter of a lawn mower—but they soon became part of the heated somnolence all around her. The sigh of the ocean hovered in the breeze. After a while she let her eyes close and felt the delicious mixture of hot sun and cool air contending for control of her senses.

She must have fallen asleep, for a different sort of rhythm began to rock her, and behind her closed eyes she saw confused images of people in strange places, calling out incomprehensible things to her and gesturing. A man pulled up his sleeve and showed off a dozen rosaries on his forearm. Behind him a woman with no arms was jumping up and down, braying criticisms at him.

The voice from the dream gave way to a more familiar one, coming from the beach. It was Dusty's voice. She was calling from the shore.

"Mother!" The voice was gay, laughing. "Mother!"

Rebecca opened her eyes to see two young people rushing up the beach toward her. Her sleep lingered in her eyes, making the whole scene look somewhat unreal. Dusty was dancing along the sand, her white two-piece suit showing off smooth young skin and the golden tan she had worked on all summer. Behind her, approaching more slowly, was the young man. They were both covered with water.

The sun had moved, and the boy's eyes were shadowed by his brow. He was tall, with long legs, square shoulders and a manly chest that belied his youth. He was hanging back, letting Dusty go first. His hands were at his sides. He was looking down at Rebecca.

"Oh!" She smiled. "I must have fallen asleep. How long have you children been here?"

Dusty dropped to her knees beside her mother. "We saw you out here and decided to take a swim right away. We didn't want to wake you until noon. You can't stay out here like this, Mother. You'll be burnt to a crisp!"

Rebecca looked down at her arms. They were indeed red. She did not tan easily and had not thought to put on any lotion before coming out.

"Oh, well," she said. "I needed some color anyway."

It was past time for her to speak to the young man. Dusty seemed to have forgotten her social graces, for the moment lengthened. The boy was still silhouetted against the blue waves, not moving, his eyes on Rebecca.

"You must be Mr. Delafield," Rebecca hazarded.

"Oh! Excuse me, Mother," Dusty said, flustered. "Tony, this is my mother. Mother, Tony. Forgive me."

"Not at all." Rebecca held out a hand without getting up. The young man bent to shake it.

"I'm pleased to meet you, Mrs. Lowell," he said. "Dusty has told me so much about you."

"I'm sure she has," Rebecca said with a hint of irony. "Be a gentleman, will you, and help an old woman to her feet?"

She did not know where she had found the familiarity to speak to him that way, but it seemed to charm him. He reached down to take her hand. His palm was warm, still damp from the salt water, as her fingers curled around it. She felt the hair on the back of his hand, and saw his muscles tense as he pulled her toward him.

"Thank you," she said.

The boy was silent. Her eyes were at a level with his chest. The ocean, glimpsed beyond his shoulder, looked bluer than before.

"Well, what's the plan?" Rebecca asked, looking from her

daughter to Tony and back. They made a lovely couple, the small blond girl and the tall boy with his dark hair and tawny eyes.

"We're starving," Dusty said. She glanced at Tony, who must have been saying something about it.

"Well, let's eat, by all means," Rebecca said, reaching to get the book off her chair. "It's all ready. I had the devil of a time with Ruta this morning, but..."

"Here, let me." Tony Delafield folded the chair and put it under his arm. He held out a hand for the book, which Rebecca gave up gratefully. She picked up her towel and they started toward the house.

"Are you a fan of Paul Bowles?" the young man asked.

"Yes, as a matter of fact." Rebecca smiled. "He's been a favorite of mine for many years. Since I was your age, I would imagine."

"There was a book of his on our reading list my freshman year at college," Tony said. "*The Sheltering Sky.* I never read it. I liked the title, though."

"Oh, yes, that's a good one," Rebecca said. "I haven't read it in years, but I remember it well."

"Are his short stories like his novels?" the boy asked.

"Yes... No... Not quite." Rebecca felt flustered. No one had asked her about a novel in years. "You should try them. I'm sure you'll like them. Most of them take place in North Africa. The heat and dust... They seem to have an effect on the brain. With white people, at least."

He was nodding slowly, carrying the chair. He turned the book over in his hand. She saw that the fingers were long, strong but sensitive. Everything about him said *boy,* but on the edge of virile manhood. He was walking beside her in that instant, while Dusty followed on her right. She sensed something protective about him. Enfolding, almost.

I'm imagining it, she thought, glancing from her own pale arms to the firm loveliness of Dusty, walking ahead. The young man was simply being nice to his girl's mother.

Nevertheless, she felt his attentiveness throughout lunch. Not only was he gracious and voluble in answering her questions about his family and friends, but he seemed to want to draw her out.

Many of his questions were about her own self, as opposed to her marriage or Dusty's family life.

"I know some Delafields," Rebecca said. "My mother used to see them at Northeast Harbor. Keenan and—"

"Trina," Tony helped her. "They're my father's cousins. I don't really know them. They're just names to me."

For some reason Rebecca was happy to hear this.

He ate with good appetite, just like a young man, but he had fine manners and was obviously well brought up. Dusty chaffed him about his swimming and other minor matters, and once he touched her shoulder as they joked. They did indeed make a perfect couple. They might have been matched by an expert to fit together without the slightest friction, the slightest spiritual bump.

Tony was not completely formed—that was part of his charm. One felt that something in him was hanging back from the world, not ready to commit itself to any particular future. Something tender and reedlike, yet already urgent with the male's impatience for life. No wonder Dusty was attracted to him. His eyes were almost like those of a fawn, but they penetrated.

And still—was she imagining it?—Rebecca continued to feel that personal touch, that respectful intimacy, in his questions to her. He spoke of his favorite books—*Anna Karenina* was one, *Madame Bovary* another—and seemed to solicit her approval of his taste. When Dusty chided him for one of his quirks of personality, he smiled and said to Rebecca, "Don't believe everything you hear." And he seemed determined to gain her approval, not only in her capacity as his girlfriend's mother but as a person in her own right.

"I'm terribly sorry my husband couldn't be here," she said. "He's eager to meet you."

She caught the unintended look in Dusty's eyes. Dusty was visibly glad her father wasn't here today. She obviously wanted to try Tony out on her mother first; if she could get Rebecca on Tony's side, she knew she would have a powerful weapon against any opposition her father might pose.

"Well, I understand how busy he is," the boy said. "He's an important man."

"He only thinks he is," Dusty objected. "He's really a teddy bear, underneath all his bluster."

But the boy's eyes were on Rebecca, and she felt him measuring the fact that she was married to a man of great power. Perhaps he wondered whether it was a strain for her. As indeed it was.

After lunch the children went back out for more swimming and a sail, and by the time they returned it was time for Tony to go.

"I've had a wonderful day," he said, holding out his hand. "Thank you for having me, Mrs. Lowell."

"It was a pleasure." Rebecca shook his hand. "Come back and see us. And drive carefully."

"Don't worry about that. I always go slowly." This last remark was accompanied by a sweet, strange look in his eyes. Then he was gone, walking out of the house on long legs while Dusty hurried beside him, joking with him about something or other.

Rebecca took her time clearing away the lunch things. She knew Damon would not be home until late tonight. He had called earlier to say he was dining in town. Her loneliness struck her, as it sometimes did, and she stood in the kitchen, staring out the window at the Sound.

On a whim she went back to the beach, carrying the same blanket she had had before. The sun was still high over the trees, but the light was different. Sadder, she thought. A sort of golden purple hanging over the remaining sails like a refrain that dies away in the next room. The empty beach beckoned to her.

She sat down where she had sat before—deliberately picking out the same spot. She felt a brief echo of the languor of the forenoon, but her eyes stayed open. The blue of the waves was so eloquent, so poignant.... How much the ocean had witnessed! So many eager human mornings, so many children with cries of happiness upon arrival, complaints when forced to leave. So many young lovers, those who played on the sand under the morning sun, or came after dark for guiltier meetings.

Those tumbling waves had seen it all. Not only the things that had passed before them, but those that were hoped for, dreamed of, only imagined. Was that why they seemed so sad? Or was it really sadness? Maybe it was merely the harmony of a limitless longing.

Rebecca sat for almost an hour, watching the water get bluer as the sky darkened. Then, thirsty, she decided to go back inside. But as she got up to shake out her blanket, she saw once more the image of the two laughing young people coming toward her,

Dusty's lyrical voice calling to her as the boy came behind, his eyes hidden in shadow.

Something had passed between them, she decided. Something born of his own desire to please her, to seem presentable, and of her own susceptibility. Something Dusty could scarcely have noticed. Something that had probably made no impression at all upon his busy young mind.

But enough to keep her awake tonight, she suspected.

3

It was Wednesday.

Rebecca had felt strange ever since the weekend. She was not sleeping well. Peculiar impulses, odd exultations kept her awake. She tried to lie back and watch her own thoughts march across her mind like sheep jumping a fence, but it did not work. The thoughts were too deep inside her to be held out at arm's length and examined.

What's the matter with me? she wondered.

She kept seeing Dusty coming out of the ocean with the young man. And somehow she wished she had had a son. There is intimacy and understanding in a mother's relationship with her daughter, but there is also something lacking, something that sparks a mother's fierce, contending loyalty to a boy. This was one of the many things Rebecca had missed out on in life.

She saw the boyfriend, Tony, before her mind's eye. He had held Dusty innocently, gazing at her through laughing eyes, in which a young man's touching desire not to look foolish was very visible. The son Rebecca might have wished for herself would not have been very different from this. So unlike Damon, who had never in his life had that boyish vulnerability, who was a leader of men and a rock of ambition at twenty.

Rebecca looked back on her own past. Come to think of it, there were no young men in it at all. She had never had a brother, never been close to a boy cousin. She had gone to a girls' school and, a hopeless wallflower, missed her chance to have a boyfriend during her growing-up years. Damon had come later, when she was finishing college. So she had never really been familiar with an adolescent boy. She had never thought much about them before; now they seemed exotic. Almost like creatures from another life.

Rebecca lay awake at night as usual. On Monday, she noticed

that Damon did not come home at all. She felt a surge of anger against him, though she couldn't very well confront him now, after so many years. How could he take her so obviously for granted?

She found herself reminiscing in the silent bed about her younger years. In those days she believed she could have anything, be anything. She used to float languidly on her own daydreams, never thinking to reproach herself for their fancifulness. Disappointment had not yet dimmed their luster.

As a young girl, her eyes would close at night upon the image of male arms holding her tight, male lips pressed to her own, and, like magic, all the bedclothes would metamorphose into the dream man. There was a Cinderella quality to her fantasies in those days, the more so because her waking was always like the stroke of midnight ending Cinderella's adventure.

Even the days had worn the colors of her exultation. When she got up to go to school, or to her riding lessons on the weekend, everything seemed new and fresh. The sun glinting at the window, the stirring of the lace curtain in the morning breeze—all was pungent and full of promise. The world had not yet caught its breath, not yet stifled itself, and anything could happen, anything at all.

On Tuesday Damon came home early. Perhaps he had sensed her reaction to his absence Monday night. He got into bed with her before twelve. She had already turned out her light. She felt his hand brush her shoulder, almost invitingly. She kept her eyes closed.

On Wednesday, he invited her to have lunch with him at Tre Scalini. He would sandwich her in between his morning at the firm and his afternoon meetings at city hall.

She knew why he was inviting her. He had been out in the evenings more than usual. More important, his yearly vacation with his mistress was coming up. Damon cared little about his wife's feelings, but he was sharp enough to notice when his own indifference might be offending her more than usual. Lunches like this one were his not-very-subtle way of mending fences, of keeping her under control.

It was a nice little restaurant, with fine Italian food, but Rebecca never had an appetite at noon, and even less so when she was in a restaurant. Something about all those silk suits and businessmen's tans took her appetite away completely.

"You're lucky, you know," Damon said. "I'm standing up Mayor Lazare himself for you."

"Ah." Rebecca smiled. "I'm privileged."

"I have to watch myself around him," Damon said. "He's got the manners of a coal miner and the instincts of a gutter rat. But he's not stupid. He knows how close Bob Krieg is to the governor. He's watching us all like a hawk. He's using us just as we're using him."

He sighed. "I haven't felt this tense in years. I can hardly sleep at night."

Rebecca suppressed a knowing smile. Damon's speech, an obvious plea for sympathy, turned into an involuntary admission of guilt before he could stop it. This was typical of so much conversation between himself and his wife, that they usually steered clear of references to the concrete details of life.

Rebecca never fought with Damon about his infidelity. She was a controlled person to begin with, and, as she had grown older, a certain respect for herself had made her keep herself above such things. She could do nothing about Damon's philandering, or about the humiliating figure she cut as his wife. But she could control her own behavior.

Perhaps her upbringing was coming to the fore after all these years. Her mother, though a selfish and impulse-ridden woman, had always respected herself. And her father, before his death, had been a man of impressive dignity. They were both from old Boston families, families who took themselves seriously. Ironically, Rebecca's Catholicism had come from her father, though it was he who had abandoned her and Irene.

Indeed, it had been to some extent Rebecca's dignity that had attracted Damon to her in the first place. He used to congratulate her on it during their courtship, calling her a "real woman" in comparison to the flighty girls he knew. Was he already thinking, even in those days, of what sort of woman would look good as a lawyer's wife? To this there was no answer.

At two-thirty Damon looked at his watch.

"I have to run," he said. "Would you like me to have James drop you?"

"No, thanks," she said. "I have some shopping to do."

James was the firm's limo driver. He took Damon to the LIRR, except on days when the rush hour made the trip from the firm's offices to Penn Station such a nightmare that it was easier to drive all the way home on the Long Island Expressway. Sometimes another partner or two would share the ride.

Commuting on weekdays had become harder and harder for Damon in the last decade. The apartment in town had originally been bought with this problem in mind. But as Damon's infidelity became an integral part of his domestic life, he had stayed in the city more and more. The apartment was kept scrupulously clean, but this did not prevent Rebecca from seeing signs in it of Damon's trysts with his mistress. Perhaps for this reason, Rebecca herself never slept in the apartment unless a social occasion in the city kept her too late for the long drive home.

She watched Damon get into the waiting car, which slid into the slow-moving traffic like a product dropping into a slot on an assembly line. Then she started down Fifty-eighth Street.

After only a few paces she was stopped in her tracks by the sound of a voice that was not entirely unfamiliar.

"Fancy meeting you here."

It was young Tony Delafield, looking very handsome in a dark suit and striped tie, and already holding out his hand.

"Oh!" she said, turning white. "You startled me. I didn't expect to…"

"I'm down here for an interview," he said. "A clerkship in a law firm. They'll probably tell me to drop dead, but my father claims he's put in a good word for me."

Rebecca could not help admiring him with her eyes. His crisp suit made a startling contrast to the swim trunks she had first seen him in, then the slacks and sport shirt he had put on for lunch on the Island. The beach loomed suddenly in the eyes smiling down at her, then fled away like a dream, leaving her struggling to get her bearings. For a moment she was amazed at the way people can overshoot intervals of space and time and reappear so far from their starting point, looking completely different.

She realized she was still holding the hand he had held out a long moment before. With a slight blush she let go.

"Oh, nonsense," she said. "They'll recognize an up-and-coming young man when they see one. And in that lovely suit you'll be the handsomest fellow in the room."

"You're very nice," he said. "Tell me, what are you doing in these parts?"

"I just had lunch with my husband." A rueful inflection crept into her words before she could stop it, but the boy didn't seem to notice.

"I suppose I should be sorry I missed him," he said, "but I'm not. I gather from Dusty that he isn't likely to approve of me much."

"Nonsense," Rebecca rejoined unconvincingly. "He'll like you, I'm sure." If Damon liked Tony, it would be a first.

"Listen," he said. "If you don't have anything on for the moment, why not have a cup of coffee with me? Maybe you could give me some extra courage for this interview."

Rebecca looked at her watch. Though she had other plans, the idea seemed intriguing. It would be an opportunity to get to know Dusty's beau a bit better.

"Well..." she said. Her own coyness surprised her.

"Please?" He looked as innocent as a puppy. "I'm lonely down here. I never have liked the city."

"Me, neither. All right."

He took her to a coffee shop in the same block. It was almost empty, but the jukebox was playing, too loudly, a rock song whose melody was entirely submerged by the thump of the bass.

"I read the Paul Bowles book you had on the beach the other day," Tony said.

"Already? My goodness, you are energetic." Again Rebecca heard in her own voice that gently bantering, almost maternal tone that came as though from outside her, and corresponded rather poorly with her real feelings.

"Oh, not really. I just like good books," he said, fingering the water glass on the table. "There were never any good books in our house when I was growing up. By the time I got to college I felt like somebody's country cousin."

"Don't your parents read?"

He laughed. "My father has been known to open the *New York Times,* and my mother studies *People* very closely. But no, they don't read."

"What about your sister?" Rebecca thought she recalled hearing from Dusty that he had a sister.

"Sisters, you mean. I have three."

"Three! What are their names?"

"Beth is the oldest—she's twenty-six. Then there's Judy, she's a year younger than me. Then Amy. She's sixteen."

"What's it like to have so many girls around the house?" Rebecca asked.

He shrugged. "Not so much fun. I wish I had a brother sometimes."

"Sisters can't hit as hard," Rebecca said.

"Beth did pretty well when we were small." He smiled. "But I outgrew her by the time I got into junior high. She's really not so bad," he added. "The other two are brats, though."

There was a pause. Rebecca wondered whether the girls were pretty, and whether they looked like Tony. She thought of asking him if he had a picture of them. Then she decided she would ask Dusty about them later.

"About the Paul Bowles, though," he said. "I read the first one, 'A Distant Episode.' It was very strange. I mean, the fellow just lost everything. He turned into an animal, a slave."

Rebecca struggled to remember. "Is that the one about the—the professor?"

"The professor, yes."

"Well, if you liked that one, I know you'll like *The Sheltering Sky*. There it's a woman instead of a man who does the disintegrating. I read it when I was about your age. I never forgot it."

It was a powerful, disturbing novel about a sophisticated American woman who is picked up by some nomadic Arabs in the desert and becomes the harem slave of one of them. Rebecca had been shocked, then fascinated by the woman's almost willing sacrifice of her Western ways, her descent into sexual thralldom, as she is kept a prisoner in a locked room with nothing to do all day but await the next visit of her Arab lover.

"So you're a reader," Tony observed.

"Not really. I don't claim to be literary. But I read a lot of the things one hears about."

He was looking at her steadily. She felt an impulse to mention Dusty, but something stopped her. He had steered the conversation toward things he had in common with Rebecca, and she couldn't help enjoying it.

"What else do you like?" he asked.

She shrugged. "Good movies. Art museums, sometimes—not often, I suppose. I have some Mozart records, but I'm not really musical."

"Television?" he asked.

"Now and then."

"Public TV?"

She shook her head. "Too English for me."

She felt herself blush. She watched a lot of television during her lonely evenings without Damon. Mostly she watched talk shows. Despite their cacophonous absurdity, the shouting of opinions on controversial subjects, which brought one not an inch closer to the truth, made her feel connected to the human race. Once in a while she would play an old movie she particularly liked, but increasingly she found it difficult to concentrate on such things. More and more she seemed to live life inside herself, paying almost no attention to what was around her.

"What about you?" she asked.

He shook his head, smiling. "I don't want to talk about me."

She looked down at his long fingers, cradling the cup of coffee that the girl had brought a few moments ago.

"That's an odd remark. I thought men loved to talk about themselves."

Again he gave her that odd, intent look.

"Not me," he said. "Though Dusty might tell you differently. The fact is that not much of interest has happened to me yet. School, college, a lot of loud friends... Often I think about it all, and it seems like nothing. I don't think life has really touched me yet."

This admission, coming from a young man, might not have surprised Rebecca were it not for something—or rather someone—he had left out. She could hardly bring it up, for it would make him feel tactless.

"You're being too hard on yourself," she said.

"Honest is more like it," he rejoined. "Sometimes I feel as though I've done very little with my life."

"The fact is," she said, "you have your whole life ahead of you."

There was a silence.

"I'm sorry I said that," Rebecca said. "It's a pretty heavy burden to bear, isn't it? Having your whole life ahead of you... I suppose it's thoughtless for old folks like me to envy younger people. Youth is not a picnic, after all."

He leaned forward.

"You say things very well," he said. "And you're right." He smiled wistfully. "I wish all adults saw things as you do."

She laughed. "Is that what I am? An adult... I'm afraid so."

"It doesn't sound like a compliment," he observed. "But I meant it as one."

"You're very kind."

She looked at her watch. "I really have to be going," she said. "It's been delightful seeing you this way. What a small world it is! Here you are right in the middle of Manhattan. It amazes me, the way people have the ability to be in two places at once. To me, you're still out on that beach, running toward me with Dusty beside you. Or at least you were until half an hour ago."

He had helped her with her chair, and they were almost to the door. A new song had come on the jukebox, a slow one, and this time the bass did not completely obscure the words.

Baby, I need you so much....

Rebecca smiled briefly at the eternal sentiment of youth.

When she looked at Tony, she saw that he seemed troubled.

"It's not so amazing," he said. "I knew you'd be here today."

She raised an eyebrow. "How?"

"Dusty told me. She told me you would be having lunch with your husband today. I called your housekeeper to find out which restaurant."

As they left the coffee shop, the noise of the traffic replaced the music. Rebecca heard a screech of brakes and the blurt of a horn. She looked up into his eyes.

"Then why did you...? What about your interview?" She already knew how pointless this question was.

He shook his head. "There's no interview. I wanted to see you."

"Me? Why on earth?"

He smiled. "You shouldn't have to ask that."

Rebecca turned pale.

"You can't be serious."

He moved closer. He was tall enough that his chest was on a level with her face.

"That's a silly thing to ask. I've never been more serious in my life."

"But..."

Her daughter's name came to her lips, and with it Dusty's blond hair, her trusting face. Then the white woman in the novel, waiting in her cage for her handsome Arab captor to come back to her... Her hands shook.

"I won't press," he said. "Try not to think too badly of me. But I had to tell you now. I would have burst otherwise."

She looked up into his face. The pain in it impressed her. He was serious.

"I'm very flattered," she said, struggling to muster the easy tone she had managed earlier. "But you'd better go home and forget about this."

He laughed. "No chance."

She stepped back a pace, but it only made him seem nearer. Pedestrians surged around them like fish in a stream.

"What about you?" he asked. "Will you forget?"

"For your sake, I will," she said. "Don't you realize what you're saying? What you're putting at risk? There are more people than just yourself to think about."

"I've already thought about that," he said. "Too much. But it didn't work."

Rebecca frowned. He seemed to have been through stages she knew nothing about, and made his decision long since. Now he was asking her to leap over all the intermediate stages and join him in his passion. Time speeded up in his urging. She felt cornered.

"I have to go now," she said. "Please don't speak of this again."

She felt something in her hand. It was his wrist. She had taken hold of it without realizing it. Hastily she let go of him. The traffic seemed much louder now.

"I'll do anything you want," he said. "But you have to know. That's why I had to see you. Just knowing that you know—it will help me."

Rebecca was trembling. The hand that had been around his wrist felt burned. She looked this way and that, avoiding his eyes.

"Shall I get you a cab?" he asked.

She shook her head, more in confusion than in refusal. She looked at him one last time and saw Dusty in her mind's eye.

Then she turned on her heel and walked away. The Don't Walk sign stopped her at the corner of Fifth Avenue, and she didn't have the presence of mind to turn left and get out of his sight. She waited, surrounded by pedestrians. Their voices rang hollow in her ears.

"They can't win a game to save their lives...."

"They're all on cocaine, anyway."

A bus whined heavily. A truck's brakes screeched, sending a shock through Rebecca's body. At last the light turned green.

She stepped into the street, feeling the wetness of an unseen puddle soak the toe of her shoe. She hurried on, but paused halfway to look back. Tony had not moved. He was gazing at her from his place on the sidewalk. She heard the impatient mutter of a pedestrian urging her forward. She faced front and crossed the street.

4

Only two weeks remained before the party. Rebecca was kept busy by a thousand errands. She shopped for a new dress. She decided she needed new napkins, and went to half a dozen stores before finding something at a place on Fifth Avenue called Métisse. She noticed that the living room upholstery was looking soiled and had it cleaned on a rush basis by a firm in town. Then she tried the napkins on the table, and the tablecloth looked shabby. She bought a new one, only to find that, with all that new napery on the table, the dining room chairs looked dull. She called the upholstery cleaner back and had them cleaned as well.

She worried about her looks. She understood this new involvement with Mayor Lazare was important to Damon. She went to Sally and asked about a new perm for the occasion. She bought some fresh makeup. She fought the feeling that her own frumpiness would hurt Damon with his political associates. She had the desperate feeling of trying to make herself over in two breathless weeks, after letting herself go for twenty years.

She thought little of Tony Delafield. When she did, she reddened and shook her head. His infatuation was absurd in itself and an insult to Dusty. Rebecca was too offended for her daughter to feel flattered on her own account.

The whole episode seemed unreal as she recalled it. Despite his obvious passion, Tony had seemed like a character in a play. This made his behavior more distressing.

She would have to get Dusty to stop seeing him. This thought, the tail end of her ruminations, stood out with impressive clarity. Obviously she could not allow her daughter to continue to dally with him under the circumstances, much less to marry him. The situation was outrageous.

But things would have to be handled delicately. Dusty was

clearly attached to Tony; all her behavior suggested that she considered him a serious marriage prospect. Things had gone far. Perhaps too far already.

On the other hand, Dusty trusted her mother. This meant that a very subtle, very judicious refusal to approve of Tony, on Rebecca's part, might carry weight. Enough weight to break up the relationship? Perhaps not. But enough to plant a seed of doubt. And with time, with growing up, with the inevitable presence of other boys, Dusty might make her choice elsewhere.

Yes, in that way things would work out. Why was it, then, that this very notion troubled Rebecca so deeply? As though the very fact of separating her daughter from this boy must ratify the hidden, the unspeakable truth about him. It all maddened Rebecca.

Ever since her fateful encounter with Tony she had been alone. Damon kept going to more and more meetings, calling to cancel lunch, then dinner, then evening plans. Dusty had not called since the day of Tony's visit for lunch, when she had asked Rebecca what she had thought of Tony. Rebecca, unfortunately, had spoken highly of him, saying she thought he was a fine young man. At the time she was under the sway of his friendly interest in her, and her absurd wish that she herself had a son. She could not have known what was coming.

When Rebecca ran out of things to do, she wandered around the house like a caged animal, as though waiting for something. She read magazines, watched talk shows, but found she could concentrate on them only to the extent of noticing how empty were the lives of those who confided their secrets in public. How little self-respect there was in the world of women! How dependent they were on men for almost every impression, every emotion.

In the end she turned off the television. It was an even more insulting mirror of herself than the one in the dressing room.

Once the phone rang when she was sitting in silence in her bedroom. She picked it up.

"Hello?"

The caller said nothing. There was silence on the line, just lengthy enough to betray a human intention on the other end. She was about to say hello again when she stopped, brought up short by the crazy idea that it was *him* calling. She held the phone to her ear, listening to the secret silence. Then she hung it up.

A wrong number, she decided. A burglar casing the house. A breather, waiting for the sound of fear in her voice before starting in on her. Waiting for the tremor in which he would find his compliance.

At this thought, Rebecca's hand began to shake. She got up, wandered the bedroom, then the whole house. It seemed to close around her like that plastic shrink wrap they put around items in the store. She could not breathe.

She kept thinking it was her duty as a mother to separate Dusty from this boy. What a scandal if they were to marry, and she, the mother, knew his awful secret! This thought gave her no peace.

Perhaps because of it, her insomnia was worse than ever. She began to toss and turn almost as soon as she lay down. A soft, recurrent thrum, almost like the beating of her own heart, kept her mind working when it should sleep. Rumination about Dusty was a curse. She could not stop thinking about it.

Her fatigue was beginning to color things with a strange uncanny light. Nothing seemed quite real. Familiar things looked sharp but distant, like objects viewed through eyeglasses with the wrong prescription. When she reached out a hand to touch a light switch or a knickknack, her arm seemed a mile long.

One afternoon, desperate with fatigue, she took a sleeping pill and lay down at noon, hoping to sleep until three. She tossed and turned for an hour, the upset in her senses fighting off the effect of the pill. Then she drifted bumpily into sinister dreams, like a somnambulist staggering down a flight of stairs.

In her dream she was back in her parents' cottage by Lake Angela. She had swum out to the float with David Plummer, the boy from down the lake, and they were sunbathing together. In reality David had never noticed her existence, but in the dream he was taking off his suit, lying nude on the float, and his hand was creeping up her rib cage, fondling her breast.

The float was rocking crazily, and the movement throbbed deep inside her—one, two, one, two—until the ringing of the phone woke her. She seized the receiver without thinking. But it occurred to her that it was the anonymous caller again, and she stifled the "Hello" on her lips. It came out as a gasp that echoed in the silence on the line.

"Mother? Is that you?"

It was Dusty.

"Oh! Hello, dear." Rebecca spoke through halting breaths.

"Are you all right? Did I get you at a bad time?"

"No. No, sweetie. I was just coming in from outside. How are you?"

"Great." This was a word Dusty rarely used, and it impressed Rebecca. "Mother, could I bring Tony over for dinner on Friday night?"

"Friday?" Rebecca tried to remember what was on for this weekend. "Let me go down to the kitchen and check my calendar...."

"I already spoke to Daddy. He loves the idea. He said he was definitely going to be home, anyway." Dusty sounded excited.

"Really?" Rebecca ran a hand over her brow. "Well, that settles it. By all means bring Tony over. But don't feel you have to dress up. We're—"

"I know. Just simple folks. Don't worry about it. How about six o'clock?"

"Whenever you get here we'll start the party." Rebecca mustered her usual humor with difficulty.

"Terrific. I love you, Mother."

After hanging up, Rebecca lay back and considered the situation. The lingering effects of her sleeping pill had vanished, and she found herself occupied with thoughts of surprising cunning. She was glad that Damon was to meet Tony. For one thing, it would remind the young man that Dusty had a powerful, protective father. That Rebecca had a husband whom she loved, who loved her, a man not to be trifled with. Why, she could even show some extra affection to Damon, just for the boy's benefit. And Damon, of course, routinely showered Rebecca with little hugs and smiles and caresses. This would make a good impression.

But there was more. It was likely that Damon would not be thrilled by Tony. After all, he had never liked one of Dusty's beaux yet. And Tony was too undecided, not ambitious enough to suit Damon. Damon would come down against him. This would impress Dusty. (Of course, there was always the possibility that Damon's opposition would make Dusty dig in her heels about Tony, but Rebecca chose not to think about that at the moment.)

Rebecca hoped for an uncomfortable evening, an evening in

which the family would seem united by its own structure, shutting out Tony. For the family did have, after all, a structure. It was perhaps not the healthiest or closest family in the world, but even its weaknesses gave it a certain intimacy. This would make Tony feel like an outsider, an interloper.

It did not work out that way. Tony showed up wearing a handsome sport jacket and tie, and looking, after all, quite manly. Damon invited him into his study for a drink, and the two conversed in quiet voices while the women busied themselves in the kitchen.

By the time dinner was served, Rebecca easily guessed that Damon had taken a liking to Tony. Unexpectedly, it was Tony's very gentleness, his boyishness, that had somehow touched Damon. Unlike Dusty's other suitors, who were so obviously cut from the same masculine cloth as Damon, Tony was less formed, more innocent. And Damon apparently found this attractive.

"I'm going to put in a good word for this young man with some friends of mine," Damon said proudly. "He needs a bit of a push, that's all."

Despite her exasperation, Rebecca could not help feeling a prohibited thrill of pride, as though it were she herself who had brought the young man home for Damon's approval.

True, she saw signs of tension in Damon when he saw Tony and Dusty together in an affectionate posture. But he seemed to overcome his own emotion, mustering a booming fatherly enthusiasm that Rebecca found more than a little out of character for him.

The evening was spent in considerable warmth and levity, with Rebecca herself the only one a little remote. Dusty was clearly thrilled that her father liked Tony.

"Aren't they great together?" she asked her mother in the kitchen. "I'm so relieved. You know how Daddy is."

Damon, for his part, found a moment alone with Rebecca to murmur, "Quite an improvement over her usual type, isn't he? I like him."

Rebecca had resigned herself to this progress of things when her worst fear suddenly came to pass.

She was upstairs after dinner, just coming out of her bedroom, when she bumped into Tony.

"I'm sorry," he said. "Dusty said the bathroom was right here. But I'm not good at finding things."

"Oh, it's this crazy old house." Rebecca smiled, turning on the hall light. "It's right around that corner there—right where no one can find it. You're not the first, believe me."

She was edging past him, perhaps half expecting what was to come, when he touched her hip and stopped her.

"This is killing me," he murmured.

And he kissed her with stealthy tenderness, on her lips. The kiss was chaste, but the young scent of him suffused her.

She stood frozen as he withdrew from her. She heard the bathroom door close. She descended the staircase on trembling legs.

So it was all a lie, then. This lovely evening, this mutual admiration, this happy family welcoming a daughter's beau with open arms.

All a lie. And the awful truth, the truth Rebecca had spent a week struggling with, was on her lips at this very moment.

When she reached the bottom of the stairs, she saw Dusty and Damon smiling up at her conspiratorially. The family was registering its favorable impression of the evening. Rebecca could not bear it more than an instant and hurried into the kitchen, where she waited until she heard Tony come back downstairs.

After that the evening drew toward its conclusion with all the grace of a stage play. Dusty showed Tony the old family albums. Damon smoked a cigar and told Tony about Dusty's girlhood. Tony talked about his own family, his sisters. At Damon's request he produced a photo and showed it around. When it was passed to Rebecca she stared unseeing at the faces in the image, and felt Tony's eyes on her.

Then the children said good-night and left.

And, tonight of all nights, Damon wanted to make love.

They were in the bedroom, and he put his arms around Rebecca. His hands slid down her back to her waist, and he drew her closer to him.

"It's been a long time," he said. "Too long."

The hands knew her well, though they seemed like strangers after all this time. He helped her off with her slip, removed his clothes quickly and turned out the light.

Then he came to her, expert in his caresses, but predictable, touching the same parts of her as always, lingering just the same amount of time over each contact. Yet he seemed more excited, somehow. His breath came rapidly, and almost at once he was inside her.

Rebecca felt nothing. Nothing at all. Damon might as well be a noise in the next room, so little did his touch affect her. Until, toward the end, he brushed her lips with his own, an unaccustomed sign of affection in the midst of the rising rhythms.

Suddenly a spasm came out of her, almost painful, shaking her body and bestowing itself on the soft touch of those lips, even as everything else he did remained a million miles away.

So the evening ended for Rebecca.

5

The hottest days had waited for the end of summer, and they now spread across the sky like long, slow-motion flames. The city sweltered. Stalled traffic was a nightmare in the blazing heat. There were brownouts all over the five boroughs and Long Island.

Rebecca stayed inside and kept the air-conditioning on. In recent years she had begun to find air-conditioning uncomfortably cold. But now she delighted in it.

She wanted to feel cold. The heat exploding outside was like a loud noise in her thoughts. She sought peace, silence, immobility. She scoured her bookshelves, in search of the coldest book she could find. She almost picked out *Madame Bovary,* but chose Flaubert's *Temptation of Saint Anthony,* instead. She had read it in college and hadn't opened it since. The yellow paperback looked like a museum piece, grayed by age. She felt sure it could not touch her in any way.

She sat down in the study—avoiding the solarium, which seemed too close to the heat—and read. The French did not come back to her easily, and Flaubert's peculiarly turbid style, with its rich vocabulary, was difficult for her. But she enjoyed the effort, for it seemed to free her mind from everything else.

Dusty telephoned on Tuesday with happy news.

"Tony's going to take me with his family to Aspen in October," she said. "They go every year. I'll only have to miss one Friday of school. Please, Mother, can I go?"

"I'll have to ask your father," Rebecca said. "But I'm sure you can go, dear. Just don't break any bones."

Dusty was excited in more ways than one. School was about to start. It was her senior year, and all her courses except one were in her journalism major. As far as Rebecca knew, Dusty was planning to apply to graduate school. But Dusty had been conspicuously silent on that subject since she met Tony. Rebecca couldn't help suspecting that marriage plans might get in the way of graduate school.

Dusty had met Tony's parents, who she said were a little dull but otherwise presentable, and who liked her. She had by now concluded that both her own parents liked Tony. And she herself had apparently solidified her feelings for him.

All this left Rebecca out on a limb. She had already resolved to use her own influence to get Dusty to give up Tony. But since the fateful dinner, at which Damon took so immediate a liking to Tony, she had felt that an inexorable process was under way that she could not arrest single-handedly. Dusty was even more committed to Tony now that she knew Damon liked him. She glowed with excitement.

Rebecca was the only one who knew Tony's guilty secret. As a mother, she could not countenance her daughter's marriage to such a person. Yet everyone else was applauding the match. It would seem tactless to try to pour cold water on it. And if Dusty married him...

The very idea made Rebecca shudder. She imagined family visits, holidays, grandchildren even—and always the significant look in her son-in-law's eyes, perhaps a stolen word, a forbidden caress every now and again, just to remind her of the terrible truth. And, worst of all, that very truth seething inside her own brain as she tried to play the innocent role of a proud mother.

So Rebecca hid away from the heat and from her own thoughts. She read her Flaubert, feeling her lost collegiate self coming faintly to life as she slogged through vocabulary she had once looked up in her Larousse dictionary. It was a self very different from Dusty, she reflected, a self that had never known the candid exhilaration that Dusty was feeling now. And yet, in another way, not so different.

It grew hotter and hotter, ninety-seven degrees during the last week in August, the whole city fainting. Rebecca grew colder.

Toward Labor Day the heat began to diminish. The temperature dipped below ninety, and there were reports that real cooling was on the way.

Rebecca had not seen Dusty in more than a week. The loneliness would have weighed heavily upon her at any other time, but now she wanted to be alone, to keep the world at arm's length.

On Tuesday she decided to go down to the beach with her copy of Flaubert and a blanket. She had had so little sun in the last few weeks that what little tan she had was almost gone. She wanted to put a bit of color back into her face before the party.

Damon would be home tonight for dinner. She was cooking his favorite roast and had had the meat marinating since last night. She was looking forward to his company. His news about the Hightower goings-on would distract her.

The phone rang as she was on her way down the lawn. She hurried back in and caught it on the fourth ring. It was Damon.

"Rebecca, I'm going to have to stay in town tonight. Lazare pulled a dinner meeting on us at the last minute."

"Oh," Rebecca said. "Well, I guess it can't be helped."

"I hate the idea of missing that roast," he said. "You must have been working hard on it."

She knew he was lying. His solicitude was out of character for him. He would be with his mistress tonight.

"I can freeze it," she said.

"You sound out of breath," Damon said.

"I was on my way down to the beach. I had to run back to answer the phone."

"I'll tell you what," he said. "Why don't you meet me in town tomorrow night? We can have a late supper after I finish with Lazare. That will give me something to look forward to."

Now Rebecca *knew* he was lying. She had to smile at his cajolerie.

"All right," she said.

"Good. See you tomorrow, then." Already he sounded distant, preoccupied with whatever he had on hand.

Rebecca hung up the phone, took the roast out of the refrigerator and threw it in the trash.

Then she went down to the beach.

The breeze seemed cool enough, but the sun was blazing hot. It was one of those days when the rays actually seem to bite at one's skin right through the cooling air. She thought of abandoning her plan, but finally decided to lie down, anyway. She read her book for a few moments, then closed her eyes. She had been wrestling with too many thoughts these past weeks, all of them leading to dead ends.

At length she lay back and put her arms at her sides. She had been lying just like this, asleep, the day Dusty had first brought Tony here to lunch....

Dreams began to billow inside her, full of sand and heat. She saw Saint Anthony against a biblical sky, opposing his faith to the tauntings of a thousand demons, tormented by his own bad conscience, which endlessly repeated, *"Even your resistance to temptation is nothing but pride in disguise!"* She saw the Moroccan desert and the bus carrying Paul Bowles' heroine, the bus leading deeper and deeper into the Arab world, where eventually she would throw off her pride and live quietly as a caged slave, waiting for her master to visit her for sex.

The dreams hovered briefly as images, then traced themselves on the surface of her mind like arguments. One owed it to oneself to fight off the demons; one had been brought up that way. And one's upbringing was like a cornerstone planted in the earth. On the other hand, the earth was only sand, really, shifting sand that slipped away under one's feet. And the very ramparts to which one clung were already eroding away in the wind, solid only as sand themselves....

Rebecca began to sink deeper into sleep. She felt relief. Let the sun burn her skin, then. She did not care. She only wanted to sleep. And she would sleep alone tonight.

She heard a faint sound in the sand and felt a shadow fall between her and the sun. Then the touch of soft lips on her own. A touch she recognized.

She opened her eyes a crack. The young man was crouched over her, quite delicately, touching her only with his lips. The sun hid behind his face, which was a silhouette, incredibly close yet featureless.

"I knew you would come."

He kissed her again, and then, tenderly, moved his lips across her cheek, along her brow, and down into the hollow of her neck.

A sudden breeze flipped the paper cover of the book open. His kiss brushed her collarbone, then the swell of her breast. She reflected that everything had conspired to bring her to this moment, his long silence, her daughter's hopes, her own evasions, even the turgid old French in the book that had belonged to her when she was Dusty's age. And now the seething sun and salt breeze were urging her surrender. She felt his lips wanting to know her as she had never known herself.

Even your resistance is only pride....

A second breeze, stronger than the first, blew the book shut.

"Come on," he whispered. "We're going inside."

"Ruta..."

"She's not there. The house is empty. Come on, Rebecca."

It was the first time he had spoken her name. She opened her eyes now and saw his face. It was handsomer than before, rendered innocent by desire.

Her body felt innocent, too. More innocent than at any time in her life. It was getting up already, accepting his helping hand. And she followed along behind, the sin following in her mind where alone it grew, free from the innocence of the flesh, free to grow on forever.

She let him lead her into the house.

6

On Wednesday night, after a long evening spent in Alison Shore's arms, Damon Lowell came home to his Park Avenue co-op expecting to find Rebecca waiting for him.

Damon was tired. He had spent nearly six straight weeks in meetings with the mayor's attorneys and assistants, trying to devise a financial plan for the Hightower project that would work. But the mayor's people were flunkies and yes-men, so beholden to political bosses that their proposals invariably led to delays, bottlenecks and financial eviscerations of the project.

The governor was behind the project for reasons of his own and had made available some of his best people, most of whom Damon knew. But the mayor hated the governor more than anyone and intended to use Hightower as the basis of his campaign against the governor next year. He was never happy with any solution unless it could be seen as damaging to the governor as well as good for the city. In the Hightower case it was simply not possible to accomplish these two purposes at one time.

So it was a delicate, nerve-racking process. Damon had to try to nudge the mayor into a more reasonable position without telling his army of acolytes to their faces what fools they were. This was politics. Damon was no stranger to it. Over the years he had dealt with many fragile egos, both within the firm and among important clients. A lawyer's education includes a bedside manner. But he had never had to deal with such patent idiocy before, and it was hard on his nerves.

Of course, he enjoyed being the center of attention. His picture was in the newspapers at least once a week, along with stories about his skills as a "mediator" and "troubleshooter." Hightower was bringing him into contact with the power brokers in Congress as well as the White House. If the project was successful, he would be a clear choice for high appointive office, probably at the federal level.

Nevertheless, the whole thing was taking its toll on him. His nerves were so frayed by day's end that he had not been able to face the evening without seeing Alison. He had met her at her place on Riverside Drive, and they enjoyed a quiet dinner, then a brandy and sex. These trysts were less for excitement than for soothing his nerves. Alison knew it and did her part very well.

Damon felt guilty about spending so much time away from home. Dusty needed him, now that she had a serious young man. And there was Rebecca. He had noticed a distance in her lately. She seemed worried, remote. That was why he had made love to her the other week. If he could just keep things together until Dusty's school year started, he would be free and clear for his vacation with Alison. Then he would be able to get in some real relaxation.

Tonight he was looking forward to seeing Rebecca. He had a notion to make love to her again. It might get him on her good side, which was important with the party coming up. Moreover, something about their encounter last week had intrigued him. She had made love differently, though he could not tell precisely how. Something about her was more remote, and yet more physical. He wanted to see if it would happen again.

But when he left work he could not resist paying a visit to Alison. She greeted him in her negligee and they made love. It left him so tired that he fell asleep for an hour. When he awoke she gave him a drink. He called Rebecca to say he was delayed, but there was no answer. Perhaps she was in the shower, he thought.

"How's it going with Lazare?" Alison asked, sipping her brandy.

"Crazier than ever," Damon said. "I've been around temperamental clients for many years, but I've never seen logic destroyed so completely by egos before. Never."

He touched his lover's thigh with a languid finger.

"The odd thing is," he said, "that Lazare likes me. I can't figure out why. He tells me dirty jokes. He nearly begs me to play golf with him every Sunday. And he's the worst golfer I've ever seen."

"He needs a friend with clean habits," Alison joked. "You

should be happy that he's picked you. I'll bet you're the first Harvard man he's ever taken into his confidence.''

Mayor Lazare was a coarse, sensual fellow, but he possessed an enormous vitality. He seemed to play himself off against Damon's coolness of manner, and, in a peculiar way, to solicit Damon's approval. He knew Damon came from the same society as the governor—both were Harvard men, Porcellians, and members of clubs that, even now, the mayor knew better than to apply for membership to—and he liked to feel that Damon was on his side because of Hightower.

Sometimes he would take Damon aside to tell him a particularly filthy story about his own sexual past. He made it look as though he had personally bedded every female in city government over the last twenty years. Damon had to force an obliging smile. The stories made him nervous, because his affair with Alison was common knowledge, and this perhaps emboldened Lazare to speak to him man-to-man.

"It makes my skin crawl just to be in a room with him, sometimes," Damon said.

"I've heard that before," Alison said. "He's like a force of nature. That's how he got where he is. Even the people who hate him the most can't resist him.''

This remark made Damon a bit uncomfortable, though he did not know why. He turned to hug Alison. He loved the feel of her body. She was older now, she looked almost fortyish, but this was part of her charm. Something womanly and nurturing had come to join itself to the sexiness that had first drawn him to her. He had recently begun to think more seriously about divorcing Rebecca to be with Alison. He needed to be with a woman who understood him.

And if, later on, Alison was a bit too old to give him everything he needed physically, there were younger women for that. He had noticed in the last couple of years that the sight of young girls started a painful ache in his loins, as much from admiration of their youth as from mere lust. Sometimes he even felt uncomfortable when he was with Dusty, though her resemblance to Rebecca had always kept her from being attractive to him.

Well, marrying Alison was not a problem. The problem was Rebecca. She would be terribly hurt, of course. Now that Dusty was of age there was no question of custody. But he honestly did not want to hurt Rebecca. Then, too, there were his political ambitions. Divorce would have to be handled delicately. The timing would have to be just right.

To some extent, Rebecca's cooperation would be required. Perhaps even her advice. He had often depended on her tact in the past. He would need it now. But she would hardly refuse it. She was, above all, a generous woman. He had given her twenty-three good years. He had taken care of her. And she was not, truth to tell, so fine a catch. She owed him.

This thought was in his mind as he returned to the apartment. The doorman, William, tipped his cap to Damon.

"Good evening, sir."

"Hello, William. Have you seen Mrs. Lowell tonight?"

"Not tonight, sir. I came on at six, though. She might have arrived earlier."

"That must be it."

Damon took the elevator upstairs and let himself into the apartment.

"Rebecca?" he called. "Sorry I was held up. Where are you?"

The apartment was dark. He walked quickly through it, turning on lights in his passage. There was no sign of Rebecca.

Damon stood thinking. Where on earth was she?

There could not have been a misunderstanding about their plan for tonight. Rebecca had been quite clear about it on the phone yesterday.

He went into the kitchen and looked at the pad beside the phone. There was no note. He scowled. Had it not been for his belief that Rebecca was here waiting for him, he could have spent more time with Alison.

He picked up the wall phone in the kitchen and called the Long Island house. He waited, listening to the distant ring repeat itself twice, three times, four times. Then the answering machine picked up and he heard his wife's voice.

"Hello. No one can come to the phone at the moment, but if you'll leave your name and number, we'll return your call as soon as we can."

The beep sounded. Damon cleared his throat.

"Hello, this is me," he said. "I'm in town. I thought you'd be here. Are you there?"

Silence. No one picked up the phone.

"Rebecca, are you there?" Damon allowed an edge of anger to sound in his voice. Still no one picked up.

"Rebecca, this is..." The machine hung up, interrupting him.

What was going on? Was Irene sick again? Whatever it was, he was far too tired to deal with it now. This had been a killing day. He would take a shower, try Rebecca one more time, and then go to bed.

But the phone suddenly rang, sending a shock through him. He had not let go of the receiver. He brought it to his ear.

"Hello?"

"Daddy?"

It was Dusty.

"Dusty! What are you doing calling us at this hour?"

"I was just hoping to talk to Mother." Dusty sounded upset. She had never been good at hiding her feelings. Something was wrong.

"Oh. I..." Suddenly the falseness of his position struck Damon. How could he tell Dusty he didn't know where Rebecca was?

"Well, she's not here at the moment, honey," he said. "Is it something I can help you with?"

"I just called home and there was no answer," Dusty said. There was a quiver in her voice. "I really wanted to speak with her."

Damon shrugged and shook his head. God damn, Rebecca!

"Well, to tell you the truth I don't know where she is. I got in just a minute ago expecting to find her, and she wasn't here. We were supposed to have dinner." He looked around him at the empty kitchen. "I called the house, and she doesn't pick up. There's nothing but the machine."

There was a silence.

"You mean she didn't leave you a note or anything?" Dusty asked.

"Nothing. I don't understand it myself."

"I—so you don't know where she is?"

Damon smiled. "I'm sure she's all right. She probably just made a plan and forgot to tell me about it. She'll turn up. Why don't you get some sleep, and I'll have her call you in the morning. From wherever she is."

"Well..."

"Don't worry, Dusty. I'll take care of everything. You just get some sleep."

Reluctantly his daughter followed his advice. Damon spent another ten minutes worrying about his wife, then took a shower, swallowed an Ambien and went to bed.

He slept poorly and woke up with burning eyes at seven. He somehow recalled Ruta's home phone number and dialed it on the bedside phone. Ruta knew nothing of her mistress's whereabouts. She was just dressing to go to the house to begin work for the dinner party.

Damon called the house two more times while he was dressing, then went to the office. A mountain of work was waiting. He had a lunch date with Tom Blackman and the others. This would be a long day, and he had slept little.

He told his secretary to get his wife on the phone. His first meeting kept him forty-five minutes. Then he touched the intercom.

"Nancy, did you find Mrs. Lowell?"

"No, sir. There's no answer in town, and I spoke to the housekeeper at your home, and she said she hasn't seen Mrs. Lowell."

At these words Damon realized for the first time that he had better start covering up. If something was wrong—something embarrassing—he could not have his secretary knowing about it.

"That's all right," he said. "I know where she is. I'll call her myself."

A few minutes later, when he had a moment alone, he called Ruta at the house.

"Isn't there any sign of her?" he asked. "No note?"

"Not that I can find, sir. Didn't she tell you where she was going?"

Again the prudent instinct to cover up seized Damon. Despite his worry, he knew he must move cautiously.

"We just got our signals crossed," he said. "Go on with your work, Ruta. One of us will be in touch later on."

"Yes, sir." Ruta sounded dubious.

Enraged, Damon spent the rest of the morning in meetings that seemed to drag on endlessly. Before lunch he called Irene in Sarasota. She sounded suspicious, because he was not in the habit of calling her. He inquired after her health, and asked if she had heard from Rebecca recently.

"Not since last week," Irene said.

"Did she seem upset?"

"I wouldn't say so," Irene said. "She copes well, as you know."

Damon grimaced at this innuendo.

"Well, take care of yourself. I'm sure she'll be calling before the week is out."

"Goodbye, Damon." Irene's voice was not warm. She had never really liked Damon and, of course, knew about Alison.

After lunch he called Mimi Parker and asked if she had heard from Rebecca. No, she said, not since the day before yesterday. He told her he was looking forward to the party and rang off.

He called Alison to tell her he would be late tonight. At the end of the day he had himself driven out to the Island to satisfy himself. The house was silent. Ruta had finished her work and left. Dishes and other things for the party were piled all over the kitchen.

There was no trace of Rebecca.

Damon looked into her closet. He couldn't tell if anything was missing. She had a lot of clothes, like most women, and he hadn't paid any attention to them in years. The same went for her suitcases. Damon couldn't even clearly recall what they looked like.

He was standing in the bedroom, worry mingling with increasing anger in his mind, when the phone rang. For once he didn't wait to hear the caller's voice on the machine. He just picked up.

"Hello."

"Oh, Dad. It's you."

It was Dusty. She sounded more upset, if anything, than last night.

"Have you found her yet?" she asked.

"No, honey. I'm afraid not." Damon was too angry to hide the truth from Dusty. He took the cordless phone into the bathroom. Rebecca's cosmetics were on the vanity as usual. If any of them were missing, he could not tell.

Then he glanced at his own things and noticed that something was different. The silver pill case Rebecca had given him a few years ago was not on the counter as usual.

He opened the medicine cabinet. The case was on the shelf. Under it was a note. In that instant it occurred to Damon that Rebecca had put it there because she knew Ruta never opened the cabinet.

Dusty was saying something as he opened the note, but he didn't hear it.

"Just a second, honey."

Holding the phone against his shoulder, he opened the note.

Dear Damon,
I've left. Sorry for the pain.

R.

Damon stood looking at the note. His mouth hung open in disbelief. The significance of the silver case hidden away in the cabinet was just dawning on him.

Dusty's voice sounded more urgent now, almost hysterical.

"Sorry, dear," he said, holding the note. "What were you saying?"

"Daddy, Tony is gone. He's disappeared."

7

For Damon, the next three days were torture.

The worst thing about the situation was that he was alone in his knowledge of what had happened and could confide in no one. Indeed, the crucial thing was to keep the truth a secret. This was the worst possible time in his career for even a hint of marital trouble, not to mention his wife walking out on him. If word of it got out, his relationship with the mayor, and even with the firm, might be compromised.

Then there was Dusty to think about. He wondered how long he could delay telling her the truth.

He put that problem aside. He was no match for it at the moment. Instead he concentrated on creating a cover story.

"Nancy," he told his secretary, "Call the partners one by one for me, will you? Tell them that Rebecca's mother is very ill. Rebecca has gone down to Florida to help take care of her."

"I'm sorry to hear that, sir."

"Thanks."

Damon breathed a bit easier. It was a perfect story, because Irene's illness was well known to everyone in the firm.

The next concern was the mayor and the Hightower people. Damon reached for the phone a dozen times to tell his secretary to cancel the dinner party. But in the end his lawyer's instincts took over. He decided to go ahead with the party, but to tell everyone that Rebecca was hoping to be present. Then, when she did not appear, her absence would bring sympathy Damon's way. He could actually use it to his advantage.

Damon knew a reliable detective agency, Hamlin Associates, which had been used by the firm over the years. He spoke to Dick Hamlin, the president, and explained the situation.

"Rebecca is gone," he said. "There's no possibility of foul play. She—left a note. But I need to know where she is."

"Did she give you any warning?" Dick asked.

"None at all," Damon said. "She's been slightly moody, but that's pretty normal for her."

"Was she angry about anything? Did you quarrel?"

"No. We haven't had a quarrel in years," Damon said with a touch of pride in his tranquil marriage. "That's why this has me worried."

Dick sent an operative to look at the house and the apartment. The fellow was very thorough and discreet. He found evidence that Rebecca had taken some clothes and cosmetics. She seemed to have packed in a hurry.

She had also taken ten thousand dollars from their joint savings account and had been into the safety deposit box, taking some jewelry and the negotiable securities that were in her name.

Damon told Dick Hamlin to find Rebecca and report on her whereabouts, but to make no effort to bring her back. Damon himself would handle that.

Now Damon had no choice but to tell Dusty the truth. He called her that same night, after the detective left.

"I don't know why, honey, but she's gone away," he said. "She took some money and some clothes. I wouldn't worry too much about it. I suspect she simply had some things she wanted to think over and wanted to be alone. I'm sure she'll get in touch soon. I'll keep you informed."

Dusty seemed shaken, almost out of control. She had no news about her boyfriend. He was still missing. Damon did not take this very seriously.

"Have you spoken to his parents?" he asked.

"Yesterday," she said. "They don't know anything. His mother is frantic. I can't understand it."

"Well, keep me informed," Damon said. "If I can help in any way I'll be happy to."

"All right, Daddy."

Damon had not attached any significance to the coincidence between his wife's disappearance and that of young Tony Delafield. He saw it as a confusing factor that he had to continually brush aside, mentally, in order to clear his mind for the more immediate challenge posed by Rebecca's absence.

By now he was beginning to understand the implications of her departure. Things had been wrong in their marriage, very wrong. He had been remiss as a husband. He had taken Rebecca more and more for granted in the past few years. He had scarcely bothered to conceal his relationship with Alison. Rebecca's life had been hard and getting harder. She had lost her father when she was still a girl, and now her mother, to whom she was attached, was very ill. She was herself getting older. Middle age was never easy for a woman. She had not complained when Dusty left for college, but Damon had noticed that Dusty's absence seemed to have taken something out of her. She seemed lonely.

These reflections soothed Damon, for they helped him to understand an event that, at first, had seemed insane, incomprehensible. Now his lawyer's mind could grasp Rebecca's state of mind, could account for it and deal with it.

And the more he felt he understood it, the more sure he was that, sooner or later, she would be back.

"She's simply not the sort of woman to walk away from a marriage and a daughter without a backward glance," he said aloud to himself as he paced the apartment. "That's not Rebecca."

Some sort of extreme inner pain must have driven her away. But her need for love, for her family, would bring her back. He was sure of it.

"It's only a matter of time," he repeated to himself. "A matter of time."

In the meantime he had to face something he had never dreamed of facing: the first painful days as an abandoned husband. Rebecca left a hole in his life. There was the dinner party, for one thing. Even now there were calls coming in that Rebecca would have answered. Calls from the guests, calls from the florist, the caterer. He had to have Ruta and Nancy take care of it. He had no illusion that they could handle it as well as Rebecca.

Then there were the physical facts of her absence. The house was empty, so was the apartment. His bed was empty. The sound of his wife's voice, a soothing background to his busy and exhausting days, was gone. The sight of her pale, somewhat worried face greeting him in the evenings was a thing he missed.

The coffee she made in the mornings wasn't there. It was Rebecca who set the thermostats, Rebecca who paid the bills that were now piling up in the foyer. Rebecca who turned the lights off at night. Rebecca who made his dinner when Ruta didn't. Rebecca who picked out his tie in the morning, who brought in the newspaper. Rebecca who rubbed his back in the evenings—when he was home, that is.

Now Damon had to do everything for himself. And new things kept popping up every day. He was forced to measure his loss anew with each fresh discovery. He realized how deeply rooted Rebecca was in every part of his daily life, because all those roots had been severed at once.

"Damn," he muttered to himself each time an unpaid bill or an empty cupboard reminded him of his dilemma. "Damn!"

Underneath his endurance, a smoldering anger began to make itself felt. No moment for a sudden loss is opportune, but Rebecca had chosen the worst possible time. There was the party, for one thing. She had left him holding the bag. And there was Dusty, who was frantic about her young man and would no doubt have been on the phone to Rebecca six times a day if Rebecca were here. Not to mention the whole Hightower business and the stress Damon was under.

"Great timing," he muttered, shaking his head as he struggled with the little stovetop espresso pot she had always made his coffee in. "Just great."

Though Damon tried to deny his anger, he felt himself deciding that one day he would make Rebecca pay for this. Whatever she had suffered in the past was nothing compared to what she would face in the future, when she came back.

He thought of asking Alison to come over and stay with him. But he rejected this idea. In the first place it might cause talk, particularly given his cover story about Rebecca's sick mother. In the second place, Alison could not help him in that way. She had her own life, she was a professional with obligations, a full calendar. More yet, she was not the type of woman to concern herself with practical responsibilities. She had a girl Friday who handled most of her domestic arrangements, along with her correspondence, her travel reservations, and so on. Alison kept a nice apartment, it was very cozy for her trysts with Damon, but she was not a house-wifely or domestic person. Nor did she want to be.

Nine days after Rebecca's departure, the party took place as sched-uled. All the partners were there. The wives were all over Damon, covering him with sympathy over Irene.

"Damon, I'm so sorry!" said Doreen Blackman, the scent of her martinis suffusing him as she kissed his cheek.

"What a terrible thing!" exclaimed Justine Gaeth. "And just when things are so busy for you downtown." For tactlessness Jus-tine was true to form. She might as well upbraid Irene for taking to her deathbed when it was so inconvenient for Damon.

"I feel so sorry for Rebecca," said Mimi Parker. "All these years she's had this thing hanging over her head. How is she taking it?"

"Fine," Damon assured her. "She's doing very well, under the circumstances."

It was a difficult evening. Not only did Damon have to keep up the pretense that Rebecca was in Florida, but he also had to put on a bereaved face and make believe that he was distraught over Irene's condition. The fact was that he and Irene had never had any love lost between them and he couldn't understand why Rebecca was so attached to a creature as selfish and shallow as Irene.

The partners were more restrained in their commiseration, and the mayor's people, ruthless as ever, hardly mentioned it. But Da-mon could see that his instinct had been right. His cover story was working to his advantage. He cut the figure of a brave man whose wife was seeing to her responsibilities at a tragic time.

Nevertheless, by the time the party ended Damon was emotion-ally exhausted. He left Ruta and the caterers to clean up and went straight to Alison's. She was waiting for him with open arms.

"Come here, love."

She was wearing her dark silk negligee, and she looked more exciting than usual in it. Damon had stayed away from liquor all evening, and the aged bourbon he now drank sent a wave of heat through his senses. He pulled off the negligee and pushed Alison down on her bed. She was amused at his ardor, and for a moment the two of them laughed together, almost wildly, for no particular reason. Damon thought of Rebecca's pale body as he looked at the rich brown nipples of his lover, and of Rebecca's pained distant eyes as he looked into Alison's laughing, naughty ones.

"You've had a long night." Alison smiled. "Are you sure you're up to this?"

"You be the judge," Damon said.

He made love fiercely, almost as though he were using his own pleasure to get revenge on his wife. Alison seemed younger, sexier than she had been in years. Damon stayed in her a long time, pumping until her eagerness became ecstasy. When he felt her begin to come he surged forward almost cruelly, taking his pleasure in the same instant that she took hers.

Then he fell into a deep sleep with his head on her breast, his fatigue joining with the throbbing of his senses so sweetly that it almost seemed he wasn't alone after all.

8

Grace Island had an illusory, ambiguous quality. As though it could not make up its mind what sort of place it was. Or, worse, that it had no mind to make up at all.

At this time of the year the fogs were beginning to loom at odd hours of the day. They moved in over the mountains and lay like tufts of cotton candy on street corners, beaches and parks. Sometimes a patch of fog would make love to the top of a tree, or cover it so completely that the trunk seemed to disappear into the heavens like Jack's bean stalk. It was a familiar thing for a child in a school playground to disappear into a white mass while climbing to the top of a slide, then to come shooting out of the obscurity, laughing gaily, while other children shouted below.

The tops of buildings were shrouded more often than not, but sometimes you would see the thirtieth floor clearly, the windows tinted gold by the sun of midday, while the base of the building was completely hidden.

Most of the tourists were gone already, for it was after Labor Day. The hotels' rates were plummeting now, and the rooms that had been occupied two weeks ago for hundreds of dollars a day would soon be filled with traveling executives here for meetings, busy men who would only see fog if they bothered to open the curtains of their rooms. Some of the rooms, that is; most would be empty until next June.

Economically the city had a split personality. The resort hotels and condominiums were spread along the six miles of beach to the west, and these, in peak season, were patronized by wealthy tourists from all over Canada and, increasingly, the United States. On the other hand, the center of the city was a thriving place of business, with steely skyscrapers, heavy traffic, a certain amount of pollution trapped by the fog—too much, according to the local population—and inhabitants famous for their pallor, insured by the lack of sunlight except in July and August. Most of this population now lived in bedroom communities forty-five minutes away by freeway from the now costly beaches. There were slums on the east side of downtown; some were only a five-minute walk from the biggest of the hotels. Unemployment was a serious problem in the off season.

There was talk of legalizing gambling, so that casinos might bring visitors to town all year round. But the city council was conservative, having come down from generations of Catholic settlers, so nothing had been done.

The natives complained that they could not afford to live in their own city in the summer, and that they could not pay their relatives enough to come to visit at any other season, because of the fog. Not too surprisingly, it was a city in which alcoholism ran high. Suicide, too.

The Royal Grace was neither the best nor the worst of the ocean-front hotels. It had tennis courts, two swimming pools, a health club and an atrium, which had attracted some attention a decade and a half ago and then been forgotten as more splendid hotels were built. There were some two hundred rooms, most of which were now empty.

In room 617 Rebecca Lowell lay under a light blanket with Tony Delafield in her arms.

At the moment, there was almost nothing in her mind. She felt her own breathing and that of her sleeping lover's. She felt the sheets against her legs, the too-soft pillow under her head. The curtains were closed, but she knew that if they were opened there would be nothing outside the window but fog. A whiteness that not only hid things, but sapped their power of being, so that one could no longer know which way was down and which was up. The fog seemed to seep into one's skin and take away the desire to know such things.

Rebecca savored this absence of thought. Her mind had always been a busy place, full of preoccupations, decisions, plans. Now there was nothing in it but a drifting, bemused attention that found no object. She had never imagined such a state of mind to be possible. She sensed it could lead to calamity, but even her foreboding became part of the drug that paralyzed her.

The sudden awakening of her senses had something to do with these feelings, of course. For the first time in her life the independent, beautiful existence of her body had come through to her. Initially shocked by it, she had now learned to surrender to it, and to let its own rhythms carry her along.

She felt the boy in her arms, and saw his tumbled hair near her face. How fresh and young he smelled and felt! Like something newly created for this moment.

She remembered the day in Manhattan when she had told him he seemed to be in two places at once. Now it was true of her, too. She carried her old life within her, precise in every detail; yet she as the vessel was changed, like a turning kaleidoscope, and all the old certainties were scattered, lacking their old significance. She took pleasure in this process that split her from within, letting the world enter her in a new way.

She knew she was going to have to pay for this some day. No one can tear the fabric of her own existence and hope not to fall through the hole. But she felt little fear. She was learning to turn her back on prudent, preemptive thought. She had made her leap. Now she would dare to fall.

Tony woke up. Like a child, he clung more closely to her even before he was completely awake. His long arms encircled her. He buried his face against her skin.

"You're still here," he murmured. This made her smile. He was in the habit of worrying that she was a dream, and that she would be gone each time he awoke.

She kissed his forehead, then the fragrant black hair.

"What time is it?" he asked.

Together they looked at the little clock on the dresser. It read five-fifteen. The light was so ambiguous that it could have been dawn or dusk.

"Time to wake up and get moving," she said. "We can't just stay like this forever." Amazed, she reflected that they had been in bed all afternoon. All day, in fact, except for their breakfast downstairs.

"But we can wish we could," he said.

"Yes."

His knee slipped between her thighs, and his hand caressed the contour of her hip. All was warm and smooth and sleepy. Their bodies were hungry, and would soon be famished, but for this one moment they were too numbed by pleasure to move.

"Tonight we'll go out to dinner," he said, his fingertips playing with her hair. "No more of this cave-dwelling. I know just the place. The concierge told me about it this morning."

"All right."

He sat up, leaning on one elbow. "I want you to dress up," he said. "I want to show you off."

She blushed. Already she had felt the glances of the hotel clerks on her, and of the handful of guests who had seen her with Tony. He was half her age, young enough to be her son, but he did not try to hide his physical possessiveness. He touched her, put his arm around her, took her hand. And, of course, they occupied the same room, a room with only one bed.

She had tried to feel brazen and shameless about what she was doing, to throw it in the faces of others. But this was not in her. So she had avoided their eyes, let Tony deal with them. And he had risen to the occasion. He behaved like the master, the one in control. He did all the talking—quite smoothly, in fact—and made all the arrangements.

"You dress up, too," she said.

"Why not? We're celebrating, aren't we?" This was another of his little jokes. No matter how small the occasion, he always said they should make the most of it because they were celebrating. Celebrating what? Their liberation from the world.

He looked beautiful in his clothes. The dark suits, the silk ties, the slacks and sweaters—all became him perfectly. And out of them: slender, coltlike, emerging from the bathroom in his shorts, pulling them down with a hint of modesty as he came toward her. He was so young, so tender and unfinished.

He got up now and padded to the bathroom. She lay back and stretched, watching the door close on him. Again she thought of questioning her contentment, and gave up.

In the bathroom, Tony looked at himself in the mirror.

His eyes, normally so dull in his opinion, were sparkling. His hair was awry. Sleep and lovemaking were visible in his flesh, spectacularly, like a badge of honor.

He saw the familiar body, the little mole under his left arm that he had once wanted to have removed, the biceps he had thought were not big enough, the pectorals he had tried to enlarge by weightlifting. It was all the same, but looked at with new eyes. For the first time in his life he felt handsome.

All because of Rebecca. His imagination had not prepared him for her depth, her mystery. He had wanted her physically, of course—from the beginning that had been an obsession. But what he felt now was more than physical. It was as though she had called him forth into life itself.

Ever since he had turned the corner from obscure boyhood into adolescence, he had felt he was missing something, or that something was missing in him. The usual adventures—girls, petting, drinking—had made him feel out of place, out of step.

For years he thought there was something wrong with him. He even wondered whether he was homosexual. His physical experiments with the opposite sex left him cold. When, in a few cases, the trysts led to completion, the spasm he felt was empty, increasing his longing rather than assuaging it.

Dusty had been the latest in this long line of pretty, innocent, friendly girls. He had told himself she was different. This time he thought he was different as well. He thought he would marry her.

Then she had introduced him to Rebecca. He had been completely unsuspecting, coming out of the Sound that day. From a distance, Rebecca looked like a middle-aged woman asleep on the sand, a book beside her. But as soon as she woke up, as soon as she began talking, she cast a spell. His heart went out to her. He longed to touch her hand, if only to help her up from her towel. To say something, anything, so he could hear her answer.

And then, in those first five minutes, it turned into something more. He wanted to drown in that smooth, melancholy depth of her. To lose himself in her sadness, her mystery.

By the end of that first lunch he knew he must try to win her. His own impulse appalled him at first, but then it began to seem more and more natural.

She struggled hard against him, and for a while he thought he was insane to pursue her. But something about her protests that day in Manhattan, in the dingy little café, gave him hope. He could feel her weaken even as she tried to push him away.

He had gambled everything on that second afternoon at the beach, when he knew the house would be empty. He'd been by no means sure of success. Seeing her lying on the sand, her eyes closed, he had almost lost his nerve and stolen away. But then something inside him had exerted its power, forced him to dare.

And she gave in.

Since then he had lived as though above the earth. He savored every instant of his time with her. He looked back on the poverty of his dreams and measured like a drunken man the extent to which she had exceeded them.

He gave himself a last look in the mirror and turned off the light. When he returned to the bedroom she was still lying there, watching him, a slight smile on her face.

"We're late," she said. "We'd better get moving."

The sound of her voice made his senses tingle. Embarrassed, he felt himself stiffen at the sight of her. He knew she saw. Her smile became softer.

Words came to his lips, but he did not say them. Naked, he lay down on top of her and kissed her lips.

"Silly boy," she murmured. "Insatiable boy…"

The sheet stirred between them. He raised himself an inch and pulled it away. Her skin glowed in the light of the fog. He lowered himself to her.

9

Damon Lowell was learning to do more things for himself.

He brought in the paper now and made his own coffee. He sent out his laundry. He opened his mail and paid his bills.

Initially he was all the more helpless for knowing so well how he wanted things to be. Over the years of their marriage it was Rebecca who had carried out his instructions about the strength of the coffee, the amount of starch in the shirts, the type of orange juice, the doneness of the eggs. Damon's tastes had evolved over the years—no garlic pulp in the Caesar salad, a touch more Worcestershire in the clam chowder—and she had learned to keep up with them. But Damon himself didn't know the first thing about actually making the coffee, instructing the laundry, squeezing the oranges.

In the end, though, he began to figure things out. And he found it a surprisingly natural process. It was simply a retooling of his executive ability, with his own home as the focus of his efforts. He let the cleaning woman go about her usual business until he saw that certain things weren't getting done. Realizing that Rebecca had done these herself, he told the cleaning woman to take care of them, as well, and gave her a raise.

He consulted with Ruta about the cooking. He had her do the grocery shopping and noted the things she forgot to get. Sometimes he even wrote little grocery notes to himself when he was at the office, keeping them on a list in his wallet. He drew the line at entering a grocery store himself, but he did begin to notice the prices of things in the newspaper ads. He was astonished to see how expensive coffee and liquor had become. Meats were out of sight. It had not occurred to him that he was paying so much for a lamb chop dinner.

He sat down with Rebecca's calendar and Rolodex and called the furnace man, the man who took care of the lawn, the roofers who were scheduled to work on the shingles this fall. The lawn man seemed astonished to hear Damon's voice, but quickly accepted his instructions.

It was simple enough to go through all Rebecca's paperwork and see how and when she had done her various jobs. A couple of weekends sufficed for Damon to get control of her work. He could not help musing that his wife had led a rather easy life, after all. If these comparatively simple jobs were all Rebecca did with her time, she must have had a lot of leisure. (This last thought wiped the smile from Damon's face; he did not know why.)

Damon felt he was coping well. On the other hand, there was no denying that the sudden loss of a spouse leaves a man in the lurch, emotionally. Sometimes he would look at himself in the mirror when he was tying his tie and feel a sudden pull of grief, which distorted his features and made his eyes mist. The tie had always been Rebecca's job.

Often he woke up calling her name. In the mornings, making breakfast as she used to do, he felt little surges of panic, like a schoolboy whose mother is in the hospital and can't make his lunch for him. Coming home from work was a lonely business; coming home from Alison's in the middle of the night was worse. A bit of conversation was always on the tip of his tongue, until he realized there was no one to say it to. Sometimes he even found himself lying awake in his lonely bed, a trifle afraid of the darkness around him, alarmed by the ticks of the furniture or the walls settling— because there was no wife there to share his world.

During this interval he depended a great deal on Alison. He met her in the city for lunch whenever possible and spent as many nights at her place as he dared. When he was with her he tried to forget the silence of his apartment, the even more frightening emptiness of the Long Island house.

Alison was warm and understanding. She also seemed concerned about Dusty and asked whether she could do anything to help. He felt the crazy impulse to ask her to see Dusty, to talk to her, to comfort her. But he saw the absurdity of this. Men didn't use mistresses as surrogate mothers for their daughters. Not in his stratum of society.

* * *

When Alison asked Damon how he was handling the situation he stressed his disbelief.

"It just isn't like her," he said. "You think you know a person... I knew Rebecca as well as I know myself. This is not a thing she would do."

There was a pause. Alison stared straight ahead, out the window onto Riverside Drive. Damon could not see the look in her eyes. It was a remote, speculative look.

"Well," she said, "that's how it goes sometimes."

"I believe she'll be back," Damon said. "If not for me, then for Dusty. It isn't in her to do this to her daughter. Of that I feel sure."

Now Alison Shore frowned slightly. Her beautiful eyebrows, cared for lovingly and one of her best features, slanted against her smooth brown skin. As she thought of Damon's daughter, the drift of her thoughts changed.

Alison herself was nearly past the childbearing age. She had never felt a genuine maternal instinct, at least not one that she could remember.

She had seen Dusty Lowell once. A ripe, blond young creature, bubbly and smiling, but obviously vulnerable, even when seen from a distance. A connoisseur of female psychology, Alison thought she understood that something in Dusty's life had not been very secure, not even from the beginning. She wore the mantle of the golden girl rather poorly. This was just a guess made at a distance, but Damon's stories about Dusty seemed to confirm it. Though, interestingly, Damon did not seem aware of it. He saw Dusty's life as simple and uncomplicated, compared to the headaches of his own existence.

With this in mind, Alison found herself measuring the courage, or the desperation, that had allowed Rebecca to leave so powerful a husband as Damon behind. Even more imponderable was the force that had compelled her to abandon a daughter like Dusty.

On the other hand, perhaps to Rebecca, Damon wasn't so powerful. Twenty years of marriage can dim the luster of any man in his wife's eyes. And perhaps Dusty, important though she might be, could not outweigh the unseen thing that was going on inside Rebecca. How can one woman know another woman's heart?

"And your detectives?" she asked. "Have they found anything out?"

"Not yet," he said. "But Dick Hamlin assures me it won't be much longer."

Dusty was the most serious problem. Damon's cover story about Irene, which was working so smoothly with everyone else, could not be extended to Dusty, for Dusty was rather close to Irene and had already spoken to her several times about Rebecca's disappearance. He could not lie to Dusty.

Most of his contact with her so far had been by phone. Her classes were starting, and she had a lot of extracurricular obligations. Moreover, the father and daughter felt a mutual reluctance to be physically at close quarters. The reasons for this were not clear to Damon.

On Tuesday, though, they finally got together for dinner. They went to a little restaurant called Crandall's, near the campus, staffed by student waiters. Mercifully, it was a quiet place, and one's voice didn't carry.

Dusty looked the same at first; then, as Damon thought about it, prettier. He realized she had lost weight. She seemed distracted.

He started to ask about Tony, but decided against it.

"Well, I'm afraid I have nothing new to report," he said uneasily. "We don't know where Rebecca has gone. Dick is a little mystified. He can't understand why there aren't any ticket receipts or reservations on her credit card accounts."

There was a silence. Dusty was looking away.

"Oh, he'll find her, all right," Damon assured her. "It's only a matter of time. These detectives have ways...."

He could see this line of thought was not reassuring her, so he took a sip of his martini and gathered himself.

"Sweetie, I don't want you to be too worried about this," he said. "The fact is that I haven't been the best husband in the world. My work takes up a lot of my time and makes me preoccupied even when I'm not at the office. What with this Hightower business, I've been worse than ever."

The image of Alison rose up in his mind. He wondered if Dusty could read his thoughts. In any case, he could not bring himself to refer to it. So he concentrated on accusing himself as an inattentive husband, and in defending Rebecca in absentia as a woman who got fed up and went away for a while to be by herself.

"I can hardly be angry with her," he said. "She had plenty of provocation. But I want you to know, honey, that she would never have left you unless she simply had no choice. She loves you with all her heart."

"Then why hasn't she written me?" Dusty asked. They were her first words since Damon had broached the painful subject.

Damon had no answer for that one.

"She must have a good reason," he said. "Don't hold it against her."

"And *where* did she go?" Dusty seemed angry.

"I don't know," Damon said. "I'm trying to find out."

"And what will you do when you find her?" Dusty asked coldly. "Divorce her?"

Damon turned red.

"Certainly not!" he said. "What can you be thinking of, Dusty? I love your mother. I wouldn't dream of divorcing her."

"Especially now."

"What do you mean?" Damon asked. She didn't answer. He knew she meant politics. She was sharper than he had thought. Perhaps in a veiled way she was referring also to his future plans with Alison. The cool, knowing words sounded strange on the lips of the daughter whose simplicity of heart, whose innocence, had always been her most salient feature.

"I'll probably get down on my knees and beg her to come back," he said with false humility. "I may have behaved badly, but I'm not a stupid man, honey. I know when I've been wrong."

"And what if she doesn't want to come back?" The words were an obvious challenge. He glanced worriedly into Dusty's eyes. He barely recognized her. There was something cold and cynical in her that he had never seen before.

"Well, let's try to assume she will," he said. "And even if she doesn't, she'll still be your mother. She loves you so much, honey."

Dusty looked away. The waiter was approaching, so there was an enforced interval of silence.

Why hasn't she written me?
Why did she leave?

The cruel questions haunted Damon. For the first time he felt the incurable guilt of a parent whose marriage has fallen out from under a child he loves. Only at this moment did it really dawn on him that what had happened might be damaging Dusty in a permanent way—or that his long unfaithful past might have damaged her already.

Mercifully, Dusty brightened after the waiter left. She spoke of her courses, of her friends. Senior year was exciting. She was taking her most important journalism courses, the ones she had been looking forward to for two years. This fall she would be applying for jobs and internships. At last she was on the threshold of her future.

Damon was heartened to hear her speak of her life that way. At least there was some semblance of normality about it.

But then he thought of Tony.

"What do you hear from the Delafields?" he ventured to ask.

Her face darkened.

"They don't know anything. I spoke to Mrs. Delafield last night. She's really worried. She seems to think it had something to do with their family. Something she's not saying."

There was a pause.

Damon said, "I talked with Mr. Delafield yesterday afternoon."

A composite look of embarrassment, anger and gratitude swept over Dusty's features.

"What did he say?" she asked.

"This is just between you and me—okay?" Damon said. Seeing her nod, he went on. "He holds himself responsible. He doesn't feel he has understood Tony very well, or tried hard enough. Apparently Tony has always been closer to his mother. Meanwhile, the three girls absorbed all the parents' attention, and Mrs. Delafield was always fighting with one or the other of them. Stormy relationships. In that sense Tony sort of slipped through without being noticed. But he had his own feelings. Mr. Delafield told me he suspects Tony never really wanted to go to law school at all. He was only doing it because he thought his father wanted him to. I don't know if it's true...." He looked at Dusty. "Is that what Tony told you?"

She thought for a moment. "Yes."

"Well," Damon concluded, "maybe that's what is behind all this. Tony is at a crossroads. Maybe he wanted to put his foot down and leave law school, and for some emotional reason this was the only way he could do it." Damon felt the need to reassure Dusty that Tony could not have been abandoning her.

"I suspect he'll be in touch with you one of these days pretty soon," he added in a confidential tone. "In fact, I wouldn't be surprised if it's to send for you."

He watched his words take effect. Dusty said nothing, but her eyes softened.

"Had he proposed to you?" Damon asked.

Slowly she nodded. "Yes."

"And still he went away," Damon said.

She looked away.

"The two things don't necessarily contradict each other," he said. "In fact, as a lawyer I would have to go under the assumption that they don't."

He raised his eyes toward the ceiling, as though measuring a thorny point of law.

"Perhaps he felt he had no choice," he said. "Perhaps things had piled up on him, and he simply couldn't face the beginning of school. He wouldn't be the first young man who has just walked away when he was pushed to the limit. I can remember feeling that way myself at his age." This was a lie, but it came off his lips rather easily.

"Maybe," he pursued, "he's just waiting for the right moment to ask you to join him. Maybe he wants you to graduate first. Indeed, maybe he's hesitating to ask you to make the sacrifice. Do you feel strongly enough about him to chuck everything?"

He saw the look of secret pride in her eyes. His flattery was working.

"Would you go?" he asked, cleverly.

"Oh, Daddy..."

"No, seriously. Would you?" He tried to appeal to her sense of romance.

She seemed thoughtful. "I have my own life," she said. "There are things I want to do. He knows that."

Damon enjoyed talking this way. It made him seem like an impersonal counselor instead of a concerned father. Someone who could speak to her as a grown woman, not as a child. He was sure it was softening her toward him. Also it was making her seem closer to Tony, making it seem unthinkable that Tony's departure was not part of a larger scheme to marry her, to be with her.

"Part of love is sacrifice, after all," he said. "Maybe he feels that he can't marry you until he makes his professional choice. Maybe he thinks it would be unfair to you. After all, it was as a prospective attorney that he first introduced himself to you. Perhaps he feels he's been dealing with you under false pretenses. He may be hesitating to confront you with his decision about the future. Maybe he even doubts you'll still want him."

Dusty was silent. She was listening intently.

"You know," Damon said, "if I had thought that way twenty-five years ago, things might never have got to where they are. I should have thought more seriously, more probingly about things. I had no passionate desire to be a lawyer. I was only doing it because I thought it was expected of me. That was my—what do they call it?—that was my mind-set. But I was passionate about your mother. I wanted her more than anything in the world. But, looking back, I wonder if she ever knew what my real priorities were. Perhaps if I had stopped to think a little, I would have entered into marriage with a better attitude."

His daughter was still silent.

"Rebecca is an extraordinary woman," he said. "I daresay her leaving when she did only proves it. But I'm afraid that, during our marriage, I allowed her to feel ordinary. I allowed her to feel that I thought she was ordinary. A man's work takes so much out of him.... It took too much out of me. There wasn't enough left for Rebecca. Or for you, I'm afraid."

He sighed. "Maybe all this is the best thing that could have happened. Maybe Tony saw the same thing waiting for him that has happened to me. Maybe, unlike me, he is getting out while there's still time. Maybe you're part of that, in his mind."

Nearly everything Damon was saying was a lie. A quarter century of experience as an attorney was shaping his words, giving them weight and credibility. His arguments were so convincing that he himself was carried away. He reached to touch Dusty's hand. He felt closer to her than he had been in years. For the first time he felt as though he was really talking to her, really communicating.

"Dad." Dusty was looking down at their joined hands.

"Yes, honey?"

"Did Tony run away with my mom?"

Darling,

You cannot know how close to my heart you are at this moment. Even though I have had to leave you—and believe me, if there had been a choice, any choice at all, I never would have left you that way, without saying goodbye, without explaining—I feel so close to you. Joined to you by something permanent, something outside time itself.

But you see, my dear, it is time that has brought about this sudden and terrible change, this necessary change. My mistake was to spend so many years pretending there was not a void somewhere in me. My pretense was what caused things to build the way they did, in silence, and finally to explode. I hid from myself too long. Now I am paying the price. It is a price I would gladly pay for myself alone. But the knowledge that my decision has harmed you, broken the family that gave you your home—this breaks my heart.

It is so terribly hard to write to you when I am in the very midst of a change that is taking me away from my old self and introducing me to someone new. Hard to be truthful with you, when the truth won't show itself clearly to me yet. But you must believe that, no matter how far I feel from my old self, I don't feel far from you. Not at all. You are with me every second...and whatever happens, please know that you have not lost me and will never lose me. I will be a mother to you forever, no matter what.

Rebecca paused, the hotel's ballpoint pen poised in her hand. She was sitting in her bed, propped against the pillows, the piece of writing paper held against the spiral-bound directory of hotel services that had been on the desk. It was not the hotel's stationery; Tony had gone out to buy blank paper.

She wore only her slip. The feel of her lover was still on her fingertips. The pen shook with tiny, regular tremors, making her handwriting look different.

She looked up. Tony sat at the desk, writing a letter of his own. He wore only his shorts. His long legs extended far under the desk. A birthmark on his back, just below the left shoulder blade, made her smile. She had kissed it a dozen times, assuring him he was perfect when he complained about it.

The square shoulders, the lean back, the tousled hair... A warm glow suffused her at the sight of her lover. But the pen still trembled in her hand. And when she looked down at the words she had written to her daughter, a wave of failure and resignation pulled at her. How could she write to Dusty? What comforting words could dull the agony that must be gnawing at her daughter's heart right now?

You have not lost me and will never lose me.... She read her own phrases again. How weak they were, how ineffectual in the face of this enormity. She noticed that she hadn't mentioned Tony. She did not intend to. She could not bear to refer directly to this sharpest point of her shame. Her intention was to send Dusty her love and her apology. That was all. She made no promise to come back or to restore the old life they had taken for granted. She simply expressed continuing, undying love.

But was that enough? Was love ever enough in the face of betrayal and abandonment?

Rebecca's own father had abandoned her and Irene when Rebecca was still a schoolgirl. She had never gotten over it. Irene had married once more after losing Frank and behaved as though he were merely a footnote to her life. Rebecca had not been so lucky. Though she rarely talked of her father to Damon or anyone else, the void he left behind him had marked her in ways she did not care to think about.

She looked at Tony. She worried for him despite herself. The dislocation that had broken her own life applied to him as well. And he was so much younger than she, so much less experienced. Even without their involvement he would have been facing the inevitable identity crisis of his age. The world expected him to be two selves at once, the boy he had been and the man he was going to be.

And so it was with Dusty. Dusty was still a girl, but soon to take on the responsibilities of a woman. And now, thanks to her mother, she was taking on a woman's greatest burden and greatest pain.

"Between two infinities," Pascal had written. Rebecca had studied that phrase in school and always found it pat and uninteresting, a banal maxim. Now she began to sense its darker meanings, multiple and dangerous, meanings one could not fathom at a stroke, but had to learn painfully, bit by bit, when one did not want to learn.

It suddenly occurred to Rebecca that in looking at Tony's naked body, seated at the desk as dutifully as that of a schoolboy sending a thank-you note, she felt an emotion surprisingly close to what she felt for Dusty. She wanted to protect, she wanted to enfold. But against some things there is no protection.

With this thought she glanced at the letter in her hands. *I don't feel far from you....* What lies! In this gray room, with the fog pressed close against the window like the breath of a lover, she felt as distant from her daughter as from the stars. How could she send messages to Dusty with cautious, apologetic nonsense in them, when it was she herself who had run away from her?

A sigh had escaped her, and Tony heard it. He pushed back his chair, leaving his own letter on the desk, and came to her.

"What's the matter?" he asked.

She let the letter fall at her side.

"I can't do it," she said. "It's impossible."

He lay down beside her and cradled her face to his chest.

"I know," he said. "Nothing could be harder."

He kissed her slowly, first on her brow, then her cheeks, as though discovering her. She had never been kissed that way before or held so sweetly. Certainly not by Damon. And now she saw that it was becoming a regular part of Tony's physical affection for her. A new habit, as it were. Just as a thousand little things become part of the fabric of a relationship, a marriage. Time was binding them closer.

But time was also slowly fraying the threads linking her to her past, to her daughter.

More tears emerged as this thought struck her.

"There, there," he said, sounding oddly like a father. "It's just that good heart of yours making a noise. Don't worry."

"Don't worry?" she moaned.

"You will do the right thing," he said. "It isn't in you to do the wrong thing, Rebecca. Why do you think I love you so much?"

There was a pause.

"Then why have I done this?" she asked. "Why have we...?"

"Because our lives were wrong without each other," he said. "We couldn't be whole, the way we were. You see, that was wrong. And, in order to correct it, we had to do another wrong. But we will correct that, too. There is always a way—when people love each other."

He held her close. "Don't despair," he said. "You'll see I'm right. It will all come out right in the end."

How delicious it was to be comforted by him that way. There was untruth in his words, but there was truth, too. In correcting the huge lie of her whole life, she had made a beginning. Surely there was more chance for salvation along this route than along the path she had been following before. Because love is surely a better road to salvation than the spiritual death of one's own self.

Such was Tony's argument. Like a good Jesuit, Rebecca pondered it, she sought the kernel of goodness on the one side and on the other. For she had learned her lessons well in the church: truth without charity was not truth.

She glanced at the letter on the sheet beside her. It was slightly crumpled, for she had lain on it without realizing it.

"It's all lies," she said. "I couldn't tell the truth. I wasn't strong enough."

"You'll rewrite it," he said. "You know how to love, Rebecca. That's what you'll put in the letter. That's what you'll send."

Rebecca looked into his eyes.

"Oh, my God," she murmured, and pulled him on top of her.

Their passion was sudden, more urgent than at any time since she had known him. But this time there was nothing erotic about it—not at first. She held him to her frantically, as though begging him to blot out everything outside them. And he was that strong, he did it for her. She filled herself with the innocence of him. It was enough, or almost enough, to silence everything else.

The letter was wrinkled and warmed by their bodies, and finally pushed under the sheets by the movements of their passion. Later she did rewrite it, though almost in the same words. And he finished his own letter, also to Dusty. Today was the beginning. Tomorrow, the day after, they might write to the others. Tony to the Delafields, and Rebecca to Damon, then to her mother. But today was the first step, the first daring to look back.

It was Tony who mailed both letters, an hour before dinner. The clerk called out to him, "Mail has been picked up already, sir. That won't go out until tomorrow."

"That's all right." Tony smiled. "Tomorrow will be soon enough. Thanks, anyway."

"Right, sir."

The clerk busied himself with some papers on his desk. Then, as Tony disappeared into the elevator, he darted a glance to the man in the chair on the other side of the lobby, who nodded briefly and looked away.

11

Mayor Lazare sat behind his desk, looking from Damon Lowell to the three other men in his office.

"You have to understand," he said, "I don't care how many of these guys there are. We have to take care of them. That's all. We have to take care of them."

The tallest of the other men, a special counsel to the governor, leaned forward in his chair.

"Mr. Mayor, if you want to know the honest truth, I don't think they're going to press it."

The mayor, a heavy man, sat back in his swivel chair, which gave a loud squeak almost like a cry of surprise. Months ago this used to bring an involuntary smile to Damon's lips.

"You don't think," the mayor said.

"The governor doesn't think so," said the counsel. "And they're all members of his party. He's on the phone with them every day of his life. I sincerely doubt that they would all be planning to come down against us on this issue without his knowing it in advance."

The mayor rocked slightly in his chair, studying the counsel. He did not trust any of the governor's men. Ever since his election, the governor had made political hay out of the city's fiscal problems, claiming in more or less obvious terms that the real talents in government were in Albany, and that the city was as corrupt as ever and simply could not be counted on to keep a leash on itself.

On the Hightower project, however, the state and city were working together. Without the governor's help the project could not be funded. It was his party that ruled the legislature. That meant lengthy, painful and mutually suspicious dealings between the mayor and the man he hated more than anyone except, perhaps, the president.

"Hang on a minute," the mayor said. He picked up his office phone. "Phoebe, get me the governor."

There were several moments of silence, the mayor looking from one face to another in the office as he waited for the governor to come on the line. The wait was a little too long, and signs of impatience were obvious in the mayor's face.

"Ron!" he said at last, a big smile distorting his normally scowling features. "Glad to hear your voice. I have Damon and Leo and the others here in my office, and we've been talking about your party colleagues."

While the others waited, the mayor went over the same ground with the governor. It was an obvious slight to Leo Coyle, who was one of the closest men to the governor and who had been sent here expressly as the governor's messenger. It was also intended to show those present that the mayor had the governor's ear whenever he wanted it.

This was one of the mayor's weaknesses—showing off his power and authority to men who didn't matter. He had an inbred need to strut before underlings. It came from his family background and his relative lack of education, not to mention his irritable ego. With the Hightower people he was worse than usual, because their Ivy League degrees made him nervous.

Unfortunately the effect was the opposite of what he sought. His back-slapping loudness made him look small and self-conscious. The more familiar he tried to be, the more foolish he looked. Damon had learned to hide his feelings during these episodes, for he knew that the mayor was terrifically sensitive to a slight.

It was surprising that so unconvincing a man had such an excellent image with the public. A posturing rascal in private, the mayor became a beloved La Guardia-like figure whenever a camera came into view. He had a pair of assistants, almost like bodyguards, who flanked him wherever he went, on the lookout for newspeople. As a result, no cameraman had ever captured the private side of the mayor, and he remained a popular figure with the public, despite his many failings as an executive. It was for this very reason that the governor had been forced to deal with him on Hightower. The project would be good for the State's image when completed; and it could never be completed without the mayor and his cronies.

Damon watched all this with amusement, but also with a psychologist's interest. The mayor was in some ways genuinely in awe of the men he worked with, though he never doubted his ability to manipulate them. He often telephoned Damon late at night, an oddly whining note in his voice, to ask for reassurance about the project's chances and to bounce ideas off him. At these times Damon sensed a childlike emotional dependence that was seemingly out of character for so brutal a politico.

Lazare was a man of loutish intensity, his ruddy face and thick body disgusting to behold, particularly after a sweaty morning and a half dozen cigars. Yet he was irresistible to many women. He was an enigma. He possessed too many qualities for one man. Perhaps, Damon mused, this was a prerequisite for all highly successful public figures.

The meeting ended with hollow assurances on all sides, and with the mayor no more satisfied after having talked to the governor than before. The governor's people were the first to leave, and the mayor dismissed his aides and asked Damon to stay a moment.

"Damon, I heard about your trouble," he said. "I just want you to know how sorry I am."

Damon, standing now, smiled.

"I appreciate that, Your Honor. It's very kind of you."

"How is Rebecca holding up?" The mayor leaned forward with a falsely concerned look on his pudgy face.

"Oh, Rebecca is a brick."

"That's good. Give her my best when you talk to her, will you?"

"I certainly will. And thank you."

"What are the doctors saying?" asked the mayor.

Damon shook his head. "The news isn't good. But of course we've known where we stood for some time."

At this point, it was doubly hard to trot through the fiction about Irene's illness, because in his briefcase Damon had a fax from Dick Hamlin. He had found out where Rebecca was, and with whom. The news had appalled Damon. He still could not take it in.

The mayor was standing with one hand held up, commanding Damon's attention. His brow was furrowed in thought. No doubt he was preparing a speech, a little *mot* for the occasion, Damon thought.

"Illness and death," the mayor said, "are the two things in this world we can have no control over. However, we can control the way we handle them when they come. We can control our own actions. That's where real men—and women—show what they're made of."

There was an embarrassed silence. Damon was chagrined not only by the mayor's speechifying, but by the false pretense on which it was based.

"And Rebecca is made of iron," the mayor concluded. "I'm sure you're grateful for her."

"That's an understatement," Damon said. "Thank you."

"If there's anything I can do... Call on me at any time."

Damon took his leave and hurried out to the car waiting for him. He had to get to Dick Hamlin's office to hear more before he went back to the firm to a meeting of the partners. He had never in his life felt so enraged. If only he could murder Rebecca! And the mayor and the mayor's men and the governor's men, along with her.

A moment after Damon's departure, the mayor's aide came back in from the outer office. He stood in silence before the huge walnut desk.

The mayor was looking out the windows, deep in thought. He turned around.

"What do you think of that?" he asked.

"Pretty good," the aide said, "for a lawyer."

The mayor nodded. "You know, I met Rebecca a couple of times. A frumpy sort of girl, looked as though she couldn't hurt a fly. This is quite a turn. Running out on a man like Damon..."

"Yes, sir."

"Do you think this had anything to do with Alison?" The mayor was, of course, on a first-name basis with Alison Shore, whom he had known for years. He knew of her long-standing liaison with Damon, as did everyone else in city government.

"We don't know," the aide said. "It wouldn't seem likely, after all these years. But maybe there was a straw that broke the camel's back."

"Find out what you can," the mayor said. "And keep an eye on him. A thing like this can get to a man. Even a man like Damon.

Underneath all that polish he must be staggering a little. I don't want his problems messing up this Hightower deal."

"Yes, sir." The aide sat down. There was a lot more business to attend to this afternoon.

12

At the cost of considerable juggling, Damon made time for a brief weekend with Alison at the Côte d'Azur, a midtown spa and hotel that billed itself as a health club but which was also a popular place for romantic weekends. It had opened recently, so no one Damon knew was likely to be there. Not that it mattered so much—everyone already knew about Damon and Alison.

He had begged Alison to rearrange her own schedule so she could spend the time with him. Since the awful news from Dick Hamlin he had not spoken to a living soul about what he had learned. Not only was there damage control to think of, but also a stinging emotional wound Damon had not expected.

He had still not figured out a way to break the news to Dusty. Their recent conversations had been strained. Dusty seemed cold and angry. She affected a brittle cheeriness punctuated by significant intervals of deadly silence, in which her face was set in a hard look of accusation. It was not pleasant to be around her. Despite himself Damon had more than once used his obligations to the mayor as an excuse not to see her.

Under the present circumstances, Damon was forced to be Dusty's main source of support as well as information. This role did not come naturally to him, because he had never been as close to Dusty as he should. He had always left to Rebecca the job of "understanding" Dusty. Now he had no choice but to deal with her. He knew that the terrible news about Tony would make things worse, perhaps unbearable.

He and Alison would not have the whole weekend together. They met Friday night at nine, after both had attended obligatory cocktail parties, Alison at a reception for some state senators being given by her textile lobby, Damon at Gracie Mansion. They were to have

Friday night, all day Saturday, and Saturday night after splitting up for business dinners.

Alison already knew about Rebecca and Tony. Damon had phoned her from the office to tell her. At the time, he was in a state of shock. For weeks he had been trying to get used to the idea that Rebecca had left. Now he was face-to-face with the unthinkable—that she had run away with a man. Her daughter's boyfriend! It was so crazy, so incredible, that Damon had so far been unable to frame cogent thought about it.

"I still can't believe it," he told Alison after they had made love. "It's simply unbelievable."

Alison turned on her side to look at him. Her expression was unreadable.

She was thinking how changed Damon looked. Something had been taken out of him. A core of balance, of assurance, perhaps. Though he was still tanned and strong, he looked like less than the man he was before this all started.

She had noticed something different in his lovemaking. The usual intimacy was not there. There was something oddly graceless and desperate about his touch. No wonder, then, that he wanted to talk about Rebecca now.

"I know I'm repeating myself," he said. "But it's just so unbelievable."

"Well, unbelievable things happen," Alison said, sipping her brandy.

Damon's anger at Rebecca flared up. "I could understand her running out on me for a while, just to teach me a lesson. Or even permanently. But to do this to Dusty! And with Dusty's boyfriend... It's just—unbelievable."

Alison said nothing.

"And to leave me holding the bag this way!" Damon exclaimed. "She runs off with Dusty's young man, and I—I of all people!— am the one who has to hold Dusty's hand. She couldn't have chosen her weapon better, if she wanted to cause both of us as much pain as possible."

Alison said nothing. She was thinking that, without realizing it, Damon had probably put his finger on something important about Rebecca.

"And the most incredible thing of all," he went on, "is that she was able to attract the boy in the first place. That I'll never understand. Rebecca is hardly a siren, after all."

He pursed his lips. His fingers were playing absently with Alison's nipple. He was thinking about Irene. When he first told her Rebecca had left, begging her to help him keep up the cover story of her illness, she had not seemed shocked, but rather involuntarily impressed by her daughter's daring.

"I never would have thought she had it in her," Irene had said, her voice cool and evaluative, and not without a palpable hint of contempt for Damon. After all, Irene had been through two husbands and was no stranger to infidelity. But she had assumed Rebecca was a different sort of woman. She was surprised and— Damon could tell—rather amused by this turn of events.

Damon put the repellent thought of Irene out of his mind.

"Christ," he said with a sneer in his voice. "Rebecca is old enough to be his mother...."

Alison put her brandy glass down on the bedside table, with a little gesture of impatience that Damon did not notice.

"Perhaps that's the attraction," she said, not very warmly.

Damon shook his head. "Incredible," he repeated. "Just incredible."

Alison sighed. "Well, it can't be all that incredible, since it's happened."

Damon looked at her. He could see he had struck a sour note with her somewhere. But he was not aware he had been repeating himself for days about how "incredible" it all was. He was too preoccupied with himself to notice.

Something about Alison's distance annoyed him. He felt she should be supporting him in this crisis.

"I still say I can't believe she had it in her," he said, aware of the challenge in his voice.

"Well, D, maybe there was more in her than you realized." Alison was not looking at him. There was a definite edge of sarcasm in her voice.

"What are you saying?" Damon raised himself to look at her.

She pondered for a moment before speaking. She lit a cigarette and took a long drag on it.

"I'm saying," she began, "that if she ran away when you thought it impossible for her to run away, that says something about her. Something that you weren't aware of. She took you by surprise. That can hardly be accidental.''

There was a pause. Damon tried to think of an answer to this.

"And," she went on, "if she stole her own daughter's boy-friend—something that you believe was 'not in her,'—then that also says something about her. About what you knew, and what you didn't know.''

Damon reddened, irked by her explanatory tone. "Are you say-ing I should have known more than I knew?" he asked. "Was I supposed to be aware that my wife was capable of a stunt like this? Why? So I could take precautions? Christ, Alison, if I knew she had this in her I would have divorced her long ago. I never would have married her.''

"Maybe she didn't have it in her back then," Alison said, tap-ping ash from her cigarette into the ashtray.

"What is this?" he asked. "Are you taking her side?"

"Not at all," she replied. "I'm just stating the obvious. She wasn't the kind of woman you thought she was. That says some-thing about the kind of marriage you had, D. It was the kind of marriage in which it was possible for you not to know something pretty important about your wife. Now she's done something rather remarkable. Perhaps that should open your eyes a little.''

Damon was staring at her hard. "I don't get it," he said.

She shrugged. "I've known you for years, Damon. You've al-ways been frank with me. You've never pretended that your mar-riage was an intimate one, or that you were particularly curious about Rebecca's inner feelings. Use your head. You're only reaping what you sowed. You and Rebecca, I should say.''

Damon tried to take this in. Her words rang true, of course, in a sense. But he could not see how he could be anything other than blameless in this whole affair. It was Rebecca who had run out on him, after all. More yet, he rebelled at the notion that there were depths in Rebecca of which he had remained ignorant. Whatever he had not known could not have been important.

"That's why I never got married," Alison concluded. "It's too limiting a relationship. You think you know the other person, but the longer you stay married, the less you know about your spouse. You use each other for security, for a warm body. And using eventually precludes knowing." She looked as complacent as the Cheshire cat in that instant, the smoke coiling about her head.

Damon measured the words on his lips for a split second, then uttered them.

"What do *you* know about it?" His voice was angry.

Alison felt the blow.

"I suppose you're right there," she said, stubbing out her cigarette. "I've never been married. That's a mixed blessing, isn't it, D?"

She got out of bed and stood looking down at him. There was something imperious in her posture, but he noticed that her breasts were sagging, as was the flesh around her hips, which she worked so hard to keep firm.

"On the one hand," she said, "I don't have anyone to kiss me hello when I come home at night. But on the other hand, I can have privacy whenever I want it. And I don't have to be anybody's helpmeet. I only have myself to answer to."

She disappeared into the bathroom. Damon lay back in the bed. He sensed what was coming, but did nothing to prevent it. Alison had enraged him with her kind words about Rebecca and her petty criticisms of him. It was a case of one middle-aged woman taking the part of another, against the man. Women today were all too inclined to gang up on men and blame them for their own problems.

Alison was clever, all right—but she thought herself even cleverer than she was. And, decidedly, she no longer had the looks to match her posturing. She was outliving her own charms.

When she emerged from the bathroom she was dressed and had her overnight bag in her hand.

"Alison, wait," he said, thinking of the weekend he would have to spend alone. Tonight was the first time he had made love in nearly a week. It had only whetted his appetite. "Don't be so hasty." But his words lacked conviction.

She brushed a strand of hair away from her eyes with a long finger. She was getting older, all right, but she had style. In that moment, her eyes flashing with irony, she was quite magnificent.

"I used to be a hasty girl," she said. "But not anymore. There's one thing about us grown women, Damon. We always know exactly what we're doing."

I want you to know above all that the last thing I have ever wanted was to hurt you.

Things happen in life. What has happened to me may seem sudden, but it was a long time in the making. Perhaps if you understand that you'll understand why, when it happened, there was nothing I could do to stop it. It was just too late.

This may only hurt you more to hear, but the fact is that I still love you. I always will. You are a wonderful person, a special person, and I will have you in my heart always, wherever I go.

In some strange, complicated way I feel that what I have done is another way of loving you. You may hate me for saying that, but still, it is how I feel.

Forgive me, Dusty, if you can. Live your life and be happy, and try to forget all this.

Dusty held the letter in her lap. Surprisingly, her hands did not shake. She had read it many times. Each time, it seemed, she was a bit more dispassionate, more controlled in her study of the words.

Her roommate was at the door.

"What's up?"

Dusty let the letter close along its fold.

"Nothing. Just a letter. How about you?"

Brit stood leaning against the dresser. She was a somewhat overweight girl, but with a pretty face and a bright personality. She had lots of boyfriends and, Dusty suspected, an active sex life. She often returned to the apartment very late, or stayed out all night.

"Listen, Susie and Jane and I are going to a party over at this friend of Jane's place. Why don't you come along? You've been cooped up here too long."

Dusty tapped the letter against the desktop. She had not been out of the apartment, except to go to class or have dinner with her father, since the letters from Tony and her mother arrived. That was almost two weeks now. On a whim she decided to go along.

"Sure," she said. "When are you going?"

"After dinner," Brit said. "No hurry. Jane will call at eight or so."

"Sounds good."

"Want to help me cook? I'm making lyonnaise potatoes." Brit was an excellent cook for a girl her age, especially when she was making one of her favorite dishes.

"I'll think about it. I might just skip dinner."

Brit glanced at the letter in Dusty's hand. "That's not about Tony, is it?"

Dusty shook her head. "No. Just family."

Dusty had told Brit about Tony's disappearance. Brit was the only friend she would trust with a piece of information like that. She knew she could count on Brit's discretion. Brit had her own secrets, plenty of them, and knew how to keep a confidence for a friend, particularly one as close as Dusty.

But there was no question of revealing to Brit, or anyone else, the terrible truth that Dusty now knew. As far as Brit knew, it was just a case of Dusty being dumped by a boyfriend—with the wrinkle that he had dropped out of sight.

Dusty was aware of the acute limitation imposed on her by her situation. She had to become more private now. She could not confide in her close friends as she had once done. The thought of them knowing about this, talking about it behind her back, was unbearable.

She put the thought out of her mind as she closed the drawer on Tony's letter.

"So, anyway, I forgot to tell you," Brit said. "Your father called. He wants you to call him. Something about dinner in the city. Tomorrow."

"All right."

"See you later, okay?"

"Okay."

Brit closed the door behind her, silently. If she was aware from Dusty's face of the significance of the letter, that silent closing of the door might have been her way of showing it. Dusty had never been good at hiding her emotions. People said she wore her heart on her sleeve.

She opened the drawer and took out the letter from her mother. She opened it an inch, as a child opens a door a crack to peek into a room.

You are with me every second.... And whatever happens, please know that you have not lost me and will never lose me.

Dusty opened the letter wider and read some more. Then, with a small tremor, she picked up the letter from Tony and held it alongside the one from her mother. She compared the fatalistic tone of apology, the limp protestations of love. Some of the language was almost the same. The language of betrayal is always the same, she mused.

The stationery was the same size. Plain white stationery. The letters had come in the same mail. The postmarks were the same. Yet neither of them mentioned the other's name. How infantile their attempt at deception! Or was it merely discretion, or squeamishness? They could not deny the awful truth, so they filled their messages with hollow excuses and left her to draw her own conclusions.

Dusty slowly brought the two letters together so that they slid into each other, her mother's handwriting disappearing behind Tony's larger characters. She folded the letters over so that they looked like a single letter with two pages.

She went out to the bathroom. She knelt before the toilet bowl and dipped the combined letters into the water, putting both hands in with them. The water felt surprisingly cold. Gradually it soaked the cheap stationery. She shredded the paper ruminatively.

hurt you...
always love...
forgive...

The little words were now adrift on crumbling shreds of paper. As she removed her hands from the water some of them clung wetly to her skin. She had to shake her fingers to brush them off. She flushed the toilet and watched them swirl down the hole.

She telephoned her father to accept his dinner invitation for tomorrow night. He was in a meeting, so she left the message with the secretary Then she went back to her room.

Later she decided to help Brit cook dinner. They joked together as usual, and Brit found Dusty, if anything, a bit more gay than she had been in the last fortnight. Yet the loss of Tony was visible in her face. She looked as though someone had died. Brit had known that Dusty and Tony were close; Dusty had even told her that she hoped to be married next spring. The two were good friends; Brit had never seen Dusty so destroyed by anything.

Dusty did an hour of studying before it came time to leave. She put on her favorite blouse, a brushed cotton with a Middle Eastern motif in the appliqué. It had been a gift from Rebecca on Dusty's last birthday.

They met Susie and Jane and walked to the party, which was at the home of a graduate student in theater, a friend of Jane's.

There were a lot of people there whom none of the girls knew, graduate students, teaching assistants, instructors, and a couple of professors whose girth, gray hair and staid manner set them apart from the younger people.

There was wine and music, and in one of the back bedrooms marijuana was being smoked. It was a noisy evening, but not a very pleasant one. The party wasn't quite jelling; Dusty sensed that the people there had had wild times together in the past and were trying without success to re-create them tonight.

She met some girls from the theater department, who seemed pleasant though a bit too aggressive. She also met three or four boys, all of whom showed an interest in her for a while before drifting away to join their friends.

Toward eleven she was introduced to a man in his early thirties, an instructor at another university, who was in town visiting some colleagues. He asked her if she wanted to smoke, but she said no, she didn't like the hangover and she had an exam tomorrow.

He was a rather tall man, balding on top, with reddish hair and long fingers with dirty nails. They talked about art briefly, then about politics. He was a member of something-or-other, he said, and he hated everything having to do with state government. He said that change could never be effected by people whose politics were conceived at that level. She thought fleetingly of her father, who was rather thick with the state government, but she did not reply. Instead she drank her glass of wine and asked for another.

The man asked Dusty if she wanted to leave with him and she

said yes. They walked through the streets, which gave off a pleasant aroma of autumn along with the smells of gasoline and restaurant food. His hand was on her shoulder. Neither of them said anything.

The place he was staying in was a brownstone. They went in the front door. She could hear a TV playing in the front room, but they went straight up the stairs. There were bedrooms in the front and back; he took her to the back one.

She thought he might offer her another drink, and she would have liked one. But he didn't. He stood behind her, massaging her breasts through her blouse. Then he lifted her skirt and put himself inside her. She found the position clumsy and difficult, because she had nothing to balance herself against. But he seemed to like it. He ground into her for a while, his hands pulling on her hips, then finished it with a series of hard grunting thrusts.

She went to the bathroom. When she came out he was lying in the bed holding a book. He asked if she wanted to join him. She lay down, thinking they were going to do it again. But he started reading the book, and after a few minutes he turned the light off.

Dusty fell asleep for a while. When she woke up the clock read three-forty. The professor was snoring. She put on her clothes and left the house, which was now dark. The block was not known to her, but she found her way to familiar streets in a few minutes and was home in her own bed by four-fifteen. She did not shower.

The only thing in her mind was the hole in the bottom of the toilet, and the way the shreds of paper mingled as they swirled down it. She had felt as though she could taste the water just by looking at it.

She fell asleep. For the first time in two weeks she slept soundly. Brit had to wake her up at eleven to remind her of her exam.

Part Two

14

"What sins have you to confess?"

Silence. In the distance could be heard sounds of the faithful before the altar, the murmur of pious voices, the tick of beads lovingly held.

"What sins have you to confess?"

"Father, I can't say it."

Another silence. The father had heard the contrition in the voice, and yet in her silence he sensed a rigid holding-back, almost a rebellion.

"My dear, you must confess."

"I know, Father."

But she did not go on. He could feel that inside her a battle raged between abnegation and something else, something that he must not be too quick to call pride.

"God refuses no sinner who repents his sins," the priest said.

"Yes, Father."

"Whom have you sinned against?"

A pause.

"Everyone." And, after a moment, "Everything."

"No sin is too terrible to confess," he said, helping her. "God is merciful. Think of the peace that awaits you when you make your confession."

She said nothing.

"Your agony will grow worse each day if you do not confess," the priest said. "If you refuse confession, you shut the doors of heaven against yourself. It is not too late. Say what is in your heart."

Still she did not give in. A connoisseur of silences, the priest now felt that hers came from a desire to punish herself by solitude, by exile.

He heard the whisper of her clothes as she leaned closer.

Then, "Forgive me, Father." And she was gone.

Grace Island was under its usual morning fog. It clung to buildings, flagpoles, even streetlights.

Tony could almost feel the fog inside his mind, clouding his vision, preventing clarity. His thoughts were as strange as this alien city.

Unbeknownst to Rebecca, he had made an appointment with an officer in a prominent Grace law firm for this morning. He had told her he had an errand and suggested she do some shopping.

Tony wanted to take action. He needed to demonstrate to Rebecca that he could take care of her, that their relationship was not a retreat from the real world, but an entry into it. This meant he had to find a job, pursue a career.

His interview had not gone well. Despite his credentials, his excellent test scores, and his first-year grades, the man he had spoken to had not been encouraging.

"Remember, this is Canada," he said. "We're only interested in clerks who are in Canadian law schools. The same goes for associates. You'd have to pass the bar here. Your American credentials are impressive but not really appropriate."

"What would you advise?" Tony asked.

"Well, I think you should go back home and finish what you started there," the man said. "Don't let that first year go to waste. Get your degree. If you still want to practice in Canada—" here a faint raising of the eyebrows suggested the fellow wondered why any American with good credentials would wish to do such a thing "—then you could take the necessary exams and get started."

Tony had thanked the man and left. The streets of Grace looked particularly uncanny as he walked back to the hotel. Sometimes the fog settled between buildings like a blanket, making it impossible to see ten feet in front of him. At other times he would turn in astonishment to see a young girl basking on a park bench in a tunnel of sunlight, her jacket thrown off because of the sun's heat.

This was a separate world whose inhabitants knew its workings, its possibilities. It seemed to shut Tony out. He and Rebecca had used it as an escape. But now he wanted it to be a home, a place to make a life. And his first attempt to fit into it had led to failure.

And more than mere failure. Mr. Blount, the man at the law firm, had unwittingly put his finger on the powerful network of relationships and influence that Tony had thrown away in coming here. Tony's father was well known to every senior professor at Columbia. He had not even needed to write recommendations for his son, or to solicit them from his fellow attorneys. The name was so well known that Tony's admission to Columbia was a foregone conclusion.

The professors who had been so kind and encouraging to Tony during his first year were all friends of his father. Several of them were involved in litigations with his firm even then. A third was one of his partners.

Tony's path toward a distinguished career in the law had been greased from the outset by his father's fame and influence. But that influence operated within a given world of lawyers. By running away from that world, renouncing it, Tony had torn himself out of it by the roots. Now it could do nothing for him.

So here he was, marooned in a foreign country, a reasonably bright young man with no prospects—whereas, at home, he had been a reasonably bright young man with all the prospects in the world.

Well, he would just have to think of something else, he thought. He would not give up Rebecca. He had made his choice.

He hurried his steps. He had the disturbing sensation of being a lost child in a strange place, desperate to get home where he would be loved and comforted. He had to see Rebecca.

When he got back to the room she was not there. He looked at the clock: eleven-thirty. They had made a date for lunch. He missed her terribly.

He sat watching the clock for a couple of minutes, then got up to pace the room. He tried to follow his train of thought from the morning's frustration to other avenues, other plans. But he could not concentrate.

He took his jacket off and hung it with the others. On the closet floor he saw his suitcase, gathering dust now, a reminder of where he had come from and what he had left behind. He took off his tie and hung it on the rack.

Then he took off his shoes and left them on the closet floor. The idea came to him to undress completely, to be naked for Rebecca when she returned. It excited him. His fingers trembled slightly as he unbuttoned his shirt. Then he unzipped his fly and the trousers came down. His breath came short as he imagined Rebecca's clothes coming off when she came home, her white silken skin, her smile as she took him to her breast.

He finished stripping and got into the bed. The wait seemed endless. He watched the hand of the clock move from eleven-forty to eleven-forty-five. She was late. Where could she be?

He was getting hungry. His morning had been a tiring one, and he had eaten no breakfast. The separate demands of his body began to vie with each other, just as contradictory trains of thought vied for control of his mind. He started to get up to dress, then lay back.

At last the key sounded in the door, and Rebecca came in.

Her eyes widened as she saw his nudity. But she did not smile. She looked upset.

"You're late," he said gently. "Where have you been?"

"Oh... Just shopping around." She forced a smile. She looked pale. "How did your morning go?"

"Not good, not bad." His desire for her was, if anything, increased by her crisp dress and the worried look on her face. For nearly an hour he had been looking forward to being naked with her, to enclosing himself in her warmth. "And yours?"

"Oh, fine."

"Come to me, then." He held out his arms to her.

She put down her purse and stood looking at him. She seemed off balance. Gingerly she removed her shoes and came to sit on the edge of the bed.

Her eyes were red.

"You've been crying," he said. "Why?"

He drew her to his face. She caressed his cheeks nervously with both hands, kissed him on his brow.

"Something has upset you," he said. "Tell me. Please, Rebecca." His voice had that soothing, fatherly tone that often came out of him when he wanted to give her pleasure, to make her happy.

She smiled weakly. "I love to hear you say my name," she said.

He held both her hands. "Tell me."

She sighed. "I've been to church," she said. "I've been to confession."

Tony felt a shock go through him. He held on to her hands for a moment, then released them.

"Confession," he repeated, as though testing the word.

She nodded.

"Why would you want to do a thing like that?" he asked.

She shook her head. "That's hard to explain," she said.

"How long has it been?" he asked.

She laughed. "A long time," she said. "Many years."

"But now you went." He was watching her more closely.

"Yes. Now I went."

His desire had left him, or rather turned into something else. He felt sheepish and somewhat silly in his nudity. Her news had put everything in a different light.

She felt his distress and kissed him on the lips. "It's nothing you should feel bad about," she said.

But he did feel bad.

He sat back, put his hands behind his head and looked at her.

"Perhaps you could have told me you were considering it," he said.

"I—yes, perhaps I should have," she said. "But I didn't want to. I'm not sure why. It didn't seem right."

"It was a private matter," he said, an edge in his voice.

"Yes, it is private," she agreed. "I imagine that's why. You see, I didn't want to bother you with it."

"Bother me?" he said. "Nothing in your heart could ever bother me, Rebecca."

"Bless you for that." She kissed him again. But he could feel that they were not going to make love. Something else had come between them.

"On the other hand, maybe it does bother me," he said.

"Oh, darling, it shouldn't." Now she was trying to make light of it, to dismiss it as a ritual without significance. But it was too late for that; she had already admitted that this was her first time in many years.

"What was it you confessed?" he asked.

She looked away. For an instant she thought of telling him the truth, that she had not been able to bring herself to confess at all. But somehow she could not do this.

"It was us, wasn't it?" He kept his hands behind his head.

She said nothing. Her eyes looked misty again.

"And what is it about us that you felt you had to confess?" The caressing fatherly tone had become faintly inquisitorial.

"Oh, Tony," she said. "You mustn't misunderstand. I could never feel bad about us. There is nothing to apologize for, to regret.... But this is—this is something else. Something I had to do."

"Why?"

She sighed. "Please, love, don't cross-examine me about it. Try to understand."

But Tony did not understand.

He pondered his own emotions. Part of him was distressed that she had withheld such private thoughts, thoughts of such gravity, from him. She should have confided them. Part of him was dismayed that she should have confided these thoughts to a stranger, a priest, instead of himself. Worst of all was the idea that she had spoken to this third party, this interloper, *about* him, about their love, their life together.

"Understand what? That it's your business?" He sat up slightly, raising his knees. They made a little wall between himself and her.

"Well, not exactly." She was smiling. "Everything about me is your business. That's why I've told you. But Tony, this is special. If you'd been brought up as I was, you'd understand."

"Understand what?"

She furrowed her brow, trying to find the right words, the right logic. She herself had not thought the thing through until this moment. She felt caught off guard.

"That confessing about us doesn't mean I repudiated us," she said. "In a sense it's the opposite. I wanted to make it—"

"Official?" He smiled.

She laughed. "Official, yes. In a sense."

But she had not done so. At the crucial moment she had held her tongue. Now it was too late to admit to that.

Tony looked thoughtful.

"Still," he said, "it was a confession. It wasn't a happy announcement. Was it?"

Rebecca sighed. "It was an announcement that I was human," she said. "And that's not a thing that I regret."

Tony looked away. Outside the window was the same thick fog, seething silently in the cool air. They had taken to leaving the curtains apart, even when they made love, because the fog was like a deep coat of white that made it impossible for anyone to see in. A cloud that concealed and protected them.

But now that privacy seemed gone.

"And what did your priest say?" he asked. "Your 'father'?"

Rebecca turned a shade paler.

"Tony, can't we forget this?"

"You mean it's between you and him?"

She sighed. "Well, yes. You have to understand, Tony, that a Catholic has a special place reserved for the priest. It doesn't mean my heart doesn't belong to you. It just means that as myself, as my own person, I choose to share my sense of my actions with God."

"And what did God say?" he asked.

Stung by his sarcasm, she thought for a split second, then answered. "Nothing."

Tony was looking toward the window.

"That doesn't sound like God to me," he said. "Did He tell you you were a sinner?"

"Oh, Tony..."

"And what about me? He must have told you I was a sinner, too."

She put both her hands on his chest in a weak gesture of protest.

"Oh, my dear," she said. "How could you be a sinner? You're too young to have had evil thoughts."

This did not seem to satisfy him.

"Yet you confess to God about what you did with me. What does that say about me?"

Rebecca began to talk, nervously and rather clumsily, about what she had done. She tried to make Tony feel that her confession was an affirmation of their love. But the more she talked, the more she could feel him receding into himself. She could almost read his thoughts. He was blaming himself for having gotten her into this spiritual crisis. He was also jealous of her faith, jealous of the priest to whom she had talked of him, of God who must know her innermost thoughts as a stern father, before Tony, her man, could know them.

But she had not confessed. The very act over which they were arguing had not even taken place. This seemed the most terrible secret of all. To have remained silent when the priest summoned her to speak was unforgivable.

Tony seemed convinced that, despite her protestations, she had, on some deep, unacknowledged level, denied him. Rebecca was of two minds. Part of her thought Tony was not trying hard enough to understand. The other part saw that, in a very small but real sense, he was right.

"Darling, I can't stand this," she said at last. "Don't shut me out any longer. Please. I can't stand it."

He was holding both her hands. He released them and ran his fingers up her bare arms to her shoulders. Then, slowly, he cupped her breasts in his palms. He began to undo the buttons of her blouse.

She looked into his eyes. He was watching her closely, measuring the meaning of her emotion. The blouse was undone now, and the bra was coming loose. He raised himself to her breast, kissing it, then sucking gently at the nipple.

She knew what he was doing. He was asking her to choose him in a new way. To give up something she had not given up before. If she denied him this, he would know she did not belong to him as he had thought.

She took his head in her hands and cradled it. He was pulling the blouse out of her skirt now. She saw the whole length of his naked body, the long legs curled a bit, like those of a child, as he held himself to her breast.

She lay down with him, and the rest of her clothes came off, tumbled in the sheets like resolutions abandoned. The rustle of the fabrics reminded her of the dim rustle of the priest's vestment behind the window of the confessional. Soon he was making love to her, and the tickle that had begun in her breast was all through the quick of her, and the sigh he had listened to was a long gasp shaking her all over.

Rebecca gave in with a shudder. She had never received him so completely, not even that first day when he came to her on the beach at Sands Point. But, even at the height of her passion, she was not sure he knew this or could feel it. He seemed to be probing for a corner that did not belong to him, that withheld itself. There was no peace in him, or in her.

His thrusts brought eager moans from her. But she was also

aware that this eagerness for surrender was not coming naturally from her, not as it had been before. The terrible heat inside her was something new, something hard and unyielding that separated her from him even as it joined her to him. Now she knew that their quarrel had changed something, made something into an illusion or revealed it as an illusion. She should not have confessed to him. Had she held her tongue, the silence could have remained complete, the screen immaculate.

15

Damon did not see Alison after their quarrel at the Côte d'Azur.

At first he thought this was simply because he was so busy. His struggles with the mayor and his men occupied his days; his anguish over Rebecca and Dusty devoured his nights.

But before long he was forced to recognize that it was pride that stood between him and Alison. The days passed without her getting in touch; each new day's silence made him more stubborn in refusing to make the first move toward her.

He could not forgive Alison for having taken Rebecca's side against him during their quarrel. She had spoken as a woman, she had closed ranks with the great sorority of wronged women when she spoke of Rebecca. This maddened Damon, particularly since he, not Rebecca, was the wronged party. It was himself—and Dusty—that Rebecca had abandoned.

So he could not forgive Alison. And he knew that, on her own side, Alison was a proud woman. He had known that about her for many years. She had a sharp edge to her, a fierce determination to have things her own way, to be treated with respect. This inner toughness had been crucial to her greatly successful career. It was also part of the way she made love. She did not yield to pleasure; she sought it and took it. He had always enjoyed this about her.

Now that they had had their quarrel, he wondered how he had made it through so many years without getting on her wrong side. She was a demanding woman, sarcastic when she wanted to be, sensitive to the least slight. And Damon himself was not the easiest man to get along with, or the most considerate. Generally speaking, he was wrapped up in himself. This had been his downfall with Rebecca, after all. He could not help wondering how Alison had stood him all these years.

In any case, she was gone now, and there was little point in pining after her. She would never apologize, never call him until he called her. And he was in no mood to mend fences. He felt she had kicked him when he was down. It was up to her to humble herself and come back to him.

So things stood, until Damon realized that his hurt pride alone could not sustain him. Alison left a hole in his life, sexually as well as emotionally. After his exhausting workdays, he had been in the habit of coming to her like a famished infant. He had never needed physical satisfaction more.

He had been alone for weeks now. He needed another woman.

He found her close at hand.

Her name was Ashley, and she worked as an administrative assistant in the county assessor's office. He had seen her several times on his way to meetings at city hall, and once noticed her name on the plaque on her desk. Now her face came to him, and he picked up the phone almost without thinking.

He called the assessor's office and asked for her by name. He was put through right away.

"Hello?"

"This is Damon Lowell. Do you know who I am?"

After a brief pause she replied, "Sure."

"I've seen you several times, but we've never been properly introduced. You're a very lovely girl."

"Oh—thanks."

"Would you like to have dinner tonight?"

This time the pause was even briefer.

"Sure. What time?"

Damon took her to an out-of-the-way Italian place in the Village where, in his more discreet days, he used to take Alison.

The girl was only twenty-two years old. She had an associate's degree from City College and a legal secretary's diploma. She had begun with a law firm two years ago, but quit because of the rock-bottom wages and the overwork. He joked about it with her; she said she would never work for a lawyer again.

She had a good figure, long in the thighs. She was fresh-looking, with auburn hair, milky skin and a freckled nose. Her eyes were a light blue, almost transparent, and it was their expression that had attracted him to her last year, when he first saw her. It was not a look of great intelligence, but of awareness, and of a willingness to dare certain things, he thought.

He was not wrong. She made love (in the apartment, in the bed he had shared with Rebecca) eagerly. What she lacked in experience, she made up for in the freshness of her body and the naughtiness of her imagination.

"Does it feel good when I do this?" she asked, crouched before him naked, her breasts standing out young and firm as she ran her fingers down his thighs.

"Yes."

"And how about this?" Her hands grew bolder. "Does this feel good?"

She enjoyed egging him on with whispered words that sounded self-conscious at first, and then, for a reason he could not fathom, remarkably sexy. Damon was struck by the difference between her and Alison, whose lovemaking was subtle, mature, but a bit too familiar to him after so many years.

He took her out again the next night—making time for her by canceling a meeting with one of the lawyers for the City—and found that he already needed her. He came out of the bathroom and saw her lying in bed naked, one knee upraised, holding out her arms to him, the slim fingers fluttering.

"Come on, baby," she said. "I want you."

He buried his face in her young breast and felt as though a door had opened to him that he had passed by too many times without bothering to notice its secrets.

She was not without the practical sort of brains that are required of any good secretary. And she had street smarts born of her childhood in the city. He wondered briefly how much sleeping around she had done, but dismissed the thought as the delights of her body took him over.

When they had finished she lay looking at him.

"They say you're a real shark," she said.

"Do they?"

"Yes, they do. I heard you would walk over your best friend to get a favorable decision."

This surprised Damon. He thought of himself as someone venerable, a man who had worked his way to a high position through brains, charm and thoroughness. A man who commanded respect.

He had never heard himself characterized as a cold or uncaring man. Naturally he had played hard in his years as an attorney; that was the name of the game, after all. Intimidation was an integral part of strategy, in the best interests of the client.

He realized that Ashley, despite her sexual playfulness, was in awe of him, or at least impressed by him. There was an odd look in those clear eyes when she listened to him talk, a grave look, which he soon realized was born of her consciousness of his importance, his power.

Flattered, he let himself indulge in a modicum of self-congratulation when he was with her. He bragged about the central role he was playing in the Hightower project, and regaled her with inside jokes about the mayor.

"Sometimes I almost feel he wishes I would tie his tie for him," Damon said. "He's that dependent."

"I thought Lazare hated Ivy League types," Ashley said. "Isn't he supposed to be the man of the people and all that?"

"Not really," Damon replied. "That's his image. In reality he's very ambivalent about educated men from upper-class backgrounds."

"Ambivalent?" Ashley asked.

Damon realized she did not know the meaning of the word.

"On one hand he resents them," he explained. "On the other hand he wishes he could be one of them. He blows hot and cold about it. For some reason he's very high on me. Calls me nearly every day. He acts as though he's afraid to make a move without my approval."

"He probably recognizes real brains when he sees them," Ashley complimented him.

"I don't know about that," Damon replied modestly. "He might not see beyond an old family name and a Harvard degree."

"Don't sell yourself short," Ashley said. "You've got the balls to go with the brains." And she closed the subject by slipping a soft hand between his legs.

Damon put himself out to find more time for Ashley during the following weeks. She offered a welcome contrast to the mental strain of his workdays. He slept better than he had in years. When, in the mornings, he saw her move naked through the kitchen of the apartment, her smooth young legs working gracefully, he had a sense of invigoration and even of home, which was doubly precious because of his solitary status.

There was the problem of hiding Ashley from Dusty, of course. Dusty came over more often now, sometimes to cook him dinner and sometimes to go out with him. There was no way to avoid this, and indeed Damon wanted it. After all, he and Dusty had been abandoned by Rebecca—Dusty no doubt more painfully than he—and all they had now was each other.

Dusty never stayed late. She always took a cab back to campus by ten or ten-thirty at the latest. Damon was aware that she didn't feel as close to him as she might have liked, and that he was not the ideal confidant for her in her grief and pain. Indeed, the embarrassing truth about Tony—of whom they no longer spoke—made it impossible for them to share their respective thoughts with the candor that might have made them grow closer.

So there was a somewhat ceremonial air about their phone conversations, their dinners, their occasional nights at the theater or the ballet. Damon was doing his duty toward Dusty, and she, for her own part, was taking care of her abandoned father.

Their evenings left him feeling frustrated, and his frustration turned quickly to desire. Often he would phone Ashley the minute Dusty had left, telling her to jump in a cab and come up right away. Only a half hour would separate the image of his blond daughter waving as she got into the elevator, from that of his sensual young mistress—barely older than Dusty—slipping into the co-op, her eyes twinkling. He would ponder the enormous difference made by upbringing, money and ambition in the two girls. It was literally impossible to think of Dusty in the same breath as Ashley. Yet they were so close in age.

Once Ashley came over wearing nothing under her raincoat, just to excite him. As the garment came off in his hands, her naked body greeting his eyes, he felt in his hands the memory of Dusty's coat, which he had taken in just the same way a few hours before. And this time he did see the similarity of the two bodies, the firmness of youth, its confident movements. For some reason this made his heart go out to Ashley. There was so much between himself and Dusty that could not be broached, so much pain to endure—while Ashley padded around the apartment with all the assurance and calm of a little girl without a care in the world, her nudity the emblem of her happy innocence.

Once Dusty telephoned when he was lying in bed with Ashley in his arms. He felt a moment's panic, not so much at the objective situation—Dusty could just as well have rung the buzzer from the lobby below—as from the dislocation of hearing his daughter's voice while his mistress's soft blue eyes rested on him. At that moment the two girls seemed too close, and Damon thought he was taking another sort of risk—not practical but, as it were, psychological—in enjoying himself with Ashley while Dusty was going through such a terrible time.

But he needed his pleasure. When he hung up the phone, having promised to meet Dusty for dinner the next night, he forgot all about her, and pressed his lips to the nipple of the girl beside him as though she were the only girl in the world.

16

Dusty went to bed with five different boys before midterms.

They weren't really boys. Two were graduate students, one was an assistant professor, and two were seniors.

Of the latter, one was a fellow named Dan Bowditch, who was well known as a womanizer. Two of Dusty's friends had dated him in the past; both had exclaimed about the heavy sexual pressure he had put on them, and Dusty suspected both had surrendered without much of a struggle.

Dan was a handsome boy, tall, sandy-haired, with lazy eyes and a smooth, rather proprietary manner. He was a business major and came from a rich family. He was intelligent and could glibly carry on conversations on all manner of topics depending on who his audience was.

The night Dusty was introduced to him he spent a quick half hour drinking vodka with her, his casual questions barely masking his interest in getting her into bed.

"So, would you like to take a walk after this?" he asked, looking at his watch.

"Yes," she said, and saw the brief glint of triumph in his eyes.

He was a reasonably good lover, slow at least, but when it was over he seemed to forget her existence. He did not offer to walk her home. She went by herself, hugging her coat around her in the unseasonably cold air.

The following week she got a call from another senior boy named Carl Weathergill. He said he was a former roommate of Dan's and that Dan had spoken highly of Dusty as a "great girl."

Dusty slept with Carl that same night at an apartment co-rented by a handful of male students on Horatio Street. It was a filthy place, full of empty beer cans and liquor bottles, and ashtrays with mountains of cigarette butts in them. There were two bedrooms, each with a double bed complete with lumpy mattress and stains on the sheets.

Carl offered Dusty cocaine and showed her how to snort it. She felt nothing for a long time. Then, as he was taking off her clothes, a sort of cruel brilliance entered her brain, and everything that happened after that was bathed in a hot sensual light that made her feel as though she was being burned through.

Carl dropped her off at her apartment, kissing her quickly on the lips.

"You're terrific," he said.

She never saw Dan Bowditch again, but Carl called her often over the next several weeks. He would pick her up at her house and take her to the apartment, where they would make love and then sit watching television or listening to music. He introduced her to crack, but after that first night he said he couldn't get any. She lay nude on the bed, watching him talk on the phone to his friends. One night he had to study, but he made love to her first.

How the graduate students got her name Dusty wasn't sure. They were better lovers than the undergraduates, but they didn't do drugs. The assistant professor was terrible in bed, but when she asked him he got some coke from one of his students and snorted with her.

She took to working hard on her studies during the day, because more and more her nights were filled with men. Brit and her other friends noticed how popular she was getting. Some of the girls envied her, but others suspected what was going on.

Brit tried to talk to her one night not long before Thanksgiving. "Dusty, are these men treating you right?" she asked.

Dusty shrugged. "Men are men."

Brit sat down beside her. "I just don't want you to get hurt," she said. "You've been hurt enough already."

"Don't worry about it," Dusty said. "I'm fine."

Worriedly, Brit went to bed.

On Thanksgiving Dusty cooked dinner for Damon in the apartment. She said she had a lot of work to do, and didn't want to make the long trip to Sands Point. Damon was not displeased, for his work was keeping him close to the office these days.

He offered her wine with dinner and told her how lovely she looked.

"You're a real young woman now," he said. "I wish your..."

They both looked away. She knew he was about to say he wished her mother could see her now. It had been nearly three months.

Damon found that an admiring paternal manner came naturally to him with Dusty. Part of his new relationship with her was his leadership role. He was the responsible one, the giver of news. It fell to him to keep her informed, in roundabout ways, about "things," and also to try to lessen the pain, to try to make the world seem like a reasonable place where justice still existed.

This was a job that had been handled by Rebecca when Dusty was a child. It was Rebecca who listened to Dusty's ceaseless questions, to her repeated "Why?" and explained the world to her. Damon, always busy, had never been available for this. When he saw Dusty he would ask her in a rather formal way about her school day or her friends, and get a monosyllabic answer. They never really conversed.

Now he had to talk, and he did so. He told her his own news, down-pedaling its importance, of course, and tried to draw her out about school. He feigned a close interest in her course work and her career aspirations. She was sending applications to graduate schools, and they talked about that. He asked her about her social life, without intruding on her privacy. They both had to continually talk around the fact that she had lost Tony, and the even more monstrous circumstances of the loss.

They discussed the problems facing young people in the present-day world—unemployment, underemployment, sexually transmitted disease, divorce, two-income families. Damon found himself speaking in a commiserating, empathic tone. He even spoke warmly about the pressures being heaped on women nowadays.

"It's a harder world than the one I grew up in," Damon said. "Sometimes I wonder how you young people can bear to face it."

"Oh, Dad." Dusty smiled. "It's not that bad. Things have always been hard."

"I'm glad to see you so cheerful about it," he said, smiling.

A new tenderness had sprung up between them. Damon found himself wanting to hover over her like a worried mother, but at the same time with a father's helplessness and ignorance of female problems. She had to constantly reassure him that she was doing fine, that she was studying hard, that she had as many friends as ever.

The subject of Tony was too painful for them to refer to directly, but once in a while Damon would ask her in a significant voice "how she was doing," and she would reassure him that she was fine, that she was "over it," that it was important to go on and not to live in the past.

Damon felt his heart go out to her when he saw how bravely she was shouldering the terrible weight he himself had to carry. After all, he was older, experienced in the ways of the world, and Dusty was still young, still incompletely formed. Damon felt an uncharacteristic surge of insight as he compared her brittle, proud display of self-sufficiency to his own more self-pitying feelings. What a strange thing youth was, he thought. Stubborn and yet adaptable. Dusty's young life would forever bear the scar, the distortion of what had happened to her, but she would go on living. And some day it would only be a small twist in her structure, perhaps invisible to her future husband, to her children. But it would be there, inside her....

Damon hated Rebecca for what she had done and was doing to Dusty. And for what she had done to him. For forcing him to learn these new and terrible feelings, for forcing him into a new world of thought and experience he wished he had never known. Somehow, some day, he hoped to get revenge.

But when he thought of Dusty and her brave adjustment to things, his anger at Rebecca took a back seat to sympathy and to hope. He wanted above all for Dusty to be all right, to overcome this misfortune. This was a new experience for Damon, this parental love that drained away all resentments, leaving only a devouring concern and love in its wake.

Gradually he realized that the ordeal he was enduring was making him grow as a man, forcing him to adapt to the world in a new way. And in this thought there was ironic gratitude for the unexpected benefits occasioned by a great loss. He hated Rebecca, to be sure, but her running away had in some ways changed him for the better. He noticed a freshness in himself, a readiness for experience and emotion, that he had not felt in a very long time.

Dusty seemed to respond to this previously unseen side of Damon. She behaved more warmly to him. She talked more openly

about things in general. She seemed to have outgrown the adolescent moodiness and reticence that had characterized her in recent
years. Sometimes she would comment on a book, a movie, or even
a political issue with an adultness that made Damon proud. Occasionally she would state an idea with a turn of phrase so thoughtful,
so grave, that Damon would feel his eyes misting all at once, and
he would have to look away.

Once in a while these turns of phrase owed something to Rebecca, who had always had a way with words. Damon tried not to
notice this similarity.

On Thanksgiving Dusty did not stay overnight. She said she had
to study for an economics exam. Damon insisted on having his own
driver take her home, despite her desire not to disturb the man on
a holiday. He kissed her goodbye at the door, saying, "Take care
of yourself, honey," and watched as she waited for the elevator.

When she was gone he called Ashley, who came over at eleven
and spent the night. Feeling her young body in his arms, he thought
of Dusty, and a strange mellow sadness added itself to his excitement. He cradled the young woman in his embrace, feeling protective and warm, and tried without success to add up the pleasures
and agonies of his existence, the injustices and the redeeming moments, the complex levels of his feelings. It was so bewildering.
He would have felt old in that moment, old and outwitted by life,
had it not been for the soft young girl moaning in his arms and
shuddering as he pushed himself deeper into her. Pride eclipsed
confusion as he brought her to her climax; and he slept heavily all
night.

After being dropped off, Dusty made a telephone call and went to
the apartment on Horatio Street. A couple of young men from another university were there, visiting friends in the city. They spent
the evening drinking, smoking dope and taking turns having sex
with Dusty. At one point, crazed by the accumulation of the drugs,
they tried a threesome. Dusty had the impression they were getting
off on each other more than on her. She left in the wee hours,
convinced they were going to do it together as soon as she was
gone.

She walked home and got into bed without showering. Between her legs she could feel the numb throbbing of sex.

The last face she saw before she fell asleep was her father's. The eyes were teary, the features drawn down by sadness as he smiled at her with paternal pride.

The next day, Friday, she studied for the economics exam she had told Damon about. Despite her hangover and the lack of sleep, her mind was clear. She concentrated well, kept orderly notes on her readings, and later got an A on the exam.

17

Christmas was coming.

Rebecca was wandering the streets, looking at the decorations as she shopped for a gift for Tony.

She kept seeing things in the stores that would be perfect for Dusty. Her maternal antennae continually directed her steps to clothing stores where they had things in Dusty's style—that faintly conservative yet sporty style that Dusty had liked since she left high school.

It was so easy to find things! She knew her daughter's body as well as her own. She knew which outfit would go with one of Dusty's favorite pairs of shoes, which skirt would match the sweater that Rebecca herself had bought for Dusty last winter.

A thousand motherly impulses pulled at Rebecca, confusing her as she passed the stores. She could almost feel the sights and sounds of home in her very skin, for Christmas was a time full of memories of home. Shopping on Fifth Avenue, meeting friends for lunch, responding to invitations, planning the party she and Damon always gave for the partners about a week before Christmas. Shopping for Damon, for Dusty, for Irene, for aunts and uncles and cousins. And most of all, looking forward to having Dusty home for a week or two.

"What do you want Santa to bring you for Christmas?" Rebecca would joke with her when the holidays approached.

"Oh, Mother," Dusty replied. "I can't think of a thing."

But Rebecca had always been able to think of something. And her choice was always right. She knew her daughter that well.

Rebecca had had trouble getting used to Dusty's absence when she left for college. She had needed her more than she realized. The closeness between them had never been very articulate, but there was a sense in which Rebecca lived only for her daughter.

Her ability to anticipate Dusty's moods, Dusty's needs, had sustained Rebecca for many years. It was the one thing she was sure of in life. Though it was she who did the protecting, the helping, the bond was perhaps more precious to her than to her daughter. Dusty could take it for granted as a fact of life; while to Rebecca it was a gift that made up for all of life's injustices.

In many ways mother and daughter were alike. They shared a chariness, a cautious attitude toward things and people. As though the approach of misfortune could be lurking behind even the sunniest of days. On the other hand, Dusty was more ambitious than Rebecca, more aware of herself, more stubborn. As a little girl, she had extended her "terrible twos" for about five years, answering "No!" to nearly every parental question—not to mention a request or admonition—and saying "Let me do it" or "I can do it myself" whenever there was a choice between doing a thing herself or accepting Rebecca's help.

"She's a free spirit," Damon had observed at the time.

"That's putting it mildly," Rebecca had agreed.

"She's like you," he had added, with his usual lack of insight.

"More like my mother," Rebecca had corrected him. "She knows what she wants, and she won't take no for an answer."

For a long time Rebecca had hoped this stubbornness would lift Dusty right out of the family and into her own life. But as Dusty got older and had to face the competitive adolescent world of her private school, she began to shrink into herself more. She shied away from ambitious undertakings and chose her girlfriends from the less popular group at school. She became quiet, and the worried look that had so long been a hallmark of her mother's personality found its way into her own face. It was somehow different there, shading the clear blond looks of a young and vibrant girl, but it was visible nonetheless.

When Dusty went to college, the two aspects of her character seemed to find a new harmony. She became active in undergraduate life, grew more intellectually ambitious and, when home on vacation, showed a poise and confidence that impressed Rebecca. She argued amicably with Damon about politics and espoused a feminism that irritated him while charming Rebecca.

Somehow by respecting Dusty's new independence, Rebecca had

felt closer to her. She was proud of her daughter and enjoyed seeing her try her own wings in life.

But now that orderly progress had been interrupted forever.

Rebecca put Dusty out of her mind as she went into a department store called Harper's. She was looking for a sweater or jacket for Tony. He had found a job as a trainee in an investment firm and would be at work all day today. She was on her own.

Tony had begun taking night classes, and was planning to change his career to investment counseling. He was very stubborn about the whole thing. He wanted income as well as a direction in life.

"I want to take care of you," he said.

"But you're already doing that," she argued.

He shook his head. "You know what I mean."

Her own money seemed to embarrass him. He encouraged her to spend less, to live more on what he earned. This amused her because it seemed so unnecessary; but it also made her proud. She was touched by Tony's determination to make their life together something serious and solid, as varied and rich and complicated as anyone else's life. She herself wanted to share down-to-earth things like worry about money with him.

And yet, somehow, the situation disturbed her. For one thing, it made her ashamed of her own money. And this embarrassed her about her age, about how much further she had come in life than Tony. She could not escape the feeling that they were both playing at being real people in a real world. Had they not left that world behind by the very nature of their flight from it? They were exiles now, as the looks on the faces of those who saw them together proved. Exiles not only from a place, not only from their families, but from a whole way of living. And everyone who came into contact with them saw it at once.

In getting a job, in pursuing a career, Tony was desperately trying to throw a veil of normality over their relationship. But it was a veil that everyone—including, most of all, Rebecca—could see through.

The full enormity of carrying through this crazy adventure to the end was now dawning on Rebecca. She was old enough to be Tony's mother. He had joked about it, saying there were lots of brothers and sisters that far apart in age. But in a few years Rebecca would be in her sixties, and Tony only a robust forty. And after that... Well, what came after that was better left alone.

Rebecca might have escaped the sharpest sting of this realization had it not been for her thoughts about Dusty. She still could not help feeling like a mother to Dusty. She wanted to be in touch with her, wanted to give her Christmas presents, to listen to her worries and comfort her. To be part of her life. And it was this impulse, the most basic of her being, that was now frustrated. The bond between herself and Dusty had been destroyed. And the destroyer was Rebecca herself.

Dusty would never forgive her. And why should she? No doubt Dusty's very sanity, at this point, hinged on a healthy outrage at her mother's crime, a healthy hatred of her mother. Rebecca's own maternal instinct told her this must be so, should be so. She would not have it any other way.

And so Rebecca was, after twenty years, a daughterless mother. This nightmare was reality. But she would never get used to it. And because of it, all life seemed illusory.

She found a sport jacket for Tony and was on the point of taking it to the cashier when she decided to think it over for one more day. Perhaps it wasn't quite Tony's style after all.

She allowed herself a stroll through the women's section on the fourth floor before leaving. She saw a skirt-and-sweater outfit that was so perfect for Dusty that she could not resist buying it. She knew she might not have the courage to send it, but she could not help herself.

Feeling more than a bit guilty, she got into the elevator and pushed the button for the ground floor.

The elevator was old and very slow. The floor numbers were indicated by a brass needle that moved in a semicircle.

Rebecca watched the needle move downward from four to three, then from three to two.

But the conveyance stopped before reaching the second floor. Not a shudder or a sound announced the malfunction. The movement simply ceased. The light dimmed, brightened, then dimmed again.

Rebecca pushed the button for the main floor. Nothing happened. She tried the button for two, then for three. Nothing.

Sighing, she tried the buttons again. Then she waited. When

nothing happened after a full minute, she overcame her hesitancy and pushed the alarm button. A shrill bell sounded somewhere up the shaft. When she stopped pushing, the bell stopped.

"Damn." She pushed the alarm button again, and yet again.

The bell sounded faraway and feeble.

She was not about to cry for help. Not yet, anyway. Her innate shyness prevented that. But she was beginning to feel something like panic.

Suddenly a voice sounded just below her.

"Hello? Are you all right in there?"

"Is someone there?" she called. "I'm stuck in here."

"I'm pushing the button out here," called the voice. "Is anything happening?"

Rebecca looked at the needle, which had not moved.

"Nothing!" she called.

"Don't worry," the voice said. "I'll get someone."

Rebecca now realized she had almost reached the second floor when the breakdown occurred. The voice had been just outside the heavy doors of the elevator.

She waited, listening to the fluttery sound of her own breathing and trying to stay calm. She had always been a little nervous in elevators, but had never been stuck in one before.

She put down her shopping bag and stood, her hands clasped together.

"Come on, come on," she murmured.

After a couple of minutes that seemed an eternity, she heard steps outside the door and voices raised in urgent conversation. Then the voice she had heard before called, "Are you all right in there?"

"Yes! I'm all right."

"Good for you. He's fixing it right now. Hang on one more minute."

Rebecca stood quietly, her fear already eclipsed by her embarrassment at having attracted the attention of strangers. Absurdly she found herself rehearsing what she would say to her rescuers when she got out of here.

She did not have more than a minute to ponder these thoughts before the elevator started with a shudder and went down to the second floor. The doors opened and she hurried out.

"Good for you. No harm done, I hope?"

A man whose face she recognized was smiling at her. She took the hand he was holding out and clasped it in mingled thanks and greeting.

"Thank you so much," she said. "I was just beginning to get worried."

A man in overalls came from the stairwell adjacent to the elevator and looked at Rebecca.

"Are you the lady who was inside?" he asked. "Are you all right?"

"She's fine." The familiar-looking man spoke for her. "No harm done."

Rebecca did her best to reassure the man in overalls, who seemed more upset than she was. He explained something about a short in the control plate, repeating himself several times. An assistant manager of the store came along to offer profuse apologies and to ask Rebecca whether she wished to lie down in the upstairs lounge.

By now Rebecca was more amused than anything else, and allowed the familiar-looking man to extricate her from the store's employees.

"Back to normal now?" he asked.

"Perfect," she said. "You look familiar to me. Haven't we met somewhere?"

"I've seen you at the Royal Grace," he said, "but we've never spoken. Sam Bittman's my name."

"I'm glad to meet you, Mr. Bittman," she said. "My name is Rebecca Lowell. Thank you for coming to my rescue."

"Oh, I didn't do anything," he said. "Isn't it funny, though? I've seen you many times at the hotel, but we probably never would have spoken if it hadn't been for a faulty elevator."

"Yes," she agreed. "Fate took a hand."

She studied his face. He had curly iron-gray hair and ruddy skin. He looked different without the reading glasses he usually wore when she saw him stopping at the desk in the hotel lobby. His eyes were bright and intelligent, and his manner was courtly and good-humored. The suit he wore was conservative, but there was something informal and attractively rumpled about his demeanor.

She noticed he was carrying a shopping bag from the store. "Have you been Christmas shopping, too?" she asked.

"Trying to, yes," he said. "Are you sure you're all right?"

"Of course. I'm very much indebted to you."

"Not at all. We're neighbors, more or less, so it was the least I could do." He noticed her own shopping bag. "Were you on your way out?"

"Yes, as a matter of fact."

"Me, too. Say, what would you think about a bite of lunch? I know a nice little place right around the corner where you can catch your breath. You still look a little pale to me."

His eyes expressed concern and friendliness, but now Rebecca thought she saw something shadowed behind his smile. She guessed that grief had played a role on the modeling of his features.

She looked down at her hands and realized they were shaking. She was more upset than she had thought.

"It's just lunchtime," he pursued. "What do you say?"

His voice was remarkably soothing. There was an old-world charm about him that made her feel safe.

"All right," she said. "I'd like that."

They took the stairs down to the first floor and went out of the store through the revolving doors. The restaurant was right where he said it was, and Rebecca recognized it from having passed it with Tony. It was a French place with checked tablecloths and Impressionist posters on the walls. At Sam Bittman's invitation Rebecca ordered a glass of white wine, which immediately soothed the tingling in her nerves.

He pointed to her shopping bag on the empty chair between them.

"Who's the present for?" he asked.

"My daughter," Rebecca said.

"Don't tell me," he said. "You were looking through the women's section and you saw something that would be absolutely perfect for her."

"How did you know?" Rebecca asked.

"Mothers," he said with a wry smile. "I'll bet you know just what she'll like and what will look good on her, and what will match her other clothes. If only I had that talent."

He pointed to his own bag. "This will probably bring more jeers than cheers," he said. "But at least I tried."

"It's for your daughter, I take it?" Rebecca asked.

He nodded.

"How old is she?"

"Twenty," he said with a little shake of his head. "And does she know it."

"Is she your only daughter?"

"Oh, no," he said. "No such luck. I've got three. But she's the most trouble, I'll say that for her. The other two are grown up and married. This one may never grow up."

Rebecca smiled. "Clothes for the not-grown-up," she said. "I think I understand perfectly. My own daughter is twenty-one."

"I used to think by the time they were twenty you didn't have to worry about them," he said. "It turned out that the real worries started at just that time."

"I'm afraid you have a point there," Rebecca said.

Again she noticed the telltale signs of sadness behind his humor. She suspected he was divorced, or perhaps a widower.

"I've noticed you often at the Royal," Rebecca said. "Does your business bring you here?"

"Every three or four weeks," he said. "I live and work back in Wisconsin, but I have some business here."

"I see."

It occurred to Rebecca that her own face must be just as familiar to him as his was to her. As must Tony's. Mercifully, though, Mr. Bittman was neither mentioning Tony nor asking her about her own long-term tenure at the Royal Grace.

He looked around at the pretty restaurant. "I don't relish being away from home at this time of year," he said, "but at the moment there's no way out of it. I'm starting a branch of my company up here, and if I don't keep an eye on things, it will fall to pieces before it even gets started."

"What sort of business is it?" Rebecca asked.

"Well, it's a consulting firm, of sorts," he said. "We show businesses how to set up a computer system that handles their inventory and billing. That's not anything new, but the system is, and the language it uses."

"Complicated, I'll bet."

"A lot of sound and fury about nothing," he said. "The end result is the simplest thing in the world. The company sends you a bill and you pay it. But we're trying to prevent the computer from getting confused and billing you twenty times over, as so often happens.''

"Yes, that rings a bell." Rebecca smiled.

"I retired from my original business several years ago," he said. "But I had been driven crazy by these computers for years before that, and I decided to use my spare time to see if I could do something about it. The odd thing is that, when you come down to it, I'm a computer idiot. But isn't that the whole point? We need to make computers that will help idiots like me, instead of helping only experts who know how to use them."

"Sounds reasonable," Rebecca said.

"It keeps me busy, anyway," he said. "But I confess I had forgotten how much aggravation there can be in starting up a company. Sometimes I wish I was home painting the garage instead of doing all this."

"I'm sure it will work out," Rebecca said. "But will you have to miss Christmas at home?"

"Oh, no." He smiled. "I'll get there by Christmas Eve. But I've got to do my shopping on the road. That's a new experience for me. Not a very pleasant one." He glanced ruefully at his shopping bag. "I'll be the one returning this to Harper's, no doubt. Sometime in January."

"Don't be so sure." Rebecca smiled again. "It might work out. What is your daughter's name?"

"Christine."

"Is she in college?"

"Yep. University of Wisconsin. She's a junior."

"Is she a sorority girl?"

He smiled. "No. As a matter of fact she's quite the other thing. If this were the sixties, she'd be marching on Washington or closing down the university. As it is, she spends her spare time protesting against nuclear power plants or toxic waste. That's her nickname for me, by the way, when she gets mad—*You're a toxic waste, Dad.*"

"That's not very kind," Rebecca hazarded.

"Oh, she means well," he said. "She just has a sharp tongue. Inherited it from her mother. Why, in my time I've been abused by four willful women, Mrs. Lowell. Christine is only the tail end.

And she wants to reclaim me, more than anything else. She considers me hopelessly old-fashioned.''

He took a photo from his wallet and showed it to her. The girl was younger in the photo—it looked like a high school yearbook picture—but one could gather from it that she was a redhead with green eyes. She was not beautiful, but the freshness of youth made her attractive. The resemblance to her father was obvious. Rebecca felt a slight pang as she handed the photo back.

"What did you buy her?" she asked.

"A dress," he said. "Would you like to have a look at it?"

He gingerly removed the box from the bag and showed Rebecca a dress that could hardly be more wrong for the daughter he had described.

"Don't tell me," he said, seeing the look on her face. "It's a disaster, isn't it?"

Rebecca smiled. "That is perhaps too strong a word," she said.

He looked at her. "I wonder if you have enough Christmas spirit to do me a big favor."

"What is that?"

"Would you come back to Harper's with me and help me find something to exchange this for?"

Rebecca laughed.

"That's small recompense for saving me from a stalled elevator," she said. "I'd be delighted."

Sam Bittman was palpably relieved and considerably more relaxed as he and Rebecca ordered onion soup and a niçoise salad. The food was delicious, and Rebecca found herself feeling remarkably at home with this self-effacing stranger.

He confirmed her suspicion that he was a widower, explaining that his wife had died three years ago. This loss was the real reason for his ambitious new career. He had been a retailer considering retirement when his wife became ill. In his grief he allowed his partners to buy him out, but after her death he decided to start a new business. He had hired a software author to help him design his new system, and had sold it throughout the Midwest before branching out to Canada.

The challenge seemed to agree with him, though Rebecca recalled that he usually looked tired when she saw him at the hotel. It was easy to see that he was running to outdistance his own grief.

Rebecca found this touching, the more so because there was a lot of grief in her own heart today.

"You seem to be handling it well," she said. "Your two older daughters have their own homes, and the younger one..."

"She doesn't hate me as much as she pretends," he said. "She just misses her mother. But you're right, Mrs. Lowell. We're surviving, as a family. In this day and age, that's an achievement in itself. Sometimes I attribute it to Margery herself. She gave us a lot before she went."

The older girls were named Gretchen and Anne. Rebecca did not catch the names of their spouses. One of them had two children, the other had a baby boy. Sam Bittman seemed terrifically proud of them all, including Christine, who was, Rebecca guessed, the most like him and the closest to his heart.

Rebecca found herself sorely tempted to talk about Dusty and her life at home. It was hard to listen to Sam Bittman's talk of his family without feeling jealous, and even harder to listen without reciprocating. Small talk always requires a common ground, she reflected. And there was a lot in common between her and this man. But she could not talk about it, because she herself had destroyed it.

For this reason her lunch was oddly double-edged, both comforting and painful. Something in her expanded as she listened to Sam talk. But she had to continually rein herself in and hide her feelings. She felt like a spy, a person whose slightest conversational response is a lie because her whole identity is a fake.

Mercifully, Sam seemed sensitive to the falseness of her position and avoided asking her any questions about herself. She became his sounding board, smiling at his stories of his family and giving little bits of advice when they were asked.

After lunch they walked back to the department store, where Rebecca helped Sam Bittman pick out a pair of slacks and a matching top that had an informal yet festive quality. His eyes lit up as he recognized his daughter's style. He paid for the outfit with a credit card, exclaiming over the provincial tax, and covered Rebecca with thanks.

"You're a lifesaver," he said. "But I warn you, I intend to take the credit for this. It will serve Chrissie right to think for once that her old man knew her as well as she knows herself. This is the first

Christmas present I've given in a decade that won't be returned on December 26. Except the candy, of course."

"I wouldn't have it any other way." Rebecca laughed. "I'm glad I could help, Mr. Bittman."

"Sam."

"Sam, then. And thanks again for rescuing me."

"No trouble at all. What are neighbors for?"

They found a cab outside Harper's and went back to the Royal Grace together. Sam Bittman shook Rebecca's hand and took his leave in the lobby. She went up in the elevator alone, not without a pang of involuntary trepidation.

By the time she turned the key in her door, she felt exhausted. Her outing had not worked out as she had planned. She was empty-handed as far as Tony's Christmas gift was concerned, and had had to thread her way through a complex and difficult lunch.

There was a *Globe and Mail* on the desk. She turned a few pages, noting the news from America, then picked up Tony's copy of *Maclean's* and tried to read an article. She found she could not concentrate. She thought of sitting down with *La Presse,* which she had bought to help her brush up on her French, but vetoed the idea.

She was debating whether to take a bath or lie down for a nap when the sound of a key in the door startled her. For an instant she wondered, absurdly, whether it could be Sam.

The door opened, and she saw Tony looking young and handsome in his dark suit.

"Well, you're home early," she said, moving forward to kiss him.

"I finished what I had to do," he said. "There was no point in sticking around."

His long arms encircled her. He smelled fresh and matinal, despite the hint of perspiration from his long morning's work. He was holding her tightly, and she felt a pulse of desire. It came from him first, powerfully, and echoed quickly in her own senses.

"Who was that man I saw you with downstairs?" he asked.

"Man?" Her eyes were half-closed; their bodies were still pressed together at the waist.

"That older gentleman," Tony said. "You were just getting out of his cab when I came back."

"Oh." She smiled. "That's Mr. Bittman. He's here on business.

I met him at the store.'' She laughed. ''Actually, I got myself trapped in an elevator, and he was the one who found me and went for help.''

''Really. Was it bad?''

''Oh, no. It only lasted a couple of minutes,'' Rebecca assured him. ''But I was glad he was there. I reciprocated as best I could by helping him pick out an outfit for his daughter.'' For some reason, Rebecca did not volunteer the truth about her lunch with Sam.

''I've seen him here before,'' Tony said.

Rebecca nodded. ''He stays here every time he comes. He runs some sort of computer business up here. Just getting started, I think he said.''

''Ah.''

He let her swing lightly from side to side, holding her pelvis tight against himself.

''Is he married?'' he asked.

''He's a widower,'' Rebecca replied. ''He has three daughters,'' she added a trifle too hastily.

''Daughters,'' Tony repeated. He sounded thoughtful.

''Yes.''

There was a silence. He looked into her eyes.

''So it wasn't too terrible for you?'' he asked.

''Oh, for a minute I was a little panicky. But that's just my nerves. There was no danger.''

''That's good. How are you feeling now?''

''Never better!''

''I'm glad to hear that.''

Tony kissed her again, more intimately this time. His hands slipped down to her thighs. Rebecca wanted to say something else, but her body betrayed her. The words died on her lips. Tony picked her up quickly and carried her to the bed.

They said no more until much later.

18

Rebecca and Tony decided to spend Christmas at a ski resort called Cally Mountain, a hundred miles from Grace Island. The weather there was predictable enough to guarantee good slopes, and the lodge, spacious and homey, was a better place to spend the holiday than a hotel in the city.

On the day of their departure they passed Sam Bittman on their way out of the Royal Grace. He had a small but heavy-looking suitcase with him—obviously a carry-on—and a shopping bag.

He was just turning away from the registration desk when they emerged from the elevator. His face lit up in a smile, and he held out a hand to Rebecca.

"Mr. Bittman," she said. "Merry Christmas. Are you off home?"

"And in the nick of time, too." Sam smiled. "I had my last meeting here in town an hour ago, and I'm getting the next flight to San Francisco. I'll be home in time for bed if all those connecting flights take off on schedule."

Rebecca touched Tony's elbow.

"Tony Delafield, meet Sam Bittman," she said. "He's from Wisconsin. I met him while I was Christmas shopping."

"Glad to meet you," Sam said. "And Merry Christmas."

"Same to you," Tony said, shaking hands. "I understand you saved Rebecca from a stalled elevator."

"Not exactly." Sam smiled. "All I did was pick up the house phone and watch the maintenance man do his work."

"I've seen you here before, haven't I?" Tony asked.

"Oh, I'm sure you have. I come here so often they save me the same room. It's not in the greatest shape, but then, neither am I. The armchair is beginning to take on the same lumps as the one back home in my living room."

There was a pause. Rebecca could feel Sam Bittman's temptation to ask Tony the usual polite questions—what he was doing here, what his relationship to Rebecca was, and so on—and his decision to remain tactfully silent. Rebecca could not help trying to cover the moment over.

"Mr. Bittman has a daughter almost Dusty's age," she said to Tony, regretting her words immediately. "What did you say her name was, Mr. Bittman?"

"Christine," Sam said. "And I've got her little present right here." He held up the shopping bag. "Mrs. Lowell saved my life in the department store," he said to Tony. "This is the first Christmas that I've been well armed to play Santa Claus."

Tony said nothing.

There was another pause, even more uncomfortable. Rebecca realized there was scarcely a question Sam could ask that wouldn't lead to embarrassing subjects. This entire meeting was a mistake. She and Tony had chosen a life that made it virtually impossible for them to have normal social relations with other people, especially Americans. There was nothing to do but get out of the moment as quickly as possible.

"Well, have a safe trip," she said. "I suppose we'll be seeing you in the New Year."

"Not much doubt of that," Sam said. "I'll be tied to this city for quite a while. But I'm beginning to enjoy it. Fog agrees with me. I guess it beats those Wisconsin snowstorms."

They took their leave, Tony shaking hands with Sam again, and left the hotel. The damp cold struck Rebecca's cheeks like a slap.

"I don't like that man," Tony said when they were outside.

"Oh, he's a decent sort," she said dismissively. "A widower with a young daughter and a new business. He seems a bit overwhelmed by everything. He's quite harmless."

Tony was silent.

"I suspect his wife's death hit him terribly hard," she added. "Why, to judge from appearances, I thought he was an old man. It wasn't until he spoke directly to me that he seemed ten years younger. That's what grief will do, I suppose." She was conscious that she was defending Sam to Tony, but she could not see any other way to respond.

"What's the matter?" she asked brightly. "What happened to your Christmas spirit?"

He gave her a sharp look that quickly turned into a smile. "Nothing," he said. "Let's hit the road."

They had rented a car through the hotel—Rebecca signing the contract, for Tony was not yet twenty-five—and it was waiting for them. The doorman put their Christmas presents and suitcases into the trunk, and they were on their way. They had no time for conversation as they made their way through the city streets toward the ferry. Rebecca read the map and gave Tony instructions. Within forty-five minutes they were driving through foothills with snowy mountain peaks on the horizon. The bilingual road signs with distances in kilometers made the landscape seem even more exotic.

"This is marvelous," Rebecca said. "I love a new adventure. It's a perfect way to spend Christmas."

She touched Tony's arm, smiling as the unfamiliar landscape slid by behind him. "There's something you don't know about me," she said. "I get as excited as a little girl on Christmas. I'll probably drag you out of bed at six-thirty."

"I always knew you were a child at heart," Tony said.

Then he added something strange. "Anyway, I'll have to keep my eye on you."

"How so?" Rebecca asked.

"You don't see your effect on people."

"What do you mean?"

"That old fart at the hotel, for one," Tony said. "He's interested."

Rebecca was taken aback. "Who?" she asked.

"The old fellow with the daughter back home," Tony said. "Bittman."

Rebecca laughed out loud. "Him? Interested in me? Tony, you're crazy."

Tony shot her a surprisingly hostile, suspicious look.

"Don't say that," he said in a warning voice.

Rebecca turned to the road ahead. The mountains were coming closer, almost imperceptibly. She wished the car could go faster so she could reach them sooner. Yet in that instant their slow approach seemed ineluctable and almost suffocating.

Rebecca watched them for a long while, saying nothing.

The holiday turned out to be a great success.

The ski resort was large and festive, with thick wood beams and Christmas decorations everywhere. Fires popped and glinted in hearths in all the lounges and tearooms, which were furnished with comfortable armchairs and inviting sofas. The place was neither too full nor too empty, and the guests had a relaxed look in their thick sweaters and knit socks.

The restaurant was a large room with a cocktail pianist who played Christmas music with a surprisingly wry humor, salting the old favorites with clever Gershwin and Cole Porter touches. At Tony's insistence Rebecca made numerous requests, and the fellow cheerfully obliged. He remembered her favorites, and greeted her with one every time she and Tony came in for dinner.

They took the easier trails together, and Rebecca watched from the bottom of the mountain as Tony took the more demanding ones himself. It was curious to watch him from so great a distance, a tiny figure curving down the slopes in utter silence, identifiable only by the red scarf she had bought him at the gift shop. He seemed remote and almost abstract as he carved his little trail down the side of the mountain. Yet as Rebecca watched he got bigger and bigger, and finally glided right to her side, his skis hissing on the packed snow.

Something about the bracing cold made her want to make love. That night she enticed him into the lodge an hour before the light waned, and they spent a long time in bed, not stirring until the dinner hour was half over. The second night Tony had sore muscles, and she massaged him slowly, unable to prevent herself from bending to kiss his back or his side. Always her caresses led to more lovemaking. She seemed insatiable, and Tony remarked on it laughingly.

"You're going to make an old man out of me."

"Nonsense," she said. "You don't seem to be slowing down."

"That's because I have you here to turn me on." He held her close, in that gentle way he had, and she kissed the crisp hair on his chest. Their bodies smelled of love, and the sheets were so warm it was hard to get up.

She enjoyed the feeling that she could excite him. Sometimes, girlishly, she played on it, stopping him when he was half dressed to make love again, or embracing him suddenly, in the knowledge that her kiss would make him want her. It had been so long since she had felt attractive!

Perhaps, come to think of it, she never had. Her only femininity, for as long as she could remember, had been her maternal instinct toward Dusty. And even that instinct implied a renunciation of her own needs, a sacrificing of all the parts of her womanhood that were not maternal. Tony, in one fell swoop, had restored that to her. Given it, perhaps, was a better expression. For she had lost something essential to her femininity even before Dusty was born. Lost, or given up by her own free will—that was the painful dualism around which her adult life turned, and the reason she had had such difficulty looking at herself in the mirror for so long.

Now she could stand naked before a mirror and watch Tony's arms curl around her from behind. She could look at his beautiful young body, strong with desire, and say to herself, *He wants me. It's me he wants.* She pondered this fact on Christmas, when, after giving Tony a sweater and a new briefcase, and receiving from him a lovely bracelet and a skirt-and-blouse outfit, she spent the whole afternoon in bed with him. This was her gift, this handsome boy and the way he made her feel. A gift worth sacrificing a lot for. Perhaps even everything.

These thoughts were in her mind, spiraling deeper toward the shadows where her real self had been so long buried, as the lovely Christmas passed before her eyes. She had never been so conscious of what she had risked, dared, as well as what she had lost. For this reason her intimacy with Tony had a sharper edge, and a hotter, more sensual feeling than ever.

On Christmas night, after a delightful dinner downstairs and a toddy before the crackling fire in the lounge, Rebecca lay naked in her lover's arms. The day sang in her senses, its many moments and impressions darting here and there inside her, making their imprints even as they slipped away, as all moments—even the best ones—must.

"I love you," Tony whispered.

"Merry Christmas," she replied.

When somnolence overcame her, a brief image of Christmas at

home, with a very small Dusty opening boxes containing dolls, toys and little girl's clothes, came to haunt her happiness. The long day with Tony had made her just tired enough to fight it off. She closed her eyes on it with a small sigh, and fell into a deep, empty sleep.

It was a Christmas party, of sorts.

The two undergraduates who had promised to score some coke had failed, but a graduate student from the English department brought some kef that his brother had smuggled in from Mexico last summer. It would be almost enough for everybody. And there was a lot of liquor.

The party was being given at a cavernous loft apartment in what was once a piano factory. There were thirty or forty people there, most of them college students, but also some rather dubious characters from the city. It was difficult to keep up drug connections without this sort of guest showing up.

Someone had tacked up a poster of Santa Claus with a hard-on. Newly arriving guests laughed briefly at the sight of it, then settled into conversation. The music was deafening.

Dusty had been brought by a student, a friend of a friend of Dan's. She barely knew the boy, though she had slept with him twice. He had begun, like most of the others nowadays, as a voice on the phone. "Hi. My name is so-and-so. So-and-so suggested you and I should meet." Then there was an apartment, with alcohol, coke or only grass—and dirty sheets, in which, nearly always, she woke up alone.

She was kept busy these days by the many calls she got. She lived a double life, working scrupulously on her studies during the day and sleeping around at night. She was careful about staying in touch with her father, for she did not want him to become suspicious. She took great care with her makeup and attire when meeting him; much more so than when keeping one of her other dates.

It was an acceptable life. Except for the hangover she had to fight off most mornings, Dusty felt nothing. It was as though she was floating on a large ocean whose waves were gentle enough for her to balance herself on their crests and see what she needed to see. She was able to read, to write papers, to prepare for exams, to make small talk with her father—without ever missing a beat. Everything was gradual. Nothing was sudden. She never lost her concentration. Her midterm grades had come in last week. She had a 4.0 average.

Tonight she had smoked some kef, perhaps unwisely, after two strong drinks. The drug was throbbing under her skin, and her fingers looked a mile away as they held the glass of liquor. She was talking to a boy she had noticed at these parties before, wondering idly whether she had ever slept with him. His name was Rick. Someone poured what looked like bourbon into the glass from a plastic half-liter bottle. Dusty was not sure the glass had contained bourbon before. She looked forward with some curiosity to her next taste.

"We need more liquor," someone said.

"People are drinking too much."

"We could take up a collection," another voice replied, possibly her own.

She smiled at the boy. But her brow furrowed when she realized it was not Rick after all, or not Rick anymore. It was a much taller boy, with brown hair and freckles, whom she did not remember seeing before.

He was asking Dusty about her studies. She was talking in vague terms about her journalism major, the same way she always talked about studies at parties. A pro forma prelude to sex. She took a long drink of the liquid in her glass—it tasted like bourbon, but she was not sure—and remembered suddenly that a moment ago he had been talking about his own work. He was some sort of graduate student. He was tall and had to lean forward a little to hear her over the noise of the stereo. Dusty noticed with interest that he seemed cold sober.

"Would you like to get a breath of air?" he asked after a while.

She agreed. They got up to leave. It was cold outside, and she had brought her warm coat. He had a short down jacket and a stocking cap that made him look, she thought, ridiculous.

The night air stung her nostrils. The boy was saying something. She felt a wave of confusion. The streetlights reflected on the wet black pavement seemed to leap at her eyes. She stopped in her tracks.

"Are you all right?" The boy seemed concerned.

"Have you got a car...?" she started to say. But before she could finish she passed out in his arms.

The next thing she knew she was in a strange apartment, and he was helping her off with her coat. She stood swaying against the door as he hung the coat in the closet.

He took her into the bedroom. There was a double bed with a comforter on it. She glimpsed a large desk with a swing-arm lamp and a computer. There were brick-and-board bookshelves with some heavy chemistry books in them.

She stumbled backward to the bed and almost fell on it. He began to help her off with her clothes. She looked up at his face. He seemed intent on the buttons of her blouse. She noticed a glow of amber in the hazel of his irises. The freckles made him look very young.

She passed out as he was lifting her hips to get the skirt off.

She woke up alone. Light glowed outside the miniblinds. She had no idea where she was.

She knew it must be some boy's apartment, but she could not remember who she had been with last night. She lay for what seemed a long time, pondering the situation. She recalled how hard the liquor had hit her. The hangover was numbing. She felt almost unable to move.

She had to pee. She forced herself to sit up. A headache she had been unaware of struck her like a brick. She grabbed her forehead and staggered into the bathroom.

There were aspirins in the medicine cabinet; she took six. She noticed that there was little else in the cabinet: a tube of Cortaid, a little bottle of cold medicine, some cough drops.

She sat down on the toilet, so absorbed by the throbbing in her temples that it took her a long time to urinate. She had not turned on the light. She noticed the shower curtain, an inexpensive but attractive vinyl with a colorful print. She wondered whether a girl-friend or mother had picked it out. It didn't look like something a man would bother to buy.

She sat for a long time, concentrating her energies on keeping the pills down. She took notice of the sensation between her legs. She could not tell whether she had had sex last night. She tried without success to recall how she got here, and the face of the person who had brought her.

She took a long, hot shower. It seemed to help her head. She emerged wearing one of the bath towels and took a brief tour of the apartment. There was a small kitchen, a front room with a small television, a collection of videotapes, and brick-and-board shelves almost to the ceiling, containing hundreds of books.

The place was neat and tidy. Even the cupboards in the kitchen, with their small supply of cans of soup, coffee mugs and dishes, were clean.

She saw a note on the counter.

There's orange juice in the refrigerator, and bread for toast, and instant coffee in the first cabinet on the left. Please make yourself at home.

She put a cup of water in the tiny microwave and waited for it to boil. The apartment was really quite attractive, she thought. Spare, but civilized in a way she was not used to. There were posters on the two spaces of wall that weren't covered with books. One of them showed Einstein, and the other might have been Nietzsche.

The couch was old, and covered with a bedspread. There was a beanbag chair. An old braided rug covered the middle of the living room floor.

When the water boiled, Dusty made herself a cup of strong coffee and took it into the bedroom. Her skirt and blouse were folded neatly on a small chair. She would have smiled at this attempt at hospitality had not the pounding in her head stopped her. She noticed her shoes, sitting on the floor beneath the chair, and realized how badly she needed a new pair. Rebecca had bought her these on a shopping trip last spring; they were worn out now.

She made the bed, wondering again what had happened in it last night, but not going so far as to examine the sheets. Then she got dressed and pinned back her hair.

She prepared to leave. She had no idea where this apartment was. She would have to find her way back to campus. She glanced quickly into her purse. It contained money, brought in anticipation of this situation.

Her coat was hanging in the closet. As she put it on she noticed a note pinned to the pocket. It was a map showing where the apartment was in relation to campus. She was only five blocks from her own place. The clock in the kitchen read nine-fifteen. She would have time to pick up her books before class.

She paused before leaving. There was a family picture tucked in among the books on one of the shelves above the TV. It showed a young man with his arm around an older woman, his mother, no doubt. He had freckled skin, short hair and a studious look. A girl who resembled him was also in the picture. His sister, Dusty guessed. They were outdoors, in front of some bleachers. The light looked like morning. The mother had sad eyes despite her smile. The boy seemed to have inherited them, but the sister looked different. Like her father, perhaps, who was nowhere to be seen.

Dusty put the little map in her coat pocket. She found an unfamiliar key there. Turning it over in her hand, she guessed that it was the key to the apartment.

Putting her coat on, she turned around and surveyed the place once more. It certainly was civilized, she thought.

Her head still throbbing, she left. There was a long dark stairway that smelled of old wood and varnish. At the bottom a bicycle leaned against the wall, and a baby stroller stood in one corner.

The morning was bright. Dusty squinted. Her head throbbed harder. But the cold air felt good on her face.

She turned east and headed for campus. The key was in her pocket.

20

On a cold, wet Friday in January, Damon was in his office at the firm, discussing the week's work with Bob Krieg.

Things were going well. Damon's hard work was paying off. The mayor had brought out Damon's written opinions on zoning and taxes before the last meeting of the major investors, and based his whole appeal on Damon's logic.

"Looks like you've got them on your side," Bob said. "On our side, I should say."

Damon smiled. "Knock wood."

"I talked to the governor yesterday," Bob added. "He's impressed with the way things are going. He's very high on you."

"Well, that's nice." Damon knew Bob was close to the governor, who had been his classmate at Harvard. If Bob said the governor was pleased, it must be true.

"The fellows are very proud of the way you've handled this," Bob added, his tone becoming a bit more formal, as it always did when he spoke of the partners as a group. "If we handle this whole Hightower thing, and it flies, it will be a feather in our cap. And you're the point man."

"I can't say it's been fun," Damon said. "I have dealt with easier people in my time. But I've enjoyed the challenge."

"I know it hasn't been an easy time for you," Bob said. "But..."

Damon was aware that the partners were watching him. It had been six months since Rebecca left. The inquiries about Irene's health had gradually died down. He often wondered how many of the partners, or their wives, had drawn their own conclusions about Rebecca's absence. His cover story could not last forever. These were lawyers, after all.

There was a knock at the door. Tom Blackman and Evan Gaeth, two of the partners, glanced in with expectant looks on their faces.

"The sanctum sanctorum," said Tom. "What are you two cooking up?"

"Just chatting about Hightower," Bob said. "Want to come in?"

He glanced at Damon inquiringly. It was Damon's office, after all.

"By all means," Damon mustered a tone of hearty welcome. "How about a drink?"

Tom and Evan came in and accepted the drinks Damon offered. His antennae told him their visit was official. They were here to pat him on the back for his efforts on Hightower, and to pump him a little on the latest developments.

Nothing about this was unexpected. Bob Krieg was the closest partner to Damon, so he was cast in the dual role of Damon's confidant about Hightower and reporter to the others on Damon's activity. As for Evan and Tom, they were the nearest in age to Damon and Bob (it was Evan who had recruited Damon for the firm two decades ago), so they were the liaison to the older partners.

They talked for a few minutes, Damon salting his conversation with precise details about the last two weeks' work. This was not the first such visit. The big boys dropped in on him at least twice a month to check up. He realized in an indirect way that Hightower was more important to the firm than any of the partners wanted to admit openly. The deal would involve a lot of billings, of course—and the firm's profits over the past couple of years were not what they might have been. But there could be more to it than that. Damon was not sure just what or why.

"Why don't we continue this over at the Grill?" Tom suggested. "I, for one, am starving."

There was a murmur of approval. So the meeting was to continue over dinner, Damon thought. Either they were checking up on him a bit more thoroughly than usual, or one of them wanted to tell him something. He resented the intrusion on his day, but he looked forward to the conversation. He prided himself on his ability to read his partners' thoughts. For twenty years he had been a step ahead of them, understanding them just a bit better than they understood him.

"Terrific," Damon said. "Let me just tell Nancy where I'm going."

The phone rang as he was getting up. He sat down to pick up the receiver.

"Damon Lowell," he said.

The voice on the phone was familiar.

"Damon?" it said. "Are you alone?"

Damon suppressed a blush.

"Oh, hi," he said, instantly affecting a lawyerly tone. "Good to hear your voice again."

It was Ashley. Damon was taken aback. How had she gotten through? Where was Nancy?

"Damon, I want to fuck."

He thought quickly. He had not seen Ashley since Tuesday. She was supposed to be away for the weekend. He had reconciled himself to not seeing her until next week. But something must have changed her plans.

He felt a stirring in his loins as he signaled to the others to hang on a moment.

"Well, how are things going?" he said heartily into the phone. "Did it all work out?"

Ashley did not answer. She was hearing the fact that he could not talk.

"Good," Damon said to the silence. "Wonderful."

Bob was looking at him. The others were exchanging a quick word, Evan leaning toward Tom. Damon could still hear the obscenity on Ashley's lips. All at once the faces of his colleagues looked incredibly old. Not only in comparison to the fresh, impudent young girl on the phone, but in a larger sense. He knew these men as well as he knew the dust on his desktop, the old leather of his chair. They had no surprises for him; neither did his work. It was all old hat, a ritual that had been polished to meaninglessness by years of repetition. But Ashley was new.

"Damon," Ashley said. "Can't you talk?"

Now it was his turn to be silent. He nodded, murmuring a bed-side-manner "Mmm-hmm" into the phone.

"Damon," she said. "I want you. Right now."

The stirring between his legs increased. She was playing on his embarrassment before the others.

"Whenever you like," he said. "Absolutely!"

"I'll be you-know-where in half an hour."

"Fine. Great."

"Are you hard? Did I make you hard?" There was an odd tone in her voice, somewhere between playfulness and an almost humorless insistence.

He hung up. The others were looking at him.

"She's nervous." He smiled. "Just got the word from the other side. Listen, let me catch up to you. I just have to drop in on her."

"On who?" Tom asked.

"Oh, just one of the Herzog people," Damon lied, using the name of a relatively recent corporate client. "I won't be long. I'll be there in half an hour or so."

He watched his partners leave the office. In twenty minutes, depending on the traffic, he would be naked with Ashley in the apartment. He could hardly wait. The naughtiness in her voice had lit a fire inside him.

The time on Grace Island was one-thirty. Tony Delafield was coming home from work early.

It was the end of his first full week back at work. He had done his research well, taking some of the files along on his vacation, and this week he had worked long hours. He knew he was impressing his superiors with his willingness to work hard, and with his brains. It was a slow start, of course, and it would not be as easy as the law career he had planned back home, but he would make it work.

He felt a new energy, a new happiness. It seemed to him that in getting through the holidays, in entering a new calendar year, he and Rebecca had finished work on the cornerstone of their life together. It had been a long autumn, full of confusing and sometimes painful feelings. But their love had been equal to the challenge.

Now they had celebrated Christmas, given each other gifts, taken a vacation together just like a real couple. It was the New Year, and this was the real world. Their love had proved its reality. From now on it could only grow stronger.

As he walked quickly through the foggy streets—the weather had turned temperate, the famous "January thaw" of which the Grace newspapers spoke—Tony measured his youthful vigor against another, more complex emotion.

At Cally Mountain he had felt close to Rebecca in a new, more powerful way. He was not sure why. When he had first met her and fallen under her spell, it was her mystery that attracted him, her depth. He had given in to it without a second thought, as though unafraid to lose his own self in his love.

He still felt that way. But now there was something grateful, almost pious in the way he nestled in her body, felt her enfold and comfort him. It was as though this warmth of hers were a rampart behind which the world's cruelty was kept at bay.

His pride would have been injured by this dependency, were it not for the unique delight of giving in to it when she held him. Of knowing, when they made love, that he was belonging to her as well as possessing her. It opened a whole new world of feeling to him.

He worried that he was giving too much, burdening her with the enormity of his own need. But he could not help it. The need was too great, the surrender too sweet.

He had tried to hide his new emotions behind sure male caresses, behind a physical mastery born of his new sexual experience. And indeed, it sometimes seemed that, as in the old saying, he played her body like an instrument. He knew its needs, its vulnerabilities, as well as he knew his own. But he was not her master.

He remembered that book by Proust she had recommended to him back in October. It was a story of obsessive love. When the man, Swann, had allowed his love for the woman to tighten its hold on him, a moment had come when it was too late to turn back, when not even his cynicism and his vast experience of women could help him. His love, as a physician would say, had become "inoperable." This was how Tony now felt about his own love. It was a scary feeling, and one he wished to hide from Rebecca. Yet it filled him with a secret pride, as though he had passed a sort of initiation.

He was a block from the Royal when he saw Rebecca being helped out of a cab by Sam Bittman.

The fog was thick, but he could see them in the light of the hotel's canopy. Bittman was holding Rebecca by the arm, bending at the waist in a courtly posture. Then, as she waited, he paid the driver. His raincoat was over his arm, and he wore glasses. Rebecca was smiling as she watched him. As he turned to her he said something, and she laughed.

Tony slowed his steps so as not to overtake them. They stood talking for a moment on the sidewalk, and Bittman held up a palm as though to see whether it was raining. Rebecca was wearing the wool coat she had bought last fall. Her eyes followed those of Bittman toward the heavens, which seemed, as so often, to lower beneath the skyscrapers and caress the city. In that instant Tony thought he saw an expression of carefree well-being in her eyes that he never saw when she was with him.

Bittman made a humorous, dismissive gesture with his hand, as if to say, "Naturally it's drizzling, it always drizzles here," and they walked into the hotel, looking happy and natural together. Bittman's arm curved as though to hold Rebecca around the shoulders. She seemed to nestle in his protection.

Tony turned on his heel and walked all the way around the block before entering the hotel.

The news in New York that evening would be all about the freezing rain, which had come on unexpectedly during the afternoon. Vehicles were sliding off the Manhattan streets and crashing into one another like bumper cars. The signposts and streetlights were glazed with ice. Telephone lines were already beginning to fall down in the outer boroughs.

Damon's cab was not able to get him to Ashley. Dusk was falling over the snarled traffic, the angry cops and faltering pedestrians as he paid the driver and went on foot the remaining five blocks. His Italian leather shoes were poor equipment for these conditions, and he nearly fell a dozen times.

In the Village the streets were no better, but Dusty was wearing sheep-lined boots with ribbed rubber soles, bought for her by Rebecca a year ago, and she was able to clump along the slick sidewalks without slipping.

She carried her book bag over her shoulder and a small purse. She had just finished her week, with Advanced Reporting as her last class. She had plenty of time for her studies, for the new semester had just started and none of the papers would be due for a long time.

The weekend lay ahead of her, empty and sinister. No one had called her during the week, so if she wanted to make a date she would have to make the first move. She wanted to get laid, but she dreaded the phone call she would have to make. Ironically, even after all she had been through, Dusty retained this remnant of lady-like demureness. It was one thing to make herself available and take the consequences; it was another to chase after men.

She wandered along East Fourth Street to Washington Square South, and past the park toward the West Village. She passed the library and the student center, and looked to her right into the park, where she was treated to the amusing spectacle of drug dealers and junkies slipping and sliding this way and that on the slick pavement as they tried to make deals. A homeless person had to grab the coat of the pedestrian he was accosting, in order to avoid falling down.

In another couple of hours the park would be closed; it was too dangerous after dark now, so the City had decided to close it at night. Several men called out to Dusty, but she kept her face and body in that New York position that warns passersby to stay away. It was getting darker and darker; reflections of the streetlights and neon signs glimmered with false cleanness from the black streets. A gasoline rainbow in the gutter added a note of grace to the impression of sharp eagerness in the air.

She had made up her mind to call Carl or Chris as soon as she was back home. *"Are you doing anything tonight?" "What's going on tonight?"* She was rehearsing her speech, and gritting her teeth for the silent acknowledgment she would feel on the other end of the line.

It would be ugly, but it had to be done. She could not spend a weekend alone. She could do anything else, but not that.

She had passed Sullivan Street and took the right turn at MacDougal. She was heading away from home now. She could not seem to make up her mind to turn back. The book bag was heavy, but she kept walking. Somehow the slippery sidewalk made it even more difficult to renounce her walk and go back the way she had come.

She went up Washington Square West and turned left into a street she had only seen once before.

The buildings looked completely alien in this darkness. She

stopped at one of them and stood looking up the steps. She felt in her pocket for the key that she had left there.

She climbed the slippery steps and looked through the glass pane at the mailboxes. She could not see the names, so she took the key out of her pocket and let herself in.

Now she looked at the names again. Aurora. Cawley. Quintero. Lange. Odd, she thought: she didn't know which one was the one she wanted. But she did know where to go.

She opened the inner door and walked up the stairs. The door she wanted was on the first landing, on the left. She stood frozen with her hand poised to knock. This was crazy, she thought. She didn't know why she was here. Time to turn back.

She knocked on the door. No one came. She put the key in the lock and turned the knob. She let herself in quickly and closed the door.

The bookshelves were the same. The family photograph tucked between the heavy textbooks still showed the young man with his arm around his mother. And there was the sister, resembling him. The bleachers behind them made a pretty background. Straight, unmoving. It looked as though time was on their side, Dusty reflected.

Dusty took off her coat, hung it in the closet where it had hung the last time, and sat down to wait.

Damon did not make the dinner with his partners. He called the restaurant to beg off, saying that his "Herzog" client needed reassuring, and that it would take some time.

He himself did not have anything to eat until he had made love to Ashley three times. She had been waiting, naked, in the apartment when he arrived, her long legs spread with the sheets bunched between them, her hard young breasts squeezed between her arms.

"So," she said. "Did I give you a hard-on?"

He was too busy taking off his clothes to answer. A moment later he was atop her, kissing her urgently as her fingers played between his legs.

He could not think of the partners now. Not while she was giving him so much pleasure. He would deal with them Monday. Besides, nothing they might have to say about Hightower could hold any surprises for him.

21

Tony and Rebecca were sitting together in a new restaurant they had found on the north side of the city. It was a continental place, with an eclectic chef who mingled Oriental and Middle Eastern flavors with his classic French dishes. It was a bit expensive for their budget, but this was Tony's birthday, and Rebecca had insisted on treating him.

"Congratulations." She smiled, touching her champagne glass to his. "And many happy returns."

"Thank you."

Tony was twenty-four years old. Rebecca reflected, not without a certain satisfaction, that he was more than half her age. And yet, the older they grew, the gap between their ages would lessen, percentage-wise. This alone made their celebration of Tony's birthday a happy moment for her.

"It's not my birthdays that matter, though," he said.

"What do you mean?"

"What I'm living for is next August 5," he said, taking her hand.

"Ah." She knew what he meant. August 5 would be the one-year anniversary of their "elopement."

"Not to mention July 11," he said.

"What's that?" asked Rebecca.

"That was the first time that I set eyes on you," Tony said.

She returned his smile. She was touched by his passion for her. In recent weeks, as things between them had become more difficult, it had become a sort of mainstay for her.

"You're so young to be so in love," she said, not quite measuring the weight of her words. "It won't last. You'll outgrow me in no time."

He squeezed her hand harder. "Don't count on it."

Rebecca laughed. "Mr. Bittman was telling me last week that

his daughter has a new boyfriend," she said. "He said he had barely reconciled himself to the last one...."

She saw a hard look come into Tony's eyes and regretted her words instantly. It was too late—Tony was letting go of her hand, leaning back in his chair. She wanted to say she was sorry, but it seemed too absurd to apologize for mentioning Mr. Bittman.

She sipped at her champagne and looked at Tony's fingers, which, despite his anger, were holding his fluted glass with an instinctive delicacy. The fingers of an artist, she thought. So long and sensitive, for a young man so rigid and willful!

"You're being foolish again," she said.

Tony looked at her darkly. "Not from where I sit."

Rebecca shook her head, feeling her cheeks flush.

"Really, Tony, we can't go on arguing this way over nothing."

"Is it nothing?" Tony asked. "I'm not so sure."

"It couldn't be *more* nothing!" she exclaimed, glancing around her at the other patrons as she raised her voice.

In her own mind the truth was obvious. Her only connection to Sam Bittman was the common bond of college-aged daughters; and even that was attenuated by the fact that every word she said to Sam about Dusty was more than half a lie.

"Really, if it weren't for Dusty..." she began, but stopped herself.

"What does that mean?" Tony asked.

She sighed. "The only reason Mr. Bittman has any interest in me at all is that he needs moral support about his daughter. He's worried about her, and he sees me as a mother who knows how to handle girls. With his own wife dead, he's grasping at straws."

The truth was that Rebecca felt a common bond of loss with Sam—bitterer, of course, on her side—and that when she was with him she allowed herself to savor the fantasy that Dusty was still a real and consequential part of her life. But she could not very well admit this to Tony.

Tony smiled ironically. "You're selling yourself short."

"And what does *that* mean?" she asked.

"That's his excuse, sure," Tony said. "But he has more on his mind than his daughter."

Rebecca managed an indulgent smile.

"My hot-blooded lover," she said. "If I didn't know better, I'd be afraid you were going to challenge Mr. Bittman to a duel."

"If it would get rid of him," Tony said, "I wouldn't mind."

"You flatter me," Rebecca observed.

"Flattery has nothing to do with it," Tony said.

Once again Rebecca felt torn between the role of a reassuring mother who calmed her lover's tantrums—and, ironically, the role of a prisoner, someone whose secret thoughts and impulses were the object of a constant scrutiny by him. And the strangest irony of all was that it was the young and beautiful man, Tony, who was jealous of the older, ordinary-looking man, Sam. Indeed, Tony seemed all the more jealous because of the fact that Sam *was* older. Sam's very ordinariness, his lack of an obvious sexual appeal, was somehow central to Tony's suspicion.

And there was, in a twisted way, some truth behind this. Sam was a non-threatening, domestic figure, someone who represented the hearth and home Rebecca had given up to be with Tony. He filled her with a sort of nostalgia, the more so because he was down-to-earth in his personality and apparently a good father. He made a stark comparison to Damon, who was so smooth, so remote and perfidious. One could read Sam's emotions on his face. She felt she could be herself when she was with him, she could be easy and spontaneous—which was no longer the case when she was with Tony.

Tony's jealousy had robbed him of one of his attractions: his ability to enfold her, to be the strong one, indeed the understanding and seductive one, as he had been on the beach on Long Island when he seemed to read her mind, to know what she desired.

Now he required constant reassurance. And, stubborn as a child, he refused it when she offered it. He trailed after her emotionally, jumping on her slightest mentions of Sam until, despite herself, she ended up blurting out Sam's name in innocent ways that instantly became provocations.

The role of nursemaid did not appeal to Rebecca. It was not for this that she had sacrificed so much for Tony. Not only did it introduce an unwelcome element of conflict into their relationship, but a note of boredom, as well.

Rebecca looked at the handsome, stubborn face of her young

lover. The champagne bottle sat in its cooler between them, an emblem of a celebration that was once again clouded by conflict.

"Tony, you've got to stop this," she said. "It's ridiculous, and it's getting out of hand."

He leaned forward intently. "Do you want to end it?" he asked.

For an instant Rebecca misunderstood him. A vision of freedom, and of loneliness, flashed inside her mind.

"What do you mean?"

"Marry me, Rebecca." He took both her hands, not noticing the look in her eyes. "It's time. You have no reason to wait any longer. This is what's causing all our problems. Get your divorce. Let's get married this spring. Then everything will be sorted out."

Rebecca considered this carefully. She had, in fact, been dragging her feet. She had told Tony that her worry about Dusty was delaying her plans for a divorce from Damon. She was not ready to cut the knot until she had in some way made peace with Dusty. But so far Dusty had answered none of her letters. And she lacked the courage to contact Damon in an effort to approach Dusty.

She wondered if it could be true that her reluctance to divorce Damon was at the heart of Tony's recent behavior. Part of her wanted to do what Tony wished, to get married right away, so as to put an end to this false position. But another part of her hung back, worried about Tony and about the recent conflict in their relationship. She wanted to feel more at home with Tony before she took the final step. Yet, in this new year, she only felt more exiled with him.

"Give me a little more time," she said, holding his hands.

"Time," he said with bitterness, as though speaking of an old enemy.

And Rebecca could not help admiring his insight. Time, indeed, was not on their side. Not as she had once hoped.

22

Damon Lowell lay in the middle of the bed he had shared with Rebecca for twenty-three years.

Ashley was astride him, her shoulders thrust back, her fingertips fluttering against his chest as he worked toward his climax inside her.

"Baby," she moaned. "Give it to me, give it to me...."

She often repeated little cajoleries that came faster and faster as orgasm approached. "Come on, come on..." or "All the way, all the way..." It had excited Damon early on, and now she never failed to do it.

He felt himself begin to come. He grasped her thighs with both hands.

"Yes!" she cried, hunching over him, her hair hanging down over his face. Damon had arched his pelvis to push deeper into her, and held it now, though he clearly recalled hurting his back in a position like this at least a decade ago, probably with Alison.

The girl sighed and shuddered for a long time. When she had finished and was curled up beside him, he felt proud.

After a while she lit a cigarette—he had told her the habit was bad for her, but everyone at the office smoked, she said—and sat up against the pillows. He rested his face against her hip. The long thighs he so much admired were under the sheets. He heard the little tap of her finger as she butted the ash of the cigarette into the ashtray.

She looked down at him and smiled.

"You were great," she said.

"So were you." He breathed in the smell of her. She was wearing the perfume he had given her, and it mingled provocatively with the aromas of sex.

They were silent for several minutes. She finished her cigarette and lighted another.

"Tell me about your wife," she said.

Damon lay back against the pillow, his eyes on the ceiling.

"That again," he said. "What is there to tell?"

By now Ashley had learned the basic facts of his existence, as could scarcely be avoided. She knew he had a daughter, for he had often had to get her into or out of the apartment depending on a visit of Dusty's, and she had sometimes been present when Dusty telephoned. She was also aware—it was public knowledge, after all—of his long relationship with Alison Shore. He suspected that Ashley wondered whether it was really over.

But most of all she was curious about Rebecca. She had seen Rebecca's face in the family photos scattered around the apartment. (Damon had not removed them, in part because he lacked the leisure to do it, and in part because he clung to the hope that she would soon return to him.) She had seen the furnishings, the knick-knacks that Rebecca had picked out. After all, everything in the apartment, from paintings to pots and pans, bore the trace of Rebecca's taste. And she had seen Rebecca's clothes, for Rebecca's closet was separate from Damon's, and Rebecca had not sent for the clothes and Damon had, of course, not removed them.

Ashley was intently curious about the structure of Damon's private life, the forces that had held it together and the stresses that had broken it apart. Up to now she had been tactful in asking questions about it. But her sexual intimacy with Damon had at once emboldened her and sharpened her interest.

"Why did you break up?" she asked.

Damon reached to touch her breast. "Forget about that," he said. "It doesn't matter."

"No, I'm interested."

He looked up at her. "Why?"

"Because it's part of you," she said. "Anything that's part of you interests me."

This speech annoyed Damon. He did not take Ashley seriously enough to want to bother explaining things to her, as he once had to Alison. That was an experience he had had enough of—at least for the moment. He did not want emotional attachments to women. They only led to conflict.

But Ashley, so intense in her sexuality, was correspondingly intense in her emotional life. He had not anticipated this, but now it was undeniable, a trade-off he had to accept if he wished to continue seeing her. She had become attached to him in a way that was not yet clear to him. And thus she was curious about his other attachments.

Nevertheless, her question seemed an invasion of his privacy. He remained silent.

Ashley sat up straighter.

"I heard she left you," she said.

Damon turned toward her. "Who told you that?"

She shrugged. "It's around. I heard it from a girl at the office."

"God damn it," Damon said, reaching for his drink. "This town makes me sick. A man can't go to the toilet without their knowing about it at city hall."

There was a pause.

"Well, did she?" the girl asked, stubbing out her cigarette.

Damon grimaced, looking at her as he swirled the brandy in his glass.

"I don't think that's your business," he said.

"Please, Damon. Just tell me this one little thing. I mean, it's pretty basic."

She touched his chest. "I have a right to know some things, don't I?"

Damon curled his fingers around her hand. He did not want to lose her. She was a good lay. She was filling an important gap in his life right now. But nothing could pain him more than talking about Rebecca.

"Perhaps," he said. "But just now it's very painful for me to talk about. Maybe later on..."

"I heard a funny story...." she said with a hesitation that seemed feigned.

"What?"

"That she left you for somebody much younger," she said. "A boy, really..."

Damon felt a surge of rage.

"What?" he asked. "Who told you that?"

"Like I say," she said, not looking at him, "it's around. It's what people are saying." Her tone was not as tactful as he would have liked. In fact, there was a note of challenge in it.

Damon got out of the bed and stood looking down at her.

"I want you to go now," he said.

She sat looking up at him. Her hands were clasped around her knees, and her young breasts stood up fresh and firm between her arms. He could see the outlines of her thighs under the sheet. Her beauty only seemed to increase his anger.

"What did I say wrong?" she asked.

"Never mind. Just... Let's call it a night. I have a long day tomorrow."

She did not move.

"Why don't you divorce her?" she asked.

Damon grimaced again. He clenched his fists. The girl's blunt curiosity maddened him.

"Ashley," he said, mustering a semblance of patience. "That's not your affair. Now, I'm asking you to leave. For tonight. We will perhaps discuss these things at a later time. But right now I've got to get some sleep."

"I thought I was staying the night," she said.

He took a deep breath. He noticed that his hands were shaking. He hated the fact that his emotion was visible to this worthless girl.

"Please, Ashley. I can't get into a quarrel now."

Suddenly she lay back against the pillow, her arms above her head. Her body slipped deeper under the sheets.

"What if I don't want to leave?" she asked coyly. "What if I want to play?"

Damon was trembling.

"You must go," he said. "No games tonight. I have a busy day tomorrow."

She frowned. She was on the verge of creating a scene. She did not like being dismissed. More yet, she knew her curiosity about Rebecca had provoked him, and she was tempted to press the issue rather than to obey him. He sensed the danger in this.

At last she sighed.

"All right," she said. "But you're a poop."

Damon breathed a sigh of relief. "Yes, I'm a poop," he said.

She dressed quickly. He watched her fanny disappear under the panties, then the jeans she had worn. Christ, she was beautiful, he thought. One had to know what those thighs were capable of to appreciate their shape. The same was true of the rest of her. Her body was like a big, smooth secret. Sometimes he felt that even when he was inside her he did not find the key to that secret. It lurked in the shadows of her very shallowness.

When she had put her sweater on and was holding her coat over her arm, she came back to him. He was still lying naked in the bed. He had been too absorbed in watching her to get up and put on his robe.

She crouched on the floor beside him. She put her hand on his thigh.

"She did you wrong," she said. "I would never do that, Damon. Not in a thousand years." She sounded very serious. Her eyes expressed, or feigned, candor and commitment.

"I know that," Damon said. He tried to make his voice sound as sincere as hers, though he assumed they were both lying.

"One thing you're going to find out," she said, bringing her face close to his, "is that I am for real. As she was not."

She kissed him deeply, her tongue caressing his with catlike urgency. Her hand moved downward to touch him.

"Remember that," she said.

She stood up to leave. He accompanied her to the front door. He watched as she waited for the elevator, just as he had watched Dusty so many times. Ashley kept her eyes on him until the doors opened, then strode through them, her body full of youth and purpose.

Damon shook his head and sighed as he went back into the apartment. A few moments later he was under the sheets again, asleep on Rebecca's side of the bed.

23

His name was Cameron Burch. He was a graduate student in chemistry.

Dusty found this out the day she used the key he had given her to get into his apartment. He returned late from one of the labs he taught and found her sitting on his couch.

There was a brief conversation during which he told her about himself and she tried to recall his face from the first time they met. She thanked him for letting her sleep in his bed. In answer to her question he confirmed that they had not had sex.

She offered to do so now, but he refused.

Puzzled, she asked him why he had brought her home.

"You were pretty stoned," he said. "And you looked kind of lonely to me. I just thought you needed a place to spend the night. You kept saying you didn't want to go home."

"Really?" Dusty had no memory of this.

"Why did you leave the key for me?" she asked.

He thought for a moment, looking from her to the book-lined walls around her.

"I liked you," he said. "I wanted to give you a chance to get to know me. But not in that context."

Not in that context. Spoken like a graduate student, she thought.

He smiled. "I didn't know whether you'd want to come back," he said. "I'm glad you did."

Dusty said nothing. She glanced at the little artificial Christmas tree on the table beside the TV.

"Isn't it a little late for that?" she asked.

He nodded. "I was home for the vacation, and I had a lot of work before I left. Would you like to help me take it down?"

She helped him remove the small collection of ornaments, which fit into the cheap cardboard box in which they had been sold. The same went for the set of lights.

"What did you get for Christmas?" she asked on an impulse.

"Nothing exciting." He smiled. "Clothes, mostly. My mother is very big on sweaters. She thinks I'm not smart enough to keep myself warm."

He was wearing a sweater that looked new.

"Was that one of the gifts?" she asked. There was something painful behind her curiosity, but she could not name it.

"Yes," he said.

She was near enough to him to touch the fuzzy fabric. It was warm to the touch.

He had bent the branches of the little tree toward the tip, and was removing the stand.

"Why don't you hold the box," he asked, "and I'll shove it in."

She held out the narrow box, noticing the *Made in Sri Lanka* legend as he pushed the flattened tree into it. Then she sat back and watched as he took all the boxes into the bedroom. A moment later he emerged, looking a bit forlorn.

"No more till next year," he said.

"No more," Dusty agreed.

"I hate to see Christmas go." He stood with his hands at his sides. "It's my favorite time of year."

There was a silence.

Then, "Me, too," she said.

He was looking at her. She was sitting with her legs curled under her. Her head was inclined slightly, making her look reflective and a bit frail.

"Oh, well," he said.

"Oh, well," she agreed. Her smile had faded, but now returned as she looked up at him.

After that, Dusty lived with Cameron.

She brought her computer and books over from her apartment and put them in Cameron's bedroom. He moved his own stuff into the living room, making a second desk out of cinder blocks and a piece of plywood from a lumberyard.

They took turns cooking for the first couple of weeks, then began cooking together. Dusty remembered a few of the things Rebecca had taught her about cooking and learned more from the dog-eared copy of *The Joy of Cooking* that Cameron had on his shelf.

After the first few days, Cameron came in to sleep with Dusty. He did not touch her, but she found herself cuddling up against him like a child. Often she would wake up with his arm around her, and spend a few moments studying his sleeping face. It was a soft face, a bit sad in the early light, despite the freckles that occasionally gave him a puckish appearance. His personality seemed divided between a cold attention to his work and something boyish that he had given up somewhere along the line.

She began to bring more and more of her clothes over. There was lots of room in his closet, for he had very few things of his own. She brought her stuffed animals, the giraffe her mother had given her when she was a senior in high school.

While they cooked, they would talk. She learned about Cameron's life, his early years in Illinois, his family's move to upstate New York, his college education at SUNY Buffalo, and his decision to go to graduate school and become a professor. His parents were divorced. His father was a psychologist who worked in a clinic in New Haven.

Cameron asked her about herself, but confined his questions to her major and her post-college ambitions. After a while she volunteered some information about her family, her mother's Boston lineage, her father's fame. She told him about their separation, but steered clear of the truth about her mother and Tony. It was easy; Cameron seemed curious only about the things she wanted to tell him. He asked no more.

Their conversations were not as long as they might have been, because Cameron not only had to spend a lot of research hours at the lab, but had classes to prepare, papers to correct. He worked very long hours and usually was still working when she went to bed. She enjoyed hearing the click of his keyboard from the next room as she drifted off.

On weekends they went for long walks. Neither said much. He took her to the movies. Once he held her hand in a darkened theater. She looked down at their intertwined fingers and back to the screen.

She had stopped sleeping around. She had given Cameron's phone number to Brit in case her father called, but she never went back to the apartment anymore. Brit gave her messages from the boys who had had her number from before, but Dusty did not return their calls.

She left the apartment only to go to classes and came home early to study. She would play Cameron's records in the afternoon. It was a small collection of disparate things, a few old jazz records, some folk music, a ragged boxed set of *The Marriage of Figaro*. Dusty listened to them all, savoring their pops and scratches as though they were a pedigree added to the music.

She didn't tell Brit about her life with Cameron. On the two occasions when she saw Brit she could see that Brit thought she was living with one of the graduate students she had been sleeping with. Brit looked concerned. Dusty did not enlighten her. It seemed very important to keep Cameron separate from her old life. That included her roommates and friends, as well as her father.

She saw Damon as usual. He seemed pleased with her appearance.

"You've put on a little weight," he said.

She did not answer.

"I meant it as a compliment," he said.

"Oh. Thanks."

"You look happier," he added. "I'm glad."

"That's good."

"More like the old days." Like so many casual remarks, this one brought painful associations. But Dusty did not feel the pain as acutely as she once would have.

She was not sure what she felt for Cameron. Every time she looked at his face it seemed divided somehow, fragmented. Part of it was the way he looked now, and another part was the empty image of that first night at the party. A third part was the image in the photo, standing alongside his mother with the bleachers in the background. She saw all these faces, but she could not put them together into one. His life seemed separated from hers by a wall as thick as it was invisible.

On the other hand, he smiled every time he came into the apartment and saw her waiting there. And at night she slept in his arms, knowing he would never try to make love to her. By now she needed him terribly and dreaded the day when time or circumstance might take her away from him.

Gradually he told her more about his family. He did not like his father (who had remarried), but he seemed fond of his mother, who was now working as an insurance agent. She didn't have to contribute much to his expenses, because he had a teaching fellowship. He seemed relieved about this.

His younger sister was named Emily. He spoke of her with easy mockery, calling her a "punk." He also spoke of his older brother, a sales representative for a motorcycle company, who was married and had two small children.

Cameron did not communicate much about his inner feelings. He was hanging back, allowing himself to have rather little reality to Dusty, as a way of not pushing her. When Brit called with a message from her father, Cameron passed her the phone and did not ask what the call was about.

The silence between them was as precious to Dusty as the bits of conversation in which they discussed insignificant things. She liked the way he held himself back. The more so because, when she woke up the next morning, she would be clinging to him under the comforter on his bed.

One night he came home late from the university and found her curled up in front of the TV. A movie was on, *Bunny Lake Is Missing*. She had turned it on in the middle, waiting for him to come home, and got absorbed. When he arrived he looked at the TV screen. Carol Lynley and Keir Dullea, the brother and sister, were playing like children in a darkened place. The brother, insane, believed their game was real. The sister played along desperately, trying to fool him into thinking she had not discovered the truth.

"You look like her," Cameron observed, pointing to Carol Lynley.

"Really?" she asked. "She looks so sad. Everybody always said I looked happy."

He corrected papers while Dusty watched the rest of the movie. Then she took a shower and washed her hair. When she emerged in her terry-cloth robe, he was lying on the bed, still in his clothes, staring into space. He looked tired. She lay down on the bed beside him and turned to put her head on his shoulder.

There was a long silence. He had taken her hand and was toying gently with her fingers, as he sometimes did.

"You're all I've got," she said.

There was a silence.

He turned to face her. She smelled fresh and soapy. Her hair had moistened the pillow. The robe had pulled away from her breast, and he saw the golden skin, the brown nipple, in the shadow.

"Me, too."

He pushed the robe back over her breast. She scrunched closer to him and he held her.

She fell asleep that way, in her robe. When she woke up the next morning the comforter was over her and Cameron was gone. For the first time since she could remember, she felt happy.

24

Ashley was becoming a real problem.

She was possessive of Damon. She demanded more and more of his time. Her sexual aggressiveness, so charming in the beginning, had now revealed its alliance with a dogged, insatiable personality that was completely out of place in a mistress.

Damon was torn. On one hand he had no patience for this foolishness, particularly in light of the pressures he was under. His professional life was at a turning point, and he had his own emotions to deal with. He had no time for the tantrums of a mistress young enough to be his daughter. Ashley's immaturity made her antics all the more irritating.

On the other hand, the only thing that had kept Damon going since his breakup with Alison was Ashley. The freshness and sensuality of a young girl in his bed was an adventure, continually renewed and unpredictable, which seemed to take years off his life. He had to admit that, in a way, even her tantrums were keeping him young, making his life exciting. And his ego got a boost from her jealous pursuit of him.

But Ashley's preoccupation with Rebecca was getting out of hand. She knew, unfortunately, the essentials about Rebecca's departure with a younger man. She had also been able to gather from Damon's hints, and from the gossip mill, that Rebecca was anything but a loose woman. She was the last wife anyone would have expected to walk out on a powerful and respected man like Damon. Ashley could not let go of this enigma. She worried it like a dog with a bone.

"You're carrying a torch for her, aren't you?" she would probe Damon. "Why don't you admit it? That's why you haven't divorced her. That's why you haven't even gotten rid of her clothes. What was it about her that got under your skin? You can tell me."

Damon tried to explain. "The only reason I haven't gotten a divorce," he said, "is Dusty. This is a very delicate time for her. The loss of her mother came as a terrible blow."

"So?" Ashley asked bluntly.

"So, I don't want her to feel that her link to Rebecca is cut off forever. I don't want her to feel that the family is definitively shattered."

It was a lie, but it had verisimilitude. Rebecca had been very close to Dusty. She was not the kind of woman to abandon her only daughter. Damon wanted to keep up the pretense of a whole family, a family to which Rebecca would return, for Dusty's sake.

His lawyer's mind thought it a good alibi. But it did not satisfy Ashley. She kept insisting that he himself remained attached to Rebecca. "You've got a thing for her," she said. "I can tell."

Ashley had once confided to Damon that her father had abandoned the family when she was a child. Damon was easily able to understand Ashley's fixation on him as an older man in light of this avowal. But it did not seem to shed light on her obsession with Rebecca.

Once Ashley wondered out loud, "I don't understand how such a frump could have you twisted around her little finger this way."

Damon surprised himself by bridling at this insult to Rebecca. "Don't talk about her that way," he warned.

His own emotions left him perplexed. There was a grain of truth in Ashley's accusations. He did feel a painful fascination with Rebecca. Not because of the way she had been when she was with him, but because of the way she had left him. It was out of character for her. On the other hand, as a lawyer, Damon was trained to take into account all human motives, even the improbable ones. It was necessary, retrospectively, to insert Rebecca's sudden departure into her character, to make room for it. And that made her more interesting, somehow. Alison had been right when she said of Rebecca, "She must have had it in her after all."

He thought a lot about Rebecca. He wondered how she had attracted the boy, Tony. Or how he had attracted her. Rebecca was a "straight" person. She was even old-fashioned, where sexual matters were concerned. It could not have been easy for her to abandon her family for a young man. Her own daughter's fiancé!

Something, some sort of change, must have come over her. There was a Jekyll-and-Hyde quality about her flight that troubled Damon. Often, as he lay in bed, he would wonder what she was doing at this moment. Was she in bed with the Delafield boy? Was she strolling about the streets with him, or perhaps waiting for dinner with him at an agreed-upon place? What were her plans? What was she thinking?

For the first time in twenty years the notion of Rebecca's private thoughts did not leave Damon indifferent. It was like a riddle, a secret he needed to fathom before he could get on with his own life. And perhaps that life was not as solid as he had thought. Perhaps she had left a deeper hole behind her than he had assumed at the outset.

Thus Ashley was not wrong in her strident claims that Rebecca "had a hold on him." Though she might not be subtle enough to understand the reasons why, she had a woman's intuition that saw through Damon's surface. Her own fascination with the enigma of Rebecca was shared by Damon himself. The more time went by, it seemed that this was, ironically, the most intimate bond between them. This disturbed him most of all.

Then one day Damon found out his daughter was living with someone.

He had called the apartment, trying to get through to Dusty. Brit was not there, and a girl he didn't know answered the phone. When he asked for Dusty, the unknown voice said, "She doesn't really live here anymore. She only comes in to pick up her mail."

Damon said it was an emergency and asked where he could get in touch with Dusty. He was given a phone number. He called it but got no answer. Then, on an inspiration, he gave it to Dick Hamlin. Within an hour Dick had had it checked out. It belonged to a graduate student in chemistry.

Damon thought the situation over carefully. He was tempted to confront Dusty brutally with his discovery. The idea that she was leading a separate life, unknown to him, was infuriating; the more so because he was paying her bills, including rent for the apartment she was not occupying.

But then he thought better of this. After all, Dusty had been through a lot these past six months. He did not want to act in haste.

Dick Hamlin had said the boy, Cameron Burch, was a quiet and respectable student with a teaching fellowship and high grades.

After a while it occurred to Damon that this new situation might be of use to him in an unexpected way. After all, Dusty was his daughter. He was a concerned father. Every troubled girl has a right to the full devotion of her family in a difficult time.

He abandoned the plan of speaking to Dusty directly about things.

He had another idea.

25

Rebecca was sitting at the desk in the hotel room, writing a letter to Dusty.

She wrote to Dusty nearly every day. But she only sent the shortest and most innocuous of the letters, passing along insignificant news and asking pointless questions about how Dusty was doing. None of these letters was answered. Rebecca wondered how long she could force herself to continue sending them.

Meanwhile she carried on a rich and deeply personal correspondence that was never sent. She wrote down all the things she would have written as a loving and concerned mother had there never been a rift between her and Dusty. She saved the letters religiously, dating them and keeping them in a little file she had bought. She had a vague idea of a future time, a time of reconciliation, when she could give all the letters to Dusty at once. She doubted that such a time would ever come, but she herself could not go on living if the idea of it were abandoned. So she pursued this aborted communication, feeling her heart go out to Dusty in each unsent letter.

Sometimes she found herself expressing new thoughts in her letters, or rethinking old ones, almost as though Dusty had responded to her earlier letters with thought-provoking comments or questions. It was as though, in the silence of her own soul, the relationship could go on and even grow. Rebecca reflected that on some level all relationships might be this way, growing and changing and evolving, but without either party ever really speaking to the other of these changes. Aren't our efforts at communication like messages thrown over a wall to another person who can't really see us, even if he loves us? Can we even imagine how he is going to read those messages, or what their effect on him will be?

Rebecca was struck by this notion and even thought about mentioning it in her letter to Dusty. But she knew that Dusty, a down-to-earth person psychologically, would find bitter irony in it. "Any wall between you and me," Dusty would reply, "is of your own making. I never asked you to run away and leave me." So Rebecca did not write down her reflections. She finished her letter with words of love, of regret, of continuing concern, and sat staring at the small, neat handwriting, her heart sinking.

She heard a knock. She got up and went to the door.

"Tony?" she called cautiously.

A muffled voice, familiar, sounded outside the door.

"Who's there?" Rebecca called.

"It's Damon."

Rebecca's breath caught in her throat. She turned and placed her back against the door, as though to hold off an enemy. Then, on a sudden impulse, she turned around and opened it.

Damon stood in the corridor. He wore a silk suit. He had his leather overcoat over his arm. His hair was immaculately groomed, though the brisk day outside had reddened his cheeks. He looked handsome as ever, if a bit more tired, more lined.

She was on the point of asking him how he had found her, but she knew that was unnecessary. There might be surprises in the conversation to come, but that would not be one of them.

"May I come in?" he asked, not without sarcasm.

She stood back in silence to let him pass.

He came into the room. He looked outsize, as though all his power, all his stature and connections, were sweeping into the room with him.

But in the next instant she saw that his air of imperious haste was a pose. When he saw the room his wife lived in, he seemed to crumble, then to fight for control of himself.

"So," he said. "This is where you live." His irony was forced.

There was a long silence. Damon's eyes took in the evidence of Tony's presence here. The books, the sweater thrown over a chair, the man's watch on the dresser. So it's all real, he was thinking.

He turned to her.

"Dusty left her apartment without telling me," he said. "She's living with some man in the Village." He did not add that the man was a student.

Rebecca felt the blow of this news. Not the fact that Dusty was living with someone, so much as the knowledge that Dusty's life had gone on after Rebecca left. Up to now, Damon and Dusty had remained as frozen figures in Rebecca's imagination, like portraits in a history book, as though nothing had happened to them after her departure. Now she saw this was not true. Dusty had gone on. More yet, having lost Tony, she had found another boy.

Tears had come to Rebecca's eyes, but she fought them back.

"Who is he?" she asked in a quiet voice.

"Some graduate student," Damon said. "In chemistry or something. That's not really the point, is it?"

Relieved, Rebecca felt her heart beating more slowly.

"And other than that, is she—all right?" she asked.

"All right?" Damon repeated with a smile. "Yes, I suppose you could say she's 'all right.' Surviving, anyway."

"Well," she said. "Thank you for telling me. But you didn't have to come all this way."

Damon stood staring at her. "And what about me?" he asked. "Are you curious to hear my news? Haven't you wondered what's happened to me since you departed?"

The note of self-pity in his voice armed her against him. He had already played his strongest card, she could feel that.

"Sometimes," she said.

The word stung him.

"You've ruined our lives," he said passionately. "You've ruined our family. Dusty, and me, and... Aren't you curious as to how we've gone about picking up the pieces?"

Rebecca steeled herself. The image of Dusty in pieces, of Dusty destroyed was terrible. But she knew Damon. She knew what he was trying to do. Even now he was making his case like a lawyer. And, true to form, going for the throat.

"You have your life to live," she said. "I'm sorry if it's difficult."

Damon sighed. "Did you have to run away with your daughter's fiancé?" he asked. "For Christ's sake, Rebecca. If you were unhappy with me, we could have worked it out in some civilized way. Even if we couldn't stay together. But this... My God, how could you do this to Dusty?"

He gave her his penetrating look. "Dusty and I have become a lot closer since you left, you know." He squared his shoulders. "After all, we're all each other's got. She's in a lot of pain, Rebecca. I've watched her go through agonies a girl her age should never have to suffer. She'll never be the same."

These words tore at Rebecca's heart. But she found strength to doubt him. This was his way of going for the jugular—using Dusty. That was why he had come. The fact that Dusty had moved in with someone was his pretext.

"Have you met him?" she asked.

He shook his head. "She tried to keep it a secret from me," he said. "Obviously she's done it to harm herself. And to let us know how much pain she's in. I trust you're not so wrapped up in yourself that you can't see that."

Rebecca said nothing. She knew that she must hold firm at this moment, while he was here. After he was gone she could let her wounds open and cry her tears. But she could not let him see her struggles. She could not let him think he had power over her.

He raised an appraising eyebrow as he looked at her.

"My God, you've got a heart of stone," he said. "I've got to admit you surprise me. I never thought you had it in you. I thought I knew you. You're as cold as ice."

Rebecca stood in front of the bed. As usual she was wearing a skirt and blouse, stockings, jewelry. Her hair was scrupulously groomed, though it was rather longer than when she had lived with Damon. The blouse had been given her by Tony. She always looked crisp and businesslike, even when she was alone in the room in the middle of the day. This was no doubt an echo of her Boston heritage. She never let down her formality until Tony came home.

Damon was staring at her, contempt mingling with admiration in his eyes. So it was all real, he thought. The Rebecca he had been carrying in his memory, a person who had been removed from him by insane and incomprehensible events, but who remained known to him, human, was truly gone. Replaced by this cold creature who could listen to his arguments unmoved.

He took a step forward. "Was this what attracted him?" he asked. "Your coldness? Your ruthlessness?"

Rebecca recoiled an inch, then stood her ground.

"I thought young men had a weakness for mother figures," Damon sneered. "You look more like an executioner to me."

Though he had moved closer, she seemed just as distant. Who could see what thoughts were behind that calm, indifferent face?

Who could know what touched her, what had meaning for her? She was not the same woman he had known. He felt a pang of grief at his loss of her, then a rush of rage.

He glanced at the bed. Suddenly he imagined the pleasures she took there with her young lover, pleasures that occupied that same opaque, inhuman space where her thoughts now lived. The notion seared him inside like a poison. For the first time since he arrived here he felt himself losing control.

"Is that what attracted him?" he asked.

"Let me go." She was struggling. He had her on the bed, he had pushed her down somehow. He smelled a new perfume, one she had never worn before. Her body seemed different. He could almost feel its new possibilities, its new appetites. In this bed she spread her legs to welcome her youthful lover, not as she had once done with Damon—not even when they were both young—but in a different way, a way he could not imagine. The idea of this dark side of her maddened him.

"How do you do it with him?" he asked, fumbling with the buttons of her blouse.

"Damon!" She wedged her arms against his chest. He pulled the blouse out of her skirt, felt the smooth skin of her stomach and pushed the skirt up her legs. He looked at her thighs, the warm center of her accustomed to another man's sex. Rage blinded him.

"Damon! Stop this. Get control of yourself." Oddly, Rebecca sounded more annoyed than frightened. Her tone was reproachful.

This made him even more angry. "Damn you," he hissed against her neck. "Damn you to hell." Confusedly he realized how excited he was.

"Damon..." Rebecca said. "Don't..."

He put his hand over her mouth. Their struggle was silent from that moment on. And before long it was not even a struggle. Rebecca had gone limp. Damon got no more from her than if she were dead.

At length he stood up to leave. His whole body was throbbing with frustration. His breath scalded his throat. His hands shook as he fixed his clothes. He glanced around the unfamiliar room and saw the bathroom. He disappeared into it.

When he emerged he looked precisely as he had looked when he first came in. His tie was neat, his silk suit unwrinkled. He looked like the rich lawyer he was. Despite her own emotion, Rebecca felt a pulse of amusement inside herself at this thought.

He looked down at her. Her clothes were in disarray. Yet she seemed composed, remote.

"You're not worth looking at," he said. "Not worth the rope it would take to hang you."

He seized his coat and walked to the door. Opening it, he paused to look at her. "You'll burn in hell for this."

He stalked out, slamming the door behind him.

Rebecca lay on the bed in silence for a long time. At first she felt nothing at all, except the pillow under her head and the tumbled sheets bunched under her. Damon's visit was like a dream, rendered even less real by his childish rage and his weakness.

But after a while her tears began to come, and with them the gasps she had kept inside her while Damon was here. She felt crushed by what had happened. Damon's tawdry use of Dusty as his weapon of attack was based on a profound truth. Rebecca had broken Dusty's life to pieces. And, in Damon's words, Dusty was now trying to put it back together on her own.

Rebecca thought of the pile of letters in her desk, the letters she had written to Dusty and not sent. So this was what was left of her as a mother, this utter inability to comfort a daughter whom she herself had probably ruined.

Perhaps Damon was right. Perhaps she would burn in hell for what she had done. Not to him, but to Dusty.

She was lying on the still-rumpled bed, staring at the ceiling, when Tony came in.

"What's going on?" he asked, looking down at her half-clothed body.

Rebecca sighed. She tried to think of an answer, but words would not come. She wiped at the tears on her cheeks.

"What the hell is going on?" Tony asked, standing before her in his suit, his coat thrown over his arm.

Rebecca struggled to come back to herself. She looked up into the eyes of her lover. They were blazing with reproach and suspicion. Because of this, everything seemed more dislocated than ever. In Tony she saw Dusty's beau, Dusty's fiancé. Everything about him, including his anger, bespoke her own crime. How could all this have happened? The world seemed turned upside down.

Tony came to her side. He grasped both her shoulders. For a moment she thought he was going to comfort her. She needed him now, more than ever.

But he pushed her roughly down into the sheets and spoke to her in a voice trembling with anger.

"Was he here?" he asked. "Is that what's got you so upset? Tell me the truth, Rebecca."

A look of amazement came over Rebecca's features as she measured the enormity of the misunderstanding. Then she looked into Tony's eyes. Nothing but jealousy shone in them. He was waiting for her explanation. In his crisp suit, with his offended masculinity, he looked almost like Damon.

"I'm waiting for your answer, Rebecca."

He shook her, pushing her deeper into the mattress.

"Answer!" he shouted. He slapped her face, hard. It was the first time he had ever hit her.

Rebecca gazed at him with new eyes. The words she had been struggling to find died on her lips.

With contempt he looked at her body. The skirt was still around her waist, but the rest of her was bare. She had been too shocked by what had happened with Damon to get up and fix herself. Now it was too late.

"You disgust me," Tony said. "I don't know why I wasted my time with you. You're not worth it."

He pushed her roughly down into the sheets. Then he abruptly let go, as though sickened by his contact with her.

He swept from the room, slamming the door as Damon had done.

He would not come back for many hours. Probably he would get drunk. Briefly she worried that he might create a scene with Sam. The idea was crazy in the wake of what had happened here, and yet not absurd. And suddenly everything felt that way to Rebecca—insane though not absurd.

She lay for a long time pondering that notion, and the fact that she had brought all this on herself. Then she got up, went into the bathroom for a long, hot shower, and came out to pack her bag.

When Tony returned late that night, after having drunk his dinner at a downtown bar, Rebecca was gone, and so were all her things.

Part Three

26

Rebecca began by taking a bus to Beatrix, a small city about a hundred miles from Grace Island. From there she intended to take a train or bus to a larger metropolis where she could get a plane to wherever she wanted to go.

But where did she want to go? No place on earth beckoned to her. No person awaited her or would take her in. Except for Irene, of course. And Irene, for too many reasons, was out of consideration.

Beatrix was a peculiar little place, hideously ugly, with lumber mills and old, old buildings that had somehow survived the last fifty or sixty years without being torn down. There was a pungent, unpleasant smell that apparently came from some sort of processing plant associated with the lumber. Many of the streets, for no apparent reason, were very wide. The people walking along them looked sad and gray and empty-eyed. Even the cars looked old. It was a profoundly depressing town.

Rebecca got a room in a hotel but did not unpack her bags. She just wanted a day to think.

It was difficult to do that. She lay on her bed, watching the silent images on the television set and breathing in the sour smell that crept in through every crack. The unpleasantness of this out-of-the-way place only accentuated her own feeling of exile.

For the second time, she had left everything behind. It was becoming her avocation, it seemed—leaving everything behind. But this time she had run away with no destination to run to.

I have no one, she thought, pacing the floor and biting her nails. The realization brought more wonderment than self-pity. All her life she had had people. At the price of being responsible for them and to them, perhaps. Sometimes at a price that made her lose something precious of herself. But she had always had people. Not anymore.

She stayed up late, lying on the bed with the pillows propped behind her. Then she fell into a troubled somnolence that seemed nothing like sleep. The next morning she woke up early. There was no room service, so she went down the block to a little lunchroom for breakfast. The odor of the town mingled strangely, horribly with the smells of frying eggs and bacon and maple syrup. She drank a cup of black coffee and left.

She went back to her room. She just needed a little more thought, she felt. The only problem was that last night, despite considerable effort, she had failed to think. And her sleep had brought her no closer to a decision. Her mind was a blank.

She looked out the window and saw the old cars moving slowly along the street. The sky was gray, but it held a diffuse light that hurt her eyes. She turned back to the room, whose emptiness was all at once unbearable. She called the desk for a cab, giving the train station as her destination, and closed her suitcase.

The station was only a few blocks from the hotel, and even more run-down than the rest of the city. The benches and ticket windows looked as though they dated from the first quarter of the century. Rebecca studied the timetable dubiously. There were trains to most of Western Canada, and others heading east. She could go to Alaska if she wished. Or down to Seattle or Portland or California. A person could start a new life here, she mused dully.

On a whim she bought a ticket to Seattle, with connections to San Francisco. She had never seen San Francisco, though Damon had been there a dozen times on the firm's business. She had often felt a prick of resentment that he had never taken her along.

The train didn't leave for two hours, so Rebecca bought a paperback novel and sat on one of the hard, old benches, reading. Once she stood up as if to take a walk around the station, but decided not to because she had her bag with her.

If only the train would get here! She would feel better, she thought, if she could at least get into the compartment and off the ground of this place.

And finally the train did arrive. Its number came up on the timetable in ancient letters that looked as though they were being manually changed. Rebecca picked up her bag and hurried to the platform. A tired-looking conductor directed her to her car. She got in and waited nervously. She was getting hungry now, and had eaten nothing all day, but she did not want to leave the train long enough to get something to eat.

At length a woman and her son came into the compartment. The woman was about Rebecca's age; the boy was perhaps seventeen. The woman murmured a few mundane remarks that the boy did not answer. He immediately buried himself in a magazine with a picture of a girl on a motorcycle on the cover.

Rebecca waited for more passengers to enter the compartment, but none did. The woman seemed to want to speak to her, but Rebecca avoided eye contact, feeling too frayed at the moment to carry on a conversation. The boy sniffed as he turned the pages of his magazine. His knees were raised, his back curved forward so that he seemed closed upon himself.

Finally there were signs of imminent departure. No announcement was made, but porters moved back from the train, a conductor walked briskly down the aisle, and Rebecca heard compartment doors being closed.

The train gave a small shudder. Another page of the boy's magazine turned with the sound of a dry leaf. The mother shifted in her seat, anticipating the beginning of the journey. Encouraged by the moment, she was about to speak to Rebecca.

But Rebecca was on her feet, her bag in her hand. The astonished woman watched her leave the compartment. A moment later Rebecca was in a phone booth on the platform, asking the operator for help with long distance. The train was still poised on the tracks, about to leave but not yet budging.

Rebecca felt her hand tremble around the receiver. She dialed the code for the United States. She knew it well, having studied the little directory at the Royal Grace with the fantasy of calling Dusty. She knew from the same source that she could make a call from Canada using her American calling card.

"Directory assistance."

"For Wisconsin, please. Madison, Wisconsin."

A moment later she was dialing the number she had been given. She chewed her lip nervously.

I have no one. No one in the world.

The phone rang three times, then a fourth. The train had not moved. Her place in the compartment was waiting for her. She was about to hang up.

"Bittman here." The voice sounded startlingly near.

"Sam, is that you? This is Rebecca. Rebecca Lowell."

There was a small pause, long enough to make her heart sink. But she stood her ground.

"Rebecca! Well, isn't this a surprise. You sound as though you're next door. Where are you?"

As she watched, the train began finally to move.

"A long way away," she said. "Canada."

"To what do I owe...?" His voice was cautious, decorous as ever. But it trailed off.

She tried to find words to say, and failed.

There was another pause. She was so upset that she nearly hung up on him.

"When can I see you?" he asked in a different voice.

"Right away!" She almost cried out the words. "I mean, as soon as I can get there. Do you really want to?"

"I'll be counting the hours. But what about you? Do you really want to?"

"Yes," Rebecca said, her eyes misting suddenly as the train slid faster along the track.

"Good," Sam said. "Good, Rebecca."

27

Cameron was the first person Dusty told. The only one, in fact. There was a time when she would have told Brit or Susan about it, or perhaps Marie, her roommate from freshman year. But now she felt a million miles removed from her old friends. Cameron was really the only person in the world she trusted.

Cameron did not let her down. He held her for a long time the first night, when she told him. He asked her about her feelings. She was not articulate about them, because she barely knew what had been happening to her these past months. It was all a dream. To some extent the dream included Cameron; to some extent he alone was real.

He helped her research the clinics in the vicinity of the university. There was no problem with confidentiality, of course. And all the clinics were above reproach, medically. But Cameron found out from one of the female graduate students that there was a clinic on Fourteenth Street where the doctor was a woman, and where the social workers were particularly caring and helpful.

Cameron went with Dusty for the initial interview. The social worker got the mistaken impression that he was the father, and asked him rather pointedly how he felt about terminating the pregnancy. Dusty explained that Cameron was not the father, but just a friend who was helping her through this. Not without embarrassment, she confided that she did not know who the father was.

The social worker gave Dusty some pamphlets that explained the procedures involved and recommended a couple of books about the deeper psychological effects of abortion. Cameron found the books at the university bookstore, and he and Dusty read them. The gist of them seemed to be that Dusty should expect some emotional fallout from the experience, perhaps coming only after several months. There might be considerable anxiety and symptoms of grief, as well as disturbances of the sexual function. Many women had abortions without thinking much about it one way or the other, only to find a few months later that they could not bear to have sex. Frigidity often ensued, lasting indefinitely and requiring psychiatric treatment.

On the day of the abortion Cameron went with Dusty. He sat alongside her for the final interview with the social worker, and, at Dusty's request, remained with her during the procedure itself.

It was not as painful as Dusty had feared, though her body felt invaded in a way she had never imagined before. The doctor was kind but businesslike, not quite as sympathetic as Dusty had expected. She explained in faintly disguised terms what she was doing, so that Dusty would not be alarmed by the sensations. There was no way to conceal the magnitude of what was happening, and the doctor did not try.

When it was over, Cameron stayed with Dusty in the recovery room and took her home in a cab. She bled freely for about two days, then the bleeding became intermittent. She stayed in the apartment, studying when concentration was possible, watching TV when it was not.

On the third day she began to cry. Cameron held her all morning and afternoon, rocking her softly against his chest and saying what he could to soothe her. By evening her sobs had stopped, and she took a pill and slept for fourteen hours.

After that she seemed like her old self, except for the tears that would creep silently into her eyes in the middle of a conversation about trivial things. Often she would laugh at something Cameron said, and her tears would erupt suddenly, almost as though she had laughed until she cried.

At first Cameron seemed as remote from her as everything else in the world. Then he came into better focus. She felt his arms as a genuine refuge, and his conversation began to make an impression on her. Proportionately, it seemed, everything else grew dim. Memory had begun to yield inside her, making room for her own survival.

The weekend after the abortion she had to see her father. She had already canceled two dinner dates, on the pretext that she had midterms and papers due. Damon would get suspicious if she put him off any longer.

Cameron watched her dress for the dinner. She chose a skirt-and-sweater outfit that she knew Damon liked. Except for a slight pallor, she looked like herself.

"Are you going to be all right?" Cameron asked.

"Sure." Her voice was brisk and a little off-putting. Only Cameron's ear, attuned now to the personality behind her outward behavior, could hear the insecurity behind it.

"I could take you and wait while you eat," he said. "I could be right outside. If you needed me."

She shook her head. "I'll be all right." Then, turning from the mirror, "How do I look?"

"Beautiful."

He walked her down the street to the cab stand. It was very cold outside. Rare flakes of snow were dancing between the buildings and around the streetlights. The air stung their faces, but a distant hint of the spring to come was palpable somehow in the empty sky.

Cameron held the door of the cab for Dusty. She got in and rolled down the window.

He leaned forward, his hands on the roof of the cab.

"Will you marry me?" he asked.

"Yes." She nodded quickly. The driver said something to her. She kissed Cameron and rolled up the window.

He stood shivering under the light snow as the cab bore her away.

28

Ashley was sitting naked on the bed, cross-legged, smoking a cigarette. Damon was propped up against the pillows, watching her.

"I'm pregnant," she said.

Damon started. He narrowed his eyes.

She was not looking at him. She took another drag at her cigarette and blew a tiny ring of smoke. She watched it dissipate in the air in front of her face, meanwhile butting the ash into the ashtray.

How different she looked tonight from the way she had looked four months ago! She was still beautiful, of course. Still the long, rich thighs, the firm breasts, the milky skin. Her hair was longer now—she knew he liked it longer—and she was using a perfume he had bought her for Christmas, Mon Baiser.

But she was different. For one thing, they had had so many quarrels about Rebecca. In a dozen more or less obvious ways Ashley had sought to bind him closer to herself, and had not succeeded as she had hoped. In her frustration she had made a shibboleth out of attacking Rebecca and accusing Damon of still carrying a torch for Rebecca. His slowness to divorce Rebecca added fuel to the fire.

During this long time of conflict, Damon's position had become more and more difficult. He could not very well tell Ashley to her face that she was a tacky, crude girl who couldn't be remotely compared to Rebecca in subtlety or in—a better expression—quality. She was not even in the same league as Alison Shore, who, whatever her weaknesses, was a real woman with a real personality.

No, he could not tell Ashley these things, for two reasons. In the first place, if he told her how he felt, he could not go on sleeping with her. He sensed that her ambition to win him was part and parcel of her attraction to him. If she believed there was no hope, she would drop him and look for greener pastures. She was an ambitious girl. She would not waste her youth on a man who only used her as a toy. She wanted something in return.

In the second place, crude and manipulative though she was, she was insecure and felt things deeply. He sensed an instability in her that kept him on edge. In the event of a definitive break—which he now saw as inevitable, though perhaps still a long way away—she might be very upset. Dangerously so.

In the meantime, she was changed. She behaved differently, she made love differently. Gone now was the girlish awe over his power and position that had flattered him in the beginning. In its place was an attitude of angry challenge that colored everything she said, including the announcement she had just made.

Perhaps because he was tired of trying to keep her under control, Damon now reacted with anger.

"How do you know it's mine?" he asked.

She darted him a quick glare. "Because I know."

There was a silence.

"Maybe you're wrong," he said.

"I'm not wrong," she replied. "I'm three weeks late."

"That's not what I meant." Damon looked past her to the skyline outside the window. "Maybe you're wrong in assuming it's mine."

"What are you saying?" she asked. "That I sleep around?"

Damon thought for a moment. "I'm not the sort of man to go through life with my eyes closed," he said. "I've never imagined I was the only one, Ashley."

She stabbed out her cigarette savagely.

"Have you been checking up on me?" she asked.

Damon measured her anger. His bluff had worked. He knew nothing about her private life, but his lawyer's instinct told him she was not keeping herself for him alone.

"What kind of man do you think you're dealing with?" he asked coolly.

She did not look at him. She chewed at her lip. She pushed a lock of hair from her eye. In that instant Damon realized that it was her tackiness that had attracted him from the beginning. He had had enough of subtle women; he wanted something simpler, more sensual, more controllable.

"What do you want me to do?" she asked.

"What any woman in your position does at a time like this," he said. "Handle it. If there's a problem with money, let me know. I'll be happy to help."

She looked at him. Reproach was in her eyes. But so was defeat.

"That's what I'm here for, after all," Damon said. "To help in any way I can."

He watched as she got up to go to the bathroom. Such beautiful thighs, he thought. Such a beautiful walk.

29

Rebecca was twelve-and-a-half years old the summer her father abandoned her.

The scene came back over and over again in her dreams, always in colors of a preternatural freshness and reality. One Saturday, she and Josey, her best friend from school, were out wandering in the state park near Concord. It was a bus ride away from home, but the girls had heard you could meet boys there and had started out early that morning. They were wearing shorts and T-shirts, but Rebecca had purloined a lipstick from her mother's huge supply, and she and Josey hung around the picnic areas with a devil-may-care manner that they hoped might attract boys.

It turned out that the stories were true. Two young boys from North Boston emerged from the shore of the pond and talked to them. They seemed interested, and the girls, between giggles, dared to encourage them. A while later Rebecca found herself near the waterfall with one of the boys, necking in the deep woods.

He was hardly older than herself and clumsy in his petting, but he was a nice boy, and his own diffidence emboldened her. She let him kiss her all he wanted. Her T-shirt had been pulled out of her shorts, and he touched her rib cage, his hand stopping at the tiny bra she had only begun wearing that spring. She helped him, the pine needles hissing under their bodies, the falls a whisper in the damp air of noon.

Later she took the bus back with Josey, feeling like a person reborn. Her body did not stop tingling all the way home. Josey was nervous and excited, but Rebecca lied about what had happened. Keeping the secret from her best friend seemed an emblem of how precious and private it had been.

When she arrived home, Irene—it was from that day, she would later recall, that she thought of her mother as Irene instead of Mom—was sitting at the kitchen table with red eyes.

"Your father has left us," she said. There was a note on the table before her, flattened out by her nervous hands and moistened by her tears. "He found someone else he loves more than us. Here. Read it for yourself." She held the letter out challengingly, like an accusation. Rebecca backed away. "No, I don't want to," she said. "Go on!" her mother cried. "This is what you have to look forward to!" Rebecca ran breathlessly up the stairs to throw herself on her bed.

Rebecca's dreams ended with that frantic uphill flight, two steps at a time, her heart pounding madly in her breast. But in her dreams she never reached the bedroom. She just kept running, away from everything and toward nothing, as the feel of the boy's kisses lingered on her lips and her mother's words rang in her ears.

She did not tell Sam about the dream, perhaps because it had become so much a part of her sleeping life that her waking mind could no longer see it.

But she told him everything else.

In February they went to a hotel in Wisconsin only a few miles from the small town where Sam had grown up. He had brought her here to show her the countryside.

"Do you see that?" Sam said. "It's all very new, geologically speaking. The glaciers sheared off the surface of the land and scooped out all the lakes. That was only a few thousand years ago. Most of the soil we're looking at is glacial drift from Canada. I wouldn't be surprised if there are minerals here from the neighborhood of Grace Island."

Rebecca pondered this strange notion. Grace Island, to her, seemed a world away from Wisconsin.

"The fact is," Sam said, "that the so-called Ice Age is not in the past at all. We're in it right now. The glaciers have come a dozen times or more, and they'll come again."

He smiled. "You know, I used to take this land for granted when I was a boy. As though all this had been here forever and would remain just as it is. But now I know how exciting a piece of land really is. Just think, Rebecca, within another hundred thousand years this landscape will be transformed all over again. With materials imported from God knows where." He breathed in the wintry air delightedly.

Rebecca laughed. "You talk about a hundred thousand years as though it were the day after tomorrow," she said.

"I guess I do get carried away," he said. "I'm fascinated by causes. Everything has a cause. But between every cause and its possible effects you have the element of chance. That's what makes life interesting."

He turned back to Rebecca. "You know," he said, "Einstein used to say that God does not play dice with the universe. I don't claim to be on his level, but I don't like that statement. Why, if God didn't throw in the element of chance in the way things work, there would be no risk. And without risk, there would be no real change." He gestured to the land. "No sudden lakes, no new hills, no interesting rocks from distant places."

His blue eyes burned inquisitively as he took in the view. She could almost feel the urgency of an adolescent in him, though it was tempered by the more whimsical intellect of a mature man.

"That's a rather daring way to look at things," Rebecca observed. "Sometimes I can't help wishing the unexpected would go away and leave me in peace."

Sam raised an eyebrow significantly. "Ah, but then you wouldn't have me, would you?"

She was silent.

"And I wouldn't have you," he concluded. "Just think of all the accidents it took to bring you to me.... And all that time I never dreamed I was going to be so lucky. But that's life."

Rebecca smiled. "I'm glad you're happy with this turn of the roulette wheel."

Sam had the unusual ability to speed up the slow passage of time in his mind, and thus to view familiar things as though they had just sprung into their present shape. He loved landmarks, historic sites, places where exciting things had happened. He found imponderable magic in looking at a grassy hill or meadow and reflecting that ten thousand Union and Confederate soldiers had given their lives under that same sun, in that same breeze, for that land. Rebecca thought this remarkable, because history had never meant anything to her before, except for the bland presence of brass landmarks or plaques on old buildings or in parks.

He loved archeology almost as much as geology. Ancient arti-
facts were as alive to him as newly made gadgets from his own
workshop. And he had an almost childlike passion for seismology.
He knew everything there was to know about fault lines, earth-
quakes and plate tectonics. He loved to say that the quiet surface
of the earth was an uneasy battle of unequal forces, one of which
would inevitably win out. Each river, each mountain, even each
continent was the result of a cataclysm in which one force won out
over another.

Rebecca was touched by the enthusiasm with which Sam admired the world. There was an innocence about him that refreshed
and delighted her. Now that she knew him better she realized that
this quality arose from an unusual strength of personality. He
showed no trace of the male's concern to be powerful, to be in
charge. He viewed life as a gift to be received with wonder, and
not as an adversary to be defeated. She had never seen this quality
in a man before. Not in Damon, certainly. And, come to think of
it, not in Tony, either.

But she found out that Sam had not always been this way. In a
sense he had only found his youth in middle age.

"I was a workaholic until Margery got sick," he told her. "Why,
I hardly even noticed my daughters when they were little. The
business kept going up and down, and I went up and down with
it, like a puppet. After Margery died I sort of hit rock bottom. I
realized that I hadn't really been living. I couldn't climb out of that
grief as a whole man unless I put the pieces of myself together in
a new way. I had been a machine without a soul. I had to start
being a person. And being smart, being in charge, getting
ahead—that has nothing to do with being a person. That was a hard
lesson to learn. Harder for a man, perhaps, than for a woman."

When Rebecca told him of her own past, she could see that he
had deduced a lot of the truth from what he had seen of her in
Canada. He seemed surprised that so controlled a woman could
have undergone so strange an adventure. But he did not disapprove.

"We think we know who we are," he said. "But so much is
going on under the surface. Sometimes there's no way out of the
old patterns except drastic action."

"I worry about Tony," she said. "In fact, I worry about everybody."

"Rebecca," Sam said, "you were a victim for a long time. Other people came to depend on you in that role. Not because they were evil, but because it was the only role they knew for you. In order to break free, you had to hurt them, yes. But which is better? To cause some pain in the short run, or to be a victim for the rest of your life? Do you think it was good for Dusty to have a mother who was so unhappy?"

"As compared to a mother who ran off with..." Rebecca murmured, looking away.

Sam put his arm around her. "That's all over," he said. "You've got to put it behind you."

As Sam comforted her, Rebecca felt the enormous irony of her situation. It was her own sin that had brought her to Sam. He was an indirect result of her own erring, her wandering from the straight-and-narrow path of life. Having abandoned her family for Tony, she had abandoned Tony for Sam himself. Sam was part of the vast destruction she had wrought. She felt like a coward, accepting reassurance from him.

"Sam," she said, suddenly urgent. "It was a sin. I know what you're saying, but in my heart it was a sin. You've got to help me—"

"Expiate it?"

She nodded, very thoughtfully. "Yes."

He hugged her close. "If that's what you need, I'm your man," he said. "Suppose you let me help you to forgive yourself for being human. As a matter of fact, my dear, that may have been your problem all along. From the very beginning."

Rebecca measured his words. Perhaps he was right. A long time ago, when she was too young to know any better, she had sinned against herself. She had done what she thought was expected of her, and lost her own soul in the process. But in order to win herself back, she had to commit a second sin, a sin that had brought harm to a lot of people. Could she hope to go unpunished for it?

It was a cruel bargain, she thought. A game with harsh, punishing rules. A game in which, as Sam would say, chance played a crucial role. If Rebecca hadn't met Tony when she did, and had the unexpected effect on Tony that she had, her whole life might have played itself out according to the pattern established during her marriage to Damon. Like one of those quiet hills that seem so permanent until the pressures under the fault lines cause it, one fine day, to split apart. *Fault lines,* Rebecca thought with a bitter smile. What an apt expression for the flaws in the human character. Her character.

She had not played the game well. She had stumbled into every pitfall. But her long, uneven journey had brought her to Sam, and for that she was grateful. He could not save her soul for her, but he was trying to help her save her life. She knew she might have to pay a high price for this, as well, but she was not afraid of that anymore.

She had written Tony within days of her departure from Grace. She was kind in her letter, blaming only herself for everything that had happened. Tony was an innocent victim. In pursuing her he had followed an impulse that was passionate, loving, but not that of a mature man choosing a mate. This was why, even without her meeting Sam, it had to turn out badly.

A week after mailing the letter she telephoned Tony. He was still at the Royal Grace. He asked her where she was. She did not deny that she was with Sam.

"I told you so," he said. "You've got to give me that one, at least."

"Yes, I guess I do."

"Well, a woman has to act her age, I suppose," Tony said. "I suppose I shouldn't have forced you to give all that up."

"Nobody forced me," Rebecca said.

There was a silence.

"Are you going to marry him?" he asked.

"I don't know," she replied. "I'm not thinking about such things now. I've been in too much of a hurry. I need to take some time to find out who I am."

There was a silence.

"I'm sorry I didn't help you in that search," Tony said.

"Oh, but you did!" Rebecca cried, regretting what she had said. "You made a great contribution to my life, Tony. I don't know what I would have done without you. I'll never go back to Damon, you know."

"I suppose that's something."

"And I want you to be happy," she said. "I want you to do

what is best for you. I hope that, in some way, our time together
will help you do that.''

Again there was silence, this time more ambiguous in the pull it
exerted on Rebecca.

"What are your plans?" she asked nervously. "Do you mind
my asking?"

"I'm going to finish out the year here, so I can get a good
recommendation from my bosses." Tony's voice was matter-of-
fact, perhaps a bit cold. "Then I'm going to go back home and
finish law school. I've written to the dean. I can start again in the
fall. I'll only graduate a year late."

"That's wonderful." Rebecca mused that a year was nothing for
a young man. By the time Tony graduated, his idyll with her would
be virtually forgotten. She wanted to leave no trace in his life. Let
him think back on her as an error of his youth—or not think about
her at all.

"Well, then…" he said.

They were both thinking the same thing. If she would never go
back to Damon, Tony would never go back to Dusty. It was too
late. That was one fact of life that could not be undone.

"Let's not say any more," Rebecca said.

"All right."

Rebecca began to hang up. Then she thought she heard Tony's
voice again and hurriedly brought the receiver back to her ear. The
click of the broken connection was all she heard.

But as she hung up the phone she thought he might have said,
"I still love you."

30

In the spring, Rebecca moved to Chicago and found a job as an editor and technical writer for a business publishing firm. She lived in an apartment overlooking Lake Michigan, a place that had once cost someone a fortune, but now became available at a reasonable rent because the building had fallen on hard times as wealthy Chicagoans abandoned the inner city.

The apartment was on the fortieth floor and had a spectacular view of an immensity of cold, choppy water that was most often gray or pea green in color, for the weather in this wind-whipped city was almost always bad.

She had chosen Chicago because of Sam. She wanted to be near his home in Wisconsin, but not near enough to interfere in his family. Sam had made no secret of his desire to marry her, but he respected her need for time alone.

"Be as independent as you can," he encouraged her. "Be what you want and do what you want. Put those pieces back together the way *you* want them to fit. And if that means that some day I get to be your husband, I'll be the lucky one."

He saw her often, for he nearly always had to make connections in Chicago for his travels. She took an unexpected pleasure in cooking, learning his favorite dishes and making new ones of her own. She decorated the apartment with simple, rather bohemian furnishings and abstract paintings. She found herself indulging tastes that had remained dormant in her when, back in New York, she had been the proper wife of a conservative lawyer.

And she visited Sam in Wisconsin. He introduced her to his daughters—with an almost embarrassing pride—as what she now was, a working woman from Chicago who hailed originally from Boston and who was getting a divorce. They were pleasant young women—the older sisters considerably more settled in their manner and viewpoint than the youngest, Christine—and they accepted Rebecca readily. Sam had told them he met her while he was on business in Chicago. The Grace Island episode, for obvious reasons, would always remain his and Rebecca's secret.

Christine, the willful daughter to whom Sam was obviously closest, took a particular liking to Rebecca. Perhaps because of Sam's distortions about Rebecca's past, Christine saw Rebecca as a strong woman who was in charge of her own destiny, a woman with her own interests and career. A passionate person.

At first Rebecca was tempted to shrug off this skewed image of herself with a laugh, and to assure Christine that in reality she was the most cautious and even cowardly of women. But more and more she felt uncomfortable with the truth about herself—with that specific truth at least—and more comfortable with Christine's version. If she was not precisely a passionate person, she had taken the same risks that a passionate person would have taken. Committed the same sins, or even greater ones.

"What I can't understand," Christine said, "is how Dad found a woman like you. He's such a fuddy-duddy. Politically, anyway. And he's a terrible sexist."

"I don't think you're being completely fair, Christine," Rebecca chided her with a smile. "Sam respects women. He may be a bit old-fashioned about the way he shows it, but I don't think I've ever felt so respected by a man before." The image of Damon pulled at her from inside as she spoke.

"You're not his daughter," Christine argued. "If you had grown up under his thumb, you might not be so quick to take his side."

"Relationships between fathers and daughters are never easy," Rebecca said. "Men don't really know how to feel about their daughters."

"That's putting it mildly," Christine said, twirling a lock of her hair around her finger, a favorite nervous gesture of hers.

"A good father—like yours—wants his daughter to be independent," Rebecca said. "But he wants to protect her at the same time. That can be a difficult balancing act. I don't think your mother's death made it any easier for Sam."

Christine smiled. "What makes you so tolerant?" she asked.

"Mistakes, child," Rebecca said. "Lots of mistakes. More than my share."

Christine sat back against the couch, looking very much at home. Rebecca's reply had pleased her in a way she did not reveal.

Thus Rebecca allowed herself to be drawn into a new relationship as Christine's friend and confidante. She sensed that Christine's politics, and particularly her feminism, had something to do with the loss of her mother. So it was easy for Rebecca to support the girl gently in her opinions while anticipating that time, and her own helping role, would soften them.

As though to bring a coda to this process of regeneration, Dusty got in touch with Rebecca that spring to invite her to her wedding. The first letter was very brief, hardly more than a note. But when Rebecca answered it with a heartfelt letter of congratulation and love, Dusty wrote back. At Easter she telephoned.

Her voice was the same. They talked for a long time, Dusty in the unseen apartment of her fiancé, Cameron, Rebecca on the sofa in the apartment high above Lake Michigan. The dislocation was complete, their former life was gone forever, and for this very reason they seemed to feel more at ease.

There were more calls, and a new version of their lifelong closeness began timidly to assert itself. Dusty was excited about Cameron and her plans for the future; Rebecca encouraged her in this and expressed pride in her self-reliance.

"He's looking forward to meeting you," Dusty said. "I've told him all about you."

Rebecca suffered the implications of this statement in silence, believing that Dusty had not told Cameron the awful truth but not entirely sure.

"Well, I can hardly wait to meet him," she said. "How is he hitting it off with your father?"

"Oh, fine," Dusty said. "They're very different, but they seem to like each other."

Rebecca felt a strange inner glow at these words.

"I'm glad," she said.

For a while they were both afraid of actually seeing each other in the flesh again; but the gentle fitting of their voices, the call and response repeated in more and more ways, gave them courage. They began to make concrete plans for the wedding that would bring them together again.

Spring in Chicago grew warmer with weak little spurts, always brushed backward by another rain, another day of freezing lake wind. In Wisconsin, snow was still on the ground. But Rebecca felt life tingling in every part of her. She could hardly wait for the summer.

She and Damon were making plans for their divorce. Her attorney in Chicago was ironing out the arrangements with Damon's personal lawyer back in New York. The situation was surprisingly amicable. Damon seemed to have exhausted his hatred for Rebecca when he visited her in Canada. Now he was polite, if a bit remote, and more concerned about Dusty's happiness than about his own failed marriage.

"I understand you've been in touch with her," he said during one of their phone calls.

"Yes," Rebecca replied.

"What do you think?"

"She sounds excited. Cameron must be a very special young man. Dusty says you've met him."

"Oh, yes. I've met him." Damon seemed guarded.

"What's he like?"

"He's quiet. Serious about his work." This was said as though to balance an unspoken criticism. Rebecca already knew that Cameron had no ambitions for a career like Damon's. No doubt Damon was having some difficulty in giving up his long-cherished wish that Dusty would have a brilliant future.

"How is he with Dusty?"

"I guess you'll find that out for yourself."

There was a barb in this last remark that made Rebecca finish out the conversation in some haste. She and Damon both knew what had happened the last time she met Dusty's beau.

For his own part, Damon was wrapped up in himself and his own life now. He had outgrown his grief over Rebecca, and was moving energetically toward the future he had planned for himself.

The Hightower project was closer to becoming a reality, at least on paper. Thanks to Damon's hard work and that of the accountants involved, the proposal had passed muster with the state legislature. It was felt that Hightower would make New York a high-profile fiscal showcase, attracting investors from other countries and offsetting the cost over the next decade. There were still problems in Washington, where opponents of the project—probably for their

own political motives—were holding up approval of federal funding. But the governor felt sure that his personal influence would
carry the day on Capitol Hill. He praised Damon's work to the
skies.

"You've been the secret weapon behind this all along," he said.
"Without you keeping all those egos at bay in city hall, the whole
idea would have collapsed a long time ago."

"That's good of you to say, Ron," Damon replied with proper
modesty.

"And don't think your work hasn't been noticed," the governor
added.

"Well, that's always nice."

"I've made sure it was noticed. Our friends at the federal level
know how to appreciate a talent like yours. By the way, did you
know that the vice president was a Porcellian at Harvard?"

Damon could feel a political appointment coming his way. No
doubt the governor was making sure that when the time came Damon would remember who had done him the favor.

Damon had begun seeing Alison Shore again. She forgave him
for his nastiness the night of their quarrel about Rebecca, and things
took up more or less where they had left off. There were rumors
around town to the effect that Alison had taken a very young lover,
almost a boy, after her rift with Damon. But the relationship had
either not worked out or been dropped when Damon got back in
touch.

Alison seemed excited about Damon's future, and it was a pleasure to be back with her. Her familiar caresses were comforting, as
was the cleverness and maturity of her conversation, which was so
often about people they knew in common. When he was with her,
his old frustration about Rebecca seemed a long way away, as if
the clock had been turned back to a simpler time. Damon felt more
in control of things.

Ashley had had her abortion, and Damon had been very kind to
her, seeing her often during the first weeks after the procedure, and
then spending a weekend with her at a Catskill resort. She seemed
a bit subdued, but otherwise her usual self. He had worried about
the effect of the abortion on her sexually, but she was as eager and
inventive as ever in bed.

Damon's new situation, which offered intimacy with both

women, bore a certain resemblance to his old life with Rebecca and Alison. He was able to intersperse Alison's more mature caresses with Ashley's passionate naughtiness, more or less at his whim. He could not help feeling he had the best of both worlds—an older woman to understand him, and a younger one to turn him on.

For Damon, as for Rebecca, the approach of Dusty's wedding was a complex and exciting event. It reminded him pleasantly of his achievements in life, his role as paterfamilias as well as his professional success. And it did not make him feel old. After all, he was intimate with a girl hardly older than Dusty, a girl who was free from the disfiguring pregnancy that would no doubt follow upon Dusty's marriage, sooner or later.

He looked forward to seeing Rebecca and her new beau, Sam, at the wedding. He knew that Sam was an older man, older than Damon himself. Damon found relief and even triumph in this. On one hand, he would no longer have to torment himself about Rebecca and the young man, Tony. On the other, he could mentally contrast his own exciting life with the rather humdrum Middle Western situation Rebecca had created for herself with Bittman. In this way, too, Damon felt his pride restored, as well as the balance in his relationship to his wayward wife. Everything was falling into place.

31

Dusty's wedding took place in the second week of June. At her own request, no one but the immediate families and a handful of close friends was invited. The ceremony would take place in the university's chapel.

Dusty planned to get a job after her honeymoon. At her insistence, they were going to live in Cameron's apartment for the time being. They would look for another place later. Dusty had many happy memories of the apartment and wanted to begin her marriage there.

Rebecca arrived a fortnight before the wedding. She had a lot of cleaning-out to do, both at the apartment and at the Long Island house. There was irony in this, because some of her things were to go to Chicago for her future, and others she was giving, like any proud mother, to Dusty and Cameron for their own place. She felt she was helping to launch two new lives, her own and Dusty's, and wiping out the past at the same stroke.

Cameron's mother and sister came from Binghamton a couple of days before the ceremony. Rebecca had lunch with them at a small restaurant in the Village. They were quiet, unpretentious people, nice to be with, though not quite as charming as Sam Bittman's daughters. She observed the physical and temperamental resemblances of Cameron to his mother, and pondered the missing figure of his divorced father (he had not been invited to the wedding), who must also have contributed some of his traits to Cameron and to his sister.

The most difficult moment for Rebecca was her first meeting with Dusty. It took place the night after her own arrival in New York. Dusty had given her directions to the apartment, and Rebecca had herself driven from her hotel down to the Village and rang the bell at seven o'clock.

When the door buzzed and she went in, she felt as though she were entering a no-man's-land of her own making. Her own crazy wanderings of the past year seemed to color the dim hallway in front of her, making it look foreign and impossible, like a location off the ends of the earth.

But Cameron was standing in the doorway of the apartment, smiling down at her from his six-foot frame and saying, "You must be Rebecca."

For a brief instant she held on to his hand and made conversation with him, afraid to go into the apartment. Then she saw the door open wider, and Dusty was coming toward her. Rebecca rushed forward and hugged her daughter hard, feeling the familiar body in her arms and not daring to look at the year-older face.

"My God," Rebecca gasped. "I've missed you so much."

"Me, too, Mommy." The sound of the old endearment, rarely used since Dusty's childhood, tore at Rebecca's heart.

There was a moment's confusion as they all flung into the little apartment, and the book-lined walls and framed prints and old furniture distracted Rebecca a bit longer from her daughter's face.

Then she truly looked at Dusty.

"Oh, you're so different," she said in an awed voice.

"Really?" Dusty asked.

The change was obvious. Dusty still looked young, but something fundamental seemed to have been taken out of her, and something else added. She was thinner; the clothes Rebecca had bought her this spring would probably not fit. She glowed, like any bride-to-be, but her girlishness was clearly a pose, covering a core of suffering for which Rebecca had to bear much of the responsibility, perhaps all. Shame coiled inside her at this realization. But Dusty was already showing her around the little apartment, holding her hand.

"Here's where I work.... Cameron's stuff is all in the other room.... Remember this picture? Brit helped me put it up. She says Cameron's taste is a little too nerdy. You know Brit."

Things were going well until Rebecca realized that she could not seem to retain anything Dusty was saying. She kept asking her to repeat herself. Then Dusty was holding out a box of Kleenex, joking, "Take the whole box, then!" Rebecca had not stopped crying since she came into the apartment.

She finally settled down when they began making dinner in the tiny kitchen. She took an immediate liking to Cameron. Though he had some of the features of a graduate student—the maturity, the slight remoteness, the careful choice of words—there was something freckled and boyish about him, too, that charmed Rebecca. And it was clear to see that he loved Dusty.

As for Dusty, she found her mother dramatically changed. Rebecca seemed at once more settled, more at peace with herself, and more energetic than she used to be. She was talkative and full of ideas, and not, as in the old days, conscious of her position. She seemed free, Dusty thought. Free and easy.

After dinner Cameron excused himself rather clumsily to pay a visit to the lab, and Rebecca was alone with Dusty. She spent a fleeting instant trying to recall the speech she had rehearsed all through the winter and spring, then blurted out, "How can you ever forgive me?"

"I've already forgiven you." Dusty's reply was quick, perhaps itself rehearsed. Yet it meant everything to Rebecca.

"I feel I've ruined your life," Rebecca said. "I'll never forgive myself."

Dusty seemed aware of the distinction between these two things, and commented only on the first.

"You haven't ruined anything. I'm going to be happy, Mother. Cameron is a wonderful man."

Rebecca wiped at her eyes. "I can see that, darling. I'm so happy for you."

They talked for a long time, sitting together on the old couch. But their exchanges of news quickly became repetitions of things they had already said over the phone in the course of the spring. True conversation was impossible. Too much had happened. The irony of the situation—two women finding happiness with men they had not known a year ago, because of what had happened between Rebecca and Tony—was not lost on them. But somewhere in the jagged course of their talk, a footing for future communication made itself felt. Rebecca found herself crying again; then laughing like a schoolgirl. Then Cameron returned and she left, exhausted, for her hotel.

Two days before the wedding Sam arrived in New York. Dusty insisted on meeting him right away, and Rebecca gave in and brought him over to the apartment. As he stood in the living room shaking hands with Cameron, Rebecca again found herself reeling emotionally from the unreality of the situation. Everyone was so remote from the positions they had occupied in the world a year ago. She could not help being reminded of Sam's fascination with the shifting plates of the earth's surface. Like those remote points of the earth that come together when one plate slides deep under another, Sam and Dusty had been brought into contact by the enormous improbability of Rebecca's adventure with Tony.

To her relief, Sam rose above the embarrassment of the moment and managed to hit it off right away with Cameron as well as Dusty. He inquired interestedly about Cameron's chemistry research and complimented Dusty on her journalism major.

"I've always admired people who know how to write," he said. "It's a talent I never had. I'd be ashamed to have you see any of my letters to your mother. They look like something an eighth-grader would have come up with."

At Dusty's request he showed them pictures of his daughters and told Dusty about Christine's admiration for Rebecca.

"She couldn't come on this trip because she has exams." he said. "She was mightily disappointed, I can tell you. But you'll be seeing her one of these days. She's dying to meet you."

In answer to Dusty's question, he told her of his plan to build a new house for himself in Lake Geneva, Wisconsin.

"I've had about enough of Madison after thirty years," he said. "I feel like starting off someplace new. But I do want to stay close enough to see the family. And there is Christine to think about— at least until she graduates from school."

He smiled at Dusty. "Your mother has kindly consented to bring some of her decorating skill to bear when the time comes. I'll be sorely in need of it, I can assure you. My tastes run to the barbarian, as Christine would say."

Though the evening passed quietly enough, there was a sense of dizzy celebration, as though they had all been picked up by a tornado and set down safe and sound. Rebecca could not believe that fate had been so forgiving as to bring her daughter back to her. And there Sam stood, deep in man-to-man conversation with Cameron about degree requirements, job applications, careers. It was all real, but it was too good to be true.

A few days before the wedding, by mutual agreement, Damon and Rebecca met for lunch. They spoke for a few minutes about their divorce, which would be final, ironically enough, the day before Dusty's wedding. Then they went on to the pleasanter subject of Dusty.

"What do you think of Cameron?" Damon asked.

"He looks like a fine young man," Rebecca said. "Not one for the social limelight, perhaps, but steady and strong."

"Yes, he seems so."

"And he's young at heart, in his own way," she added. "That's a good quality."

She blushed slightly as she realized they were both mentally comparing him to Tony as a suitor for Dusty.

She knew Damon could not be as pleased with Cameron as he had been with Tony. Cameron came from a modest suburban family. Even if he distinguished himself in his academic career, he would never be, or wish to be, a pillar of the community like Damon.

"How does she look to you?" Damon asked, watching Rebecca closely.

"Happy," Rebecca replied after a moment's thought. "Strong. I'm very proud of her."

Damon looked away, then back at her.

"So your friend is with you," he said.

Rebecca nodded. "You can meet him if you like. I hope you don't mind his coming to the wedding."

"Nonsense," Damon said. "Bring him. Any friend of yours, as they say. Besides, Dusty seems to like him," he added, without apparent jealousy.

"Yes," Rebecca agreed. "She does."

Damon looked at his wife. In a few days her marriage to him would be dissolved, and Dusty would be the last link between them. Rebecca already seemed a million miles away. The last few months had changed her. When he saw her in Canada she had seemed rebellious, determined—but not happy. Now she was calm, smiling, very much at peace with herself in a way he had never imagined possible for her. This Sam fellow must be good for her.

Damon did not have the heart to reproach her any more. He had done that in Canada, and it had not helped anything. Surprisingly enough, there was no reason not to wish her happiness now. For Dusty's sake as well as her own. He felt he was man enough to be magnanimous toward her. They had all survived, and he had his compensations.

"I'm going to miss you," he said.

"I'll miss you, too, Damon." She gave his hand a brisk squeeze. He felt a sudden sting of pain somewhere in the heart of his pride, and forced back the grimace that came to his lips.

The ceremony was intimate. The chapel dwarfed the small wedding party. Brit was the maid of honor. A young man from Cameron's hometown was best man. Damon gave Dusty away.

Sam sat beside Rebecca. Damon had met him briefly this morning. He was puzzled. Sam seemed a somewhat rough-hewn, even folksy fellow, lacking in any real charm or distinction. Was this the man who was making Rebecca so happy? It seemed incredible.

The chaplain went through the Unitarian ceremony—Rebecca had not passed on her Catholicism to Dusty, and Cameron's family was vague about religion—and did not add a sermon of his own.

When Dusty and Cameron joined hands to make their vows, Sam took Rebecca's hand.

"Do you, Dusty, take this man, Cameron, to be your lawfully wedded husband, to have and to hold, for richer, for poorer, from this day forward, in sickness and in health, forsaking all others, for as long as you both shall live?"

The words of the ritual stung Rebecca, and the tears welling in her eyes were for herself as well as her daughter. So much to promise, she thought. So much to dare in a few small words. She thought of her own promise, made so many years ago to Damon, and the way their marriage had ended.

"I do." She could not see Dusty's face. She felt Sam squeeze her hand. The next thing she knew it was over. The bride and groom were hugging everyone in turn and seemed eager to get on with their honeymoon.

As for Damon, he felt a certain superiority to everything that was happening. Something about the modesty of the proceedings, and of Dusty's future life, offended him. He had always been an ambitious man, a man who wanted to make his mark on the world. This entire ceremony seemed a rather quaint repudiation of such wide horizons. A husband with chalk on his sleeves and a tiny house full of children in some college town—that was the dream in Dusty's eyes.

Yet there was obviously a great deal of happiness in the chapel that morning. Dusty was beaming. Cameron looked proud and excited. Rebecca, tears coming down her cheeks, looked oddly beautiful.

"I now pronounce you husband and wife," said the chaplain with a smile.

As Cameron kissed Dusty, Damon could not help being impressed by the seriousness of the occasion. Dusty and Cameron had chosen each other against the grain, so to speak, and were daring to forge ahead into life despite the awful uncertainties of this era. As for Rebecca, though she had sinned against her family and her religion, she had found her freedom, or at least what she thought of as freedom. And Sam Bittman, having struggled manfully through his bereavement, had now found Rebecca. That, Damon had to admit, was a considerable find.

Obscurely, Damon felt the weight of a certain improbability in all these relationships, and the courage necessary to overcome that improbability. Everyone here today was fallible, imperfect—but everyone was trying to make the right choice. To do the best thing. Weakness and strength found harmony in the glow of love that filled all these faces. And love was indistinguishable from hope. Damon saw this and was touched.

That night, after the reception, he called Ashley and broke off his relationship with her. She listened in silence to his reasons, which were, truth to tell, rather vague to himself as well as to her.

Then, with a single expletive, she hung up the phone.

32

Rebecca and Sam went back to the Midwest immediately after Dusty's wedding. They had a lot to do. There was the house to build, and furniture to shop for, and a million details to see to.

Christine found time to spend a long weekend in Chicago with Rebecca. They went to see a David Mamet play at the Steppenwolf Theater and spent a long day at the Art Institute. Rebecca insisted on buying Christine a new outfit at Marshall Field. When Christine came out of the dressing room, Rebecca recalled helping Sam pick out his gift for her last Christmas at Harper's department store on Grace Island. Soon, perhaps, she would know Christine's body as well as she knew Dusty's.

Rebecca visited Sam often in Madison and helped him baby-sit for his older daughters' children. She shopped with Gretchen on Madison's West Side, strolled with Sam on State Street between the state capitol building and the university, and saw Christine's apartment near campus. The weather was balmy, the lakes were beautiful, and Rebecca had to smile when Sam warned her of the frigid winter that would make all these walks impossible six or seven months hence.

The irony of Rebecca's situation was beginning to be eclipsed by new habits that made the past seem more remote. She realized she was not the only woman in America whose marriage had collapsed and thrown her into a whole new world of people. Modern life imposed such dislocations on millions of people. Little was permanent anymore.

But she considered herself lucky. The Bittman family was a warm and happy one. It had welcomed her with open arms. And, most important of all, despite her own mistakes she had not lost Dusty. She spoke to her on the phone every week and never forgot to thank heaven for bringing her back.

*   *   *

After dropping Ashley, Damon spent a lot more time with Alison. Though he was glad to be rid of Ashley, there were minor echoes of the grief he had suffered when Rebecca left last year. He did not like loneliness. Besides, Ashley had been a powerful energizing force in his life, psychologically as well as sexually. She left a void.

Alison did not seem aware that anything had changed. She was her old self, full of bright ironies about the friends she and Damon had in common. Damon found himself appreciating her intelligence and personality more than ever before. Even when it had worked against him, as in their quarrel about Rebecca, he had had to respect Alison's brains and insight. She was a remarkable woman.

It occurred to him that he might like to propose to her. When the divorce papers came through from Rebecca's lawyers, the idea took on a greater weight. Alison was a rare woman, too special to languish in celibacy. He would be doing himself an enormous favor by making her his wife. And the benefit to Alison, given his political prospects, would be great. They could move to Washington together.

Damon met her for a weekend in D.C. and looked at a few houses in Georgetown with her. She seemed to share his excitement about the future. He felt a comfortable belonging when he was with her. How elegant she looked in her suit and foulard as she asked the Realtor questions about the house and the neighborhood. She was an expert on Washington already. She would be an invaluable help to Damon.

He saw Dusty and Cameron regularly during the summer. He invited them for weekends at the Long Island house. They seemed happy and comfortable with each other and with him. Rebecca had removed a lot of her things, but the house did not look so very different. It was odd to feel her ghost hovering between them in the house and on the beach. Odd, but not terribly painful. Everyone had what they wanted now, including Rebecca. Their past was different from their future, that was all.

Dusty herself seemed more affectionate toward Damon than ever before. It was as though, having finally found her own husband, she was less in awe of Damon, more comfortable with her relationship with him. Damon enjoyed this and felt closer to his daughter.

He was even learning to like Cameron. Slowly but surely they were becoming a family. The only one missing was Rebecca. And thankfully, all the blame was on her head. She was the one who had run out. In a way, Damon even felt grateful to her. Her departure had not damaged his own political career; she had liberated him from a stultifying life and helped him start down a new road.

And when, at the Old Senate Office Building in Washington, he met a young girl who struck his fancy, a legislative assistant in Senator Drake's office, he felt that the entire future was full of promise. He spoke familiarly to the girl, a strawberry blonde with freckled cheeks and no wedding ring. She seemed to know him by reputation. He told her he expected to be back in town often, and she seemed interested in that information.

At the beginning of August, Bob Krieg called Damon into his office. Bob looked serious.

"Damon, there's something I want to show you."

Bob pushed a photocopied text across the desk. It was a copy of an article that was to appear in the *Post* the next day. Damon put on his reading glasses and read it carefully.

Mistress of Lazare Attorney Says
He Worked Against Hightower

A county employee, who claims to have been the mistress of Mayor Lazare's legal advisor, Damon A. Lowell, says that Lowell covertly worked to undermine the Hightower Land Development project while remaining privy to the mayor's highest councils on the project.

Lowell, according to the woman, was working on behalf of certain unnamed associates of the governor to assure the governor's reelection next year. The Hightower project, if successful, would be a feather in the mayor's electoral cap, and a weapon in his projected campaign to unseat the governor.

Post reporters have learned that phone conversations and memos between Lowell and aides of the governor coincided with lobbying efforts in Albany and on Capitol Hill to prevent state and federal funding for the Hightower project. According to the unidentified source, Lowell communicated cost-overrun estimates and other financial information harmful to Hightower to lobbyists closely associated with the governor. "He made it his business to reassure the mayor and his aides about

Hightower while letting the governor and others know about the weaknesses of the project," said the source.

The firm of Minter, Gaeth, Blackman, Krieg and Lowell, of which Lowell is a senior partner, has denied all knowledge of the alleged "double agent" scheme. "Our firm had no knowledge of the details of Hightower," said a spokesman for the firm. "Damon Lowell was the firm's one and only representative in the matter. We find the accusation incredible. Our firm has never knowingly acted against a client's interests in its entire history."

Ken Prieto, a key aide of the mayor, told reporters the "double agent" scheme was discovered by mayoral aides several months ago, and was allowed to continue so that the mayor could "stay on top of the real opposition to Hightower."

The cloak-and-dagger counterespionage story was leaked to a *Post* reporter by the county employee, whose name has been withheld pending legal action against the Lowell law firm by the City. Meanwhile, an investigation into the matter is planned at the state level and by the bar association.

Damon looked across the desk at Bob, who did not meet his eyes.

"What is this nonsense?" Damon asked.

"It's not nonsense, I'm afraid," Bob said. "The City officially severed its relationship with us on Hightower this morning. Lazare told Roy Minter that you're not to set foot in city hall on Hightower business again. We've been fired, Damon."

Damon was puzzled.

"I don't get it," he said. "Hightower is doing well. I've been on the phone with all the principals within the last forty-eight hours."

The way Bob shifted in his chair told Damon bad news was coming.

"Damon, you and I go back a long way. I feel like I'm cutting off my own right arm in telling you this. But the partners want you to resign. Right away."

"Resign?" Damon repeated. "Are you out of your mind, Bob? Why in hell should I resign?"

"It's for the good of the firm," Bob said. "Don't think this is something I stomach easily, Damon. I argued half of last night against it, but the partners lined up against me, to a man. It's one thing to embarrass yourself, Damon. It's another thing to embarrass the firm.''

"How have I embarrassed the firm?'' Damon asked incredulously.

"For Christ's sake, Damon, we have partners and associates working on two hundred City contracts right now!'' Bob said. "How long do you think we're going to hold on to that business, now that this has come out? We double-crossed our own client. And that client was the City of New York. We're up to our eyeballs in damage control. No one slept a wink last night. You can't imagine what this could do. Our good name as a firm will be destroyed.''

Damon shook his head as though to clear away cobwebs. "But it isn't true!'' he cried. "How can a thing destroy our credibility as a firm when it's false on its face? I never schemed against Hightower. You know that. I worked my fingers to the bone on that damned thing. I soothed egos all over Albany and Washington to get the project through.''

Bob was silent.

"It isn't true, is it?'' Damon asked.

Bob said nothing. The look in his eyes was evasive.

Damon was puzzled. What was there for Bob to be evasive about?

"Is it?'' Damon repeated.

Bob did not reply.

The truth, like a fatal disease hiding behind the most innocent of symptoms, began to dawn on Damon.

"My God,'' he said. "It *is* true, isn't it?''

Bob looked away. The East River loomed outside the window behind a haze of pollution. The filthy water used to seem picturesque from this great height. Now it looked as though one could drown in it.

"You were all in it, weren't you?'' Damon asked. "You and the governor. And Roy and Tom and Evan, too. You used me as a shill for Hightower, and you were trying to scuttle it all along.''

He pondered the enormity of the deception. All his hard work, his weekly meetings with the governor's people, his endless sessions with Lazare, a man he held in contempt—all in the name of a project that his own partners intended to destroy from the beginning.

"Why?" he asked quietly.

Bob sighed. "Because if it went through, Lazare would have been a hero. He would have made it the centerpiece of his campaign for governor. We can't afford to have Lazare running the whole state, Damon. He has all the wrong friends. He would destroy everything the state government has worked for."

Damon saw the truth of this. No wonder it had always seemed out of character for all the governor's Ivy league friends—including Damon himself—to be working hand-in-glove with Lazare.

"Why in the bloody hell didn't you tell me?" he asked Bob. "Why did you let me stick my neck out that way, when it was all a charade?"

A look somewhere between embarrassment and pity distorted Bob's rosy features. "We intended to bring you in," he said. "But in the beginning you were making things look so good, there seemed no point in slowing you down. The governor wanted Lazare to get in as deep as possible, before... Well, you get the idea. The hope was that when Hightower didn't work out, the egg would all be on Lazare's face."

He shrugged. "Everything was going according to plan. But after Rebecca left you, you seemed to drop the ball. Losing Alison and taking up with that young girl... You weren't careful enough. You gossiped to the girl about Hightower. That became common knowledge. I hate to say it, Damon, but at that point we all felt you were becoming a risk. It was a security situation. We had to be extremely cautious."

Damon glanced again at the damning article in the *Post.* Yes, he had become a security risk. He had joked with Ashley about Hightower when they were in bed together. She was a county employee. Lazare's stock-in-trade was people like her. Perhaps he approached her months ago. Or, worse, she had approached him. Whatever he offered her, it must have seemed more attractive to her in proportion as Damon's affections for her decreased.

Damon tapped the article with his manicured fingernail.

"What makes you think they can make this stick?" he asked.

"Lazare is thick as thieves with the media," Bob said. "The *Post* is only the beginning. He'll plaster this all over town. And he's got enough clout left with the working-class voters to use it all to his own advantage. *Ivy League law firm in cahoots with Albany to hurt City.* That sort of thing."

Damon thought of the photo of himself that the *Post* had used all last winter and spring, the photo that would no doubt accompany the article tomorrow.

"So," Damon said. "It's too late to do anything."

"Yes," Bob said. "And no one could be sorrier than I am, Damon."

"I might have been a bit more careful if I had known the truth," Damon said, his voice tight with anger. "How can you expect a man to handle a complex situation when he himself is in the dark about the key element?"

Bob shook his head as if he were talking to a stubborn child. "As I say, we intended to bring you in...."

Damon thought of the governor, who had seemed so friendly and cooperative over the past months. The governor was much easier to deal with than Lazare, much closer to Damon in background and temperament. But now Damon recalled that the governor had always been closest to Bob Krieg, his Harvard classmate. When he decided that Hightower could be a political liability in the event of a Lazare candidacy for governor, he had confided this to Bob and the others. Not to Damon.

"God damn it!" Damon's anger flared into rebellion. "Why should I take the heat for this alone?" he asked. "I was being used myself. The least you can do for me is to circle the wagons."

Bob shook his head. Again that look of benign contempt shone on his face.

"As far as the world knows, or will ever know, you were in it alone," he said. "You were the only one who had actual contact with the governor or his people."

"My God," Damon said. "I didn't think you were that clever.

Using me as your cat's paw. I should kick myself around the block for not seeing through it long ago."

"As I say," Bob repeated, "when Rebecca left you, things weren't the same...."

Damon could not deny this. A year ago he might have seen through a thing like this. After all, he had long since learned to trust no one in his profession. In a peculiar way, he *had* lost his grip on things after Rebecca left.

He smiled ruefully at Bob. "But Lazare saw through you," he said. "He must have tumbled to it a long time ago. That's why he..."

His words trailed off as he realized he was praising Lazare for having the brains and cunning that Damon himself had lacked when he most needed them. Lazare, the political street fighter, had smelled a rat. He must have sensed that the governor was too strange a bedfellow for him to trust. Thus he saw through Damon's Ivy League exterior, Damon's breathless reports about what was happening in Albany—to the tiny possibility of betrayal. A betrayal of which Damon himself was unaware, so blinded was he by his sense of his own importance as point man, and his political ambition.

Both sides had been smart, but Lazare had been smarter. And as for Damon, he had been everybody's tool, outwitted and used on all sides. And now he was being thrown to the wolves.

"So now you expect me to resign," he said.

"It's the best thing," Bob said earnestly. "The only thing. Think how many careers are at stake, Damon."

"I only care about one career," Damon said.

"You'll land on your feet," Bob said. "It doesn't have to be as bad as it looks for you." His voice was without conviction.

"I could tell my own story to the *Post,* you know," Damon said. "And elsewhere, too."

Bob shook his head. "You've always been a good soldier, Damon," he said. "A team player. Everyone knows that. You wouldn't want to throw away the reputation of thirty years by blabbing to the media at a time like this. Your silence is your best hope."

Damon could not deny the truth of this. He had already violated the lawyer's oath of discretion in enough ways. Spilling his guts to the media would be the end of him.

There was a pause.

"And what about Hightower?" he asked.

Bob shrugged. "I talked to the governor a few minutes ago. He thinks the project will probably go through in the end. I'm afraid we all underestimated Lazare."

Damon looked at his old friend's florid face. He wished he could kill him with his bare hands.

"There's one thing that puzzles me," Damon said. "What would you all have done if I hadn't been there to use as a fall guy?"

Bob shrugged. "We would have found some other way," he said. "There's a way around everything. Isn't that what you used to say? But the thing is, Damon, you *were* there. You lost the handle."

There was a silence. Damon looked out the window. He thought of Ashley. He recalled his phone call to her the night of Dusty's wedding. He had not taken her anger seriously. That had been a fatal mistake. She was not the type of girl to be walked over without fighting back. The more so because she had aborted a baby for his sake. Looking back, Damon wished he had understood women a bit better.

"They want to announce your resignation before two o'clock," Bob said. "In fact, they sent me here, as the one closest to you, to get it. I'm to bring it back with me. God, Damon, I'm sorry."

Damon looked at the photo of Rebecca and Dusty on his desk. Months ago he had planned to replace it with one of Dusty alone, but his preoccupation with Hightower had prevented him from finding the time.

"I'm sorry, too," he said.

33

It was December, six months after Dusty's wedding. Rebecca had taken a week off from her job to help Sam plan the decoration of his new house in Lake Geneva. The location was working out well. Sam was near enough to his daughters for visits, and yet far enough to feel independent.

Christine would probably not be home next summer. She had found an internship in Milwaukee and was making plans to sublet an apartment there. Sam suspected that this had something to do with a new boyfriend who came from Milwaukee, but he kept his opinions on the matter to himself.

The house, a typical suburban model with four bedrooms to accommodate guests and grandchildren, had been built with dispatch by a construction firm with which Sam had had dealings in the past, but it was still almost completely unfurnished. In order to have it livable by Christmas, Sam had brought in the old furniture from his house in Madison. The pieces looked very colorless and bedraggled in this new location, and Sam suggested they be junked. But Rebecca insisted he keep them for the time being. Her sense of irony was pricked by the presence of this furniture, whose "ninth life" consisted of this brief tenure so far from its original home.

"It's not unlike me, when you think of it," she told Sam. Here in this Midwestern setting, so foreign to her Boston forebears and her years as a New Yorker, she was almost like a fish out of water. But not quite; for a modest suburban house like this was just what she would have wanted for herself all those years, had she had the opportunity of reviewing her choices more wisely when she was fresh out of college.

The blustery Wisconsin town, the chilly lake, the taciturn neighbors with their Jeeps and pickup trucks—it was all gloriously new to Rebecca, and she savored every facet of it. There were no pretentious Long Island neighbors or law partners to pass judgment on the furnishings Sam would choose for this house. Sam enjoyed a right Rebecca had been denied all her life—the right to be ordinary.

It was a little after one. The fire Sam had lit was still crackling in the living room. He was on his way out to work.

He gave Rebecca a kiss on the lips and a long, lingering hug.

"I don't like to leave you on a day like this," he said. "See that fire? We should be curled up on a couch in front of it all afternoon. Why should I spend that time in an office?"

Sam was touchingly romantic toward Rebecca. He coveted every moment alone with her. He cursed the new business that took him away from her during her brief visit. But Rebecca insisted he keep at it, for she could see how invigorating the challenge was for him.

"The home fires will be burning when you get back," she said, patting him on his shoulders.

"And see if you can have me a living room when I get back, too," he said, waving as he went out the door.

He had given Rebecca the power of decision where decorating was concerned. There were heavy books of wallpaper and fabric designs on the floor in front of the fire. It was a difficult job, but Rebecca wanted to decorate it in a way that would suit Sam's new life. She wanted it to be comfortable and challenging at the same time, so that when Sam came home from work he would feel he was entering upon something new, something exciting.

She heard the cold crunch of the car's tires in the driveway, which had not yet been paved. Then the engine roared and died away as Sam drove off. Rebecca sipped at her coffee and looked at the fire. She glanced at the design books, willing herself to get to work, but a throb of well-being made her sit back against the old couch and stare into the flames.

On the coffee table was her old volume of Proust, *The Past Recaptured,* which she had not opened in many years but had found when moving her own things to Chicago. She had only skimmed it in college, because the preceding six volumes of the novel were so enormous that she had no energy left for the last. Now, having forgotten most of what went before, she was reading through the last volume with great interest. She felt a bit naughty, skipping to the end like a lazy student, and this increased her pleasure.

Unfortunately the French was quite difficult. But Rebecca struggled on, using the heavy old French-English, English-French dictionary, which was itself a relic of her college days. She was using Dusty's latest letter as a bookmark, and she took it out to look at it now. Dusty was working as a part-time reporter and English teacher while Cameron began his Ph.D. dissertation. She was pregnant, as she had announced excitedly to Rebecca over the phone last month.

On a whim Rebecca got up, carrying the letter, and went to the phone. Glancing at her watch, she guessed that Dusty would not be home from work yet, but she dialed the number anyway.

"Hi, we can't answer the phone at the moment," came Cameron's recorded voice. *"Leave a message at the sound of the beep and we'll get back to you."*

Rebecca waited for the beep. For an instant she could think of nothing to say. Answering machines always made her nervous. Then she glanced at the letter.

"Hello, children," she said, a smile in her voice. "Dusty, I'm calling about the flights you mentioned in your letter. I'll pick you up at O'Hare, if that's all right. I don't want you to have to take a limo." Dusty was to visit Rebecca after Christmas, and Rebecca had made all the travel arrangements.

She hesitated. She could almost feel her invisible daughter in the silence on the line.

"Silly me," she added. "The truth is, I just wanted to hear your voice, honey. And to talk about the baby. And Christmas. Give me a call. I miss you. Kiss Cameron for me."

She hung up, feeling embarrassed. She had never been good on the phone. Something about the close contact over such huge distances was artificial and unsettling. Damon used to say that she was as primitive as her New England ancestors when it came to long-distance calls. If he hadn't restrained her, she would have shouted her responses into the receiver.

She returned to the couch with the letter in her hand. She looked once again at Dusty's handwriting, which had come to resemble her own rather closely in the last few years. There was a photo enclosed, showing Dusty and Cameron in front of the chemistry building at the university. Cameron looked very tall, and Dusty very pretty. The glow of new pregnancy was in her eyes.

Rebecca closed the letter and reopened the book. The page she had been reading was dense, with no paragraph divisions. She sighed as she thought of Proust's tortuous syntax, divided by endless dependent clauses. One had to have incredible patience to get through his longer sentences. At night, when one was tired, it was virtually impossible.

But now Rebecca recalled that last night before bed she had intentionally stopped at this page, and reminded herself to look at it again when she was awake and alert. In the middle was this sentence: *"I would need to have the courage to refuse those who came to visit me or asked me to visit them, on the grounds that I had a crucial and urgent rendezvous with myself."*

The sentence had struck her, not only because she had a vague memory of an intense young professor quoting it many years ago, but because it spoke to her now as it had not when she was a girl. Yes, she thought. There comes a time in life when one's obligation to other people must take a back seat to one's duty to oneself. Too often, in order to fit in to the world, one forgets the true shape of one's own spirit and forces it like a square peg into a round hole, gradually eroding it until there is no self left to encounter. Was this what Proust had meant? She was not sure.

She tried to find the answer now, but it eluded her. The mental effort made her tired, and she lay back on the couch with the book open against her breast.

The fire was deliciously warm. It had that concentrated heat that dying fires so often have, when the wood is all but consumed and nothing but embers heat the hearth. Rebecca glanced at the glowing coals, one of which collapsed with a sigh as she watched, then closed her eyes, lulled by the warmth.

This was the couch on which Sam's unruly daughters had turned somersaults a generation ago, ruining the cushions and cracking the arm so that Sam's wife had to have it completely reconditioned. This was the couch on which Sam had sat in the evenings in Madison, watching television with Margery and reading his newspapers and magazines. The couch he had avoided after her death, just as he avoided the bed they had slept in together.

Rebecca could almost feel a thousand family hours swirling

around her, masked by the curtain of time but real nonetheless, and insistent in some way more important than mere memory.

Everything changed. Real things were overwhelmed by the passage of the years and disappeared. Or rather, they reappeared in unlikely places and unrecognizable forms, like the mountaintops from one continent that became lake beds on another.

And people change in the same way, Rebecca thought. Her eyes half closing as the dying fire warmed her cheek, she saw herself as a girl, running through the town with Josey, getting into mischief, looking for boys. How different she had been in those days! More often than not she was the "ringleader," enticing Josey into forbidden adventures with a reckless daring soon to be expunged from her personality by time and circumstance.

And yet life comes full circle. Today she felt a tingle of adventure not so terribly different from her emotion when she met that nameless boy in the state park and went into the woods with him. A teetering on the edge of something perilous, a loss of balance one did not fear, because it was one's nature to dare, to challenge…

She could feel his hands on her shoulders and the crunch of the pine needles as she squirmed to make it easier for him.

And now she remembered what it was like to go home that night and find her mother there alone. To stand in the doorway in her forest-soiled clothes and see her mother crying, "Daddy has left us. Daddy has left us." The reckless child whose body was covered with dirt and kisses stood back, wide-eyed, making room for another to take her place, and slipped away unobserved as the crumpled letter was held out accusingly by Irene. And that child had never come back, through all the years that Rebecca played it safe, exchanging her own heart against the danger and cruelty of the world.

I had a rendezvous with myself.

Rebecca fought to stay awake, but sleep rose up around her like a wave. Dreams looped and folded within her, wordy and discursive as thoughts. She was, in a way, arguing with herself. Part of her was saying that she had lived her life reasonably and valuably, from the start. But another voice was reproaching her in no uncertain terms. *You were wrong,* it said. *You were wrong.*

The voice claimed that Rebecca had abandoned that rendezvous with herself long ago, preferring first her mother, then Damon, then the world of her friends, her obligations, and even Dusty. It was good to be a loving mother. But was it good to bury one's own soul under one's devotion to others? Even to one's daughter?

She had preferred everyone to herself—as though her own company were worthless. And then, when it was almost too late—or was it already too late?—she had broken the bonds, transgressed the law.

Yes, that was the first sin, Rebecca mused. The one she had never confessed. The one she had not thought to confess, because it was so much a part of her. The sin of throwing away one's own self in favor of the world into which one wanted to fit.

And what about the second sin? The one she *had* confessed, the one the world condemned her for the most harshly. The one that had broken the chains, thrust her into a limbo from which there seemed no escape save hellfire, and then, improbably, offered her redemption.

A person's journey through life can lead to an emptiness that only seems natural and real because we have become accustomed to our cage. And then one day, like waking up from a bad dream, we realize the prison is destroying us, and we run, we flee. And the world shouts its blame and its disapproval. But around the next corner, so long forgotten that she looks like a ghost, beckons our old forgotten self, wondering whether we have the courage to come back to her.

The second sin banishes us. With that sin, too quickly confessed, everything begins.

She heard a noise that she took to be the settling of the dying logs. It barely disturbed the sleep falling over her, and she smiled. It was good to sleep, sweet and cleansing.

When, a moment later, she opened her eyes to check the fire and saw Tony standing over her, she thought he was part of the dream, part of the argument going on inside her. And did he not belong there, after all? Was he not the key to her escape from her own past, the first step toward her rediscovery of the soul she had lost? He could rightly claim to be her leader, her liberator, the one who had shown her the way and the light.

But the look on his face showed that it was not a dream, and that he was changed. He was pale. He looked aged. He was staring down at her with hatred. And she was not surprised, somehow, to see a gun appear in his hand.

He said something, but the urgent arguments of the dream drowned him out, made his words confusing.

Then, "You did this," he said, the gun trembling in his hand. She struggled to raise herself out of the dream, to reason with him, but now she understood that it was too late, that he was, in his youth and his anger, right. It was her second sin that had brought him back.

She was smiling up at him like a sleepy mother, forgiving, when the gun went off.

34

The funeral was held in Lake Geneva, at Dusty's request. She knew that Rebecca had loved this place and hoped to live here someday. And, truth to tell, there was no other place where she could be said to belong.

Irene flew up from Florida, looking tanned and healthy despite her illness, which now seemed truly defeated by her superior staying power. Damon had met her at O'Hare and flown with her to Madison, where they had joined Sam before driving to Lake Geneva.

Dusty and Cameron had flown to Chicago and driven the rest of the way. In the car, Dusty kept hearing Rebecca's last words, on the phone, about her planned arrival at O'Hare. She had come through O'Hare today, but on the way to her mother's funeral. Rebecca's voice was still on the answering machine back in New York. Dusty was sure she would never have the courage to listen to it again.

Understandably enough, none of Tony's family was in attendance. Tony had been buried yesterday in New York.

The bodies had been found together. Tony had gathered Rebecca to his breast before putting the gun in his own mouth. There was no note. Only the spectacle, found by Sam and then shown to the police, of the two together before the still-smouldering fire.

Today was a characteristic Wisconsin winter day, cold and sunny, with a hint of future snow in some gray clouds moving up slowly to the west. The bare trees looked shamed by the sunlight, which glared in an occasional half-frozen puddle from last weekend's storm.

The service was held in the local Catholic church. Christine had come with Sam. His other daughters and their children were in Madison. Sam and Christine would drive back there tonight. Cameron and Dusty intended to join them there for a day or so before going back East. Damon and Irene would return to Chicago this afternoon for their respective flights to New York and Sarasota.

There were handshakes all around, but the mourners did not seem very comfortable with one another. Damon, visibly preoccupied, spoke only briefly to Sam. Dusty stayed close to Cameron, Sam to Christine. Damon had Irene on his arm most of the time.

The priest from Lake Geneva had never known Rebecca, but Dusty and Sam had coached him on what to say. There had been some embarrassment as they talked about her life and the cause of her death. The priest seemed to know more than he let on; they sensed disapproval in his manner.

The cemetery was picturesque, nestled on a hill just outside the town. One could see the lake as a distant blue gem behind the graves. No one in either family was buried here. It was for Rebecca alone.

The small procession drove slowly to the graveside, the cars' tires crunching on the packed snow. Everyone gathered shivering around the grave, and Dusty had the odd thought that they should hurry, for the wind was so cold that it would be warmer for Rebecca under the ground.

After the usual prayers, the priest added some words of his own. "Father, we ask your forgiveness and your blessing in sending you Rebecca. We ask your forgiveness for her sins, and your blessing on her courage. For whatever her mistakes, she knew how to recognize them. She dared to acknowledge her sins to herself and to You. Judge her for her repentance, and be merciful, through Jesus Christ our Lord."

The small crowd drifted away, bit by bit, after the coffin was lowered. Only Irene was visibly crying. For a moment Damon stood beside Sam, looking down at the grave. Then he led Irene away.

Sam was left with Dusty and Cameron. The three remained together for several minutes, joined by an unspoken impulse. The two men held Dusty's hands.

Sam let go first and walked back toward the cars. Dusty felt a throb of loss. In recent months she had come to love him almost as a father. But now their closeness seemed unreal, a thing that might have been rather than a thing that was. For it was Rebecca alone who had brought them together, and, now that Rebecca was gone, they had no real relationship, nothing but the instinctive affection that might have given them a long life together had she lived. Dusty would perhaps never see Sam again. And because of this, the loss of Rebecca seemed suddenly more absolute and more terrible.

Dusty looked down at the grave. A flake of snow, wind-borne from distant cloud or drift, came to sting her cheek. It brought the first tears. The light was brighter than before. It was the kind of day when children's cries echoed long distances in the cold. The lake, though half frozen, glowed amid the snowy hills.

"Oh, Mother..."

Dusty bent down to touch the already freezing earth. Weakness, or a sudden loss of heart, made her lose her balance, and she nearly fell forward. But Cameron caught her in time and supported her.

"Careful."

You're all I've got.

He helped her to her feet. She grasped his hand so he would know not to let her go.

Her pain ebbed as she felt the strange incidence of human flesh and of her own love. How impermanent it all was! And how improbable. Cameron himself had come into her life as a consequence of Rebecca's wanderings. Cameron, whose child was now growing inside her.

"Are you all right?" he asked.

"Yes." She was leaning on him now. They did not move, but the grave seemed to recede, as though something was already taking them away from Rebecca, toward another life.

All things come from far away, Dusty thought, feeling his arm curl about her waist. All things approach unseen and, in the end, slip through our fingers. We reach out blindly to catch them and find only ourselves. Yet in the end, the world takes pity, the wheel turns one last time, and we are not alone after all. A lucky chance, or only a dream...

The question became a soft smile on her lips as she looked down one last time at Rebecca.

Then she turned from the grave with her husband on her arm and moved back toward the waiting car.